AFTER
Perfect

AFTER
Perfect

A NOVEL

MAAN GABRIEL

SHE WRITES PRESS

Published 2021
Printed in the United States of America
Print ISBN: 978-1-64742-203-5
E-ISBN: 978-1-64742-204-2
Library of Congress Control Number: 2021910765

For information, address:
She Writes Press
1569 Solano Ave #546
Berkeley, CA 94707

She Writes Press is a division of SparkPoint Studio, LLC.

Book design by Stacey Aaronson

To Chris, who is a realist but chooses to live in my magical world.

To Jack, who is our magic.

Chapter One

"Gabriella, open the goddam door!" I hear her. My best friend, Felicity, is on the other side of the door. But I don't move. My eyes are fixated on what's on the kitchen table. It's a ticking time bomb. And I own it.

There on top of my kitchen table is the end of my story.

I need to sign it to set Simon free. I need to sign it to set *myself* free. I have cried enough. There are no more tears to be shed.

You can't really prepare for moments like this. Moments you know will change your life forever—will change *you* forever.

Simon had been the love of my life. He had been my breath. When he walked out on me six months ago, I felt my world crumble like I never knew possible.

But I did not expect this.

I stand in the middle of my Manhattan apartment, which I can no longer afford, staring intently at the thick envelope on my dining table, thinking about how I got here. How I got it all wrong. Sixteen years of my life, all but inconsequential now. This used to be a home. Our space. Our love nest. We picked every item here together, even the strange puppy sculpture tucked in the corner bookshelf, which we both thought was funny back then. It was our private joke, an example of how we each had an extension of ourselves to the other, that we were once the same heart and the same soul. Now, this room is a sad memory of what once was.

Like a robot, I mechanically look around as if someone holds the key to my existence. The white walls, which once used to be bright and shiny, now feel cold and dreary, and the curtainless windows appear naked and unadorned.

Simon moved out most of his things two months ago. I didn't ask where he was going, but I was sure it would be with her. I know him too well. He wouldn't risk it all unless he was sure that someone was going to catch him at the other end. He's meticulously careful like that.

Still in my clothes from last night, I bend my head and regard myself with disgust. I'm a thirty-six-year-old woman with more than a few extra pounds on me; my hair has not seen a salon in months; and I let my man run my life for almost two decades. I was pretty once. Boys used to follow me around in college, even though I was already with Simon back then. Being half Filipina means I will always look younger than my age, but who cares about that now? I was a valedictorian in high school. I used to be someone. Now, I'm an echo of who I once was—a faint version of my old self.

Divorce. It is such a painful reality. But it is now my truth.

I hear the blaring song *Just Like a Pill* by P!nk that is my iPhone ringtone coming from inside my room. It yanks me out of my reverie. I don't move, knowing that it's probably my mother or my best friend, Felicity, checking in on me. I hear it stop. *I need to change that goddamn ringtone.*

I can't talk to my mother right now. This, right here, is her worst nightmare. All my life, she had me convinced that I'd be happy as long as my marriage was stable, as long as Simon felt satisfied and content, as long as I did my best to be a devoted wife. It's the culture she was brought up in, and a culture she lives in. Traditional Filipinos look at women in a very old-fashioned, restricted way.

"Gabriella!" There is no denying the worry in Felicity's voice, and yet I still don't move. I'm too exhausted. It's only seven in the morning, but I can already feel the weight of the day on my shoulders.

I can't talk to anyone right now. I can't even handle my own thoughts. I put my hands over my ears. It muffles the noise around me, but it doesn't stop the hostile noise inside my head. I close my eyes in hopes that if I block what I see, I will not feel what I feel right now.

The doorbell buzzes. And I let it. It doesn't stop.

My phone comes back to life from inside my bedroom with P!nk singing at the top of her lungs. I press my hands more firmly over my ears. And I stand there frozen in time. Unmoving. The feeling bubbles inside me like heat creeping in slowly but steadily. I want to go back. I just want to crawl back to when I have Simon's arms to cradle me when things are not going as planned. Losing him was not something I ever anticipated. I always thought we were going to grow old together. Wrinkly, we even joked. I move both my hands to cover my face, hiding, ashamed of myself. At thirty-six, I'm already a failure—as a wife.

Numbness inches through me like fire and ice. I feel nothing, and yet it is everything. But my tears still don't come.

"Gabby, open the door, please . . . I know you're in there. Let me in." Felicity is pleading now. Last night, I sent her a text message after I opened the envelope. "It's really over," was all I said. She probably didn't get it until this morning, and I'm most certain that she also called my mom. Felicity and I have been best friends since high school in Virginia.

The three of us, actually—Felicity, Simon, and I—we were all inseparable once.

Minutes pass. I let this moment sink in.

"Don't make me call the fucking fire department to break this door down. It's your embarrassment, not mine." I smile in the middle of it all. I have Felicity. At least I get to keep her.

I walk slowly to the door. I didn't think there was any truth to how you deteriorate physically when you're sad. But here I am now, going through the motions of my emotional pain to physical ruin.

"I'm here. . . ."

"Don't scare me like this, Gabby!" I open the door. She bangs it wide open with her fist and grabs me in her embrace. "Gabby!" I sink my head onto her neck, letting myself go. And yet the tears don't come.

"Hi," I whisper, my head still leaning heavily on her shoulder. Felicity is a lot shorter than I am, so my body is arched uncomfortably. But I don't mind. Her scent consoles me. It is familiar. It is what I know—like Simon.

"Where is it?" Felicity asks, letting me go and walking to the kitchen table where the thick envelope lies waiting for my attention. She pulls the papers out, reads them for a few minutes, and tosses them back on the table. "That fucking dick!"

"It's over," I say with calmness. It scares me. And I can tell it terrifies Felicity too.

"You deserve better." She runs back to me for a hug, on tiptoe, trying to catch me with her small frame.

"I know . . . I heard a rumor that he proposed to her." But I don't cry as I say this. I've known about this for months, and yet I had hoped that, somehow, he would change his mind. I thought he had because something seemed to have shifted the past month. He started calling me again, checking in on me, and having brief conversations on the phone. He had been by the apartment a few times when I was around, and we had been cordial, respectful. We even cracked jokes a few times. There were moments when we would look at each other, and I could tell that somehow love still lingered somewhere between us. I was obviously wrong. I've misread Simon.

"They deserve each other!" Felicity is angry.

"What am I going to do now?" I move to the living room. I lower myself to the sofa slowly, still in shock. My reflexes are slow, like my body is shutting down.

I hear a fire truck drive by, and I give Felicity a questioning look. "I didn't call that," she says with a smirk. The noise from outside the window is proof that life goes on outside even without me. I need to be out there.

I bend my head to my chest and cover my face with my shaking hands. "What do I do now?" I ask again in a whisper, talking more to myself than to my best friend standing across from me in obvious worry.

"What the hell are you talking about?" she wails. She does that when she tries to cover up her fears. I hate that I make her feel this way. "You're starting grad school on Monday and will finally do something you've always wanted to do. Think about the cute guys you'll meet at NYU—smart creative writers." Felicity helped me get into the New York University master's in fine arts creative writing program. She has been an adjunct professor in its undergraduate communications department for more than five years, in addition to her gig at *The New York Times*, which she recently put on hold. She's still single and living the life she said she's always wanted. "Besides, it's time for you to be single in New York. You're missing out on a lot of things."

I sink deeper into the sofa, clutching its armrest tightly, but I feel nothing. I'm too exhausted. I sigh. It's the best I can do right this second. I let go of the last breath that is Simon. I let go of the life I once shared with him. And yet I'm still holding on to me. I should probably let go of her too.

Chapter Two

C rash!

I jolt backward from the sudden contact. On impulse, I close my eyes and cover my chest with both my arms. I let my things fall on the floor.

"Watch where you're going," the voice says. The words are uttered with precision and irritation. I open my eyes one at a time and I start to blink repeatedly. I am captivated by the voice, and in surprise find myself mesmerized by the face whose body I just collided with. I involuntarily shiver within. This reaction unsettles me. My brows furrow in confusion.

I'd hit him straight on the chest. It had been my fault. I've been mindlessly looking around my new environment on my first day in unchartered territory—graduate school. I didn't see him coming, which seems silly because his presence is definitely strong—even more so now that we're standing face to face. My movement, as I picture it like a movie in my head, is in slow motion, and I flutter my lashes upwards as I peek underneath to meet his eyes with mine.

An inexplicable emotion consumes my center. I feel ashamed all of a sudden.

He's a tall guy, more than a foot taller than I. Standing in front of him, with my insecure stance, I feel like a tiny waif—afraid, yet at the same time in awe. I instinctively move my head sideways, angling for a better view of his face, like an alien examining a human being for the first time. His black hair is unkempt, and yet it still looks unbelievably attractive. I'm quite sure there are ridiculous amounts of gel in it. He's wearing black jeans and a plain white shirt. And an expensive-looking black leather jacket is draped over one arm. His nose is strikingly structured, his upper lip curved atypically where I can only imagine a stunning smile can come from it, and his eyes are luminous, pulling me to swim into them. He looks no more than thirty-five, maybe even younger. He's probably also a graduate student like me.

He crosses his arms in front of his chest with the jacket covering both his forearms but based on the parts I can see, they are toned and muscular. They're the kind of arms you'd like to melt into. I shake off this ridiculous thought with a toss of my head. Nobody in her right mind should feel this much attraction toward someone she literally just bumped into mere seconds ago.

I bend my head to look away from his compelling glare.

"I'm sorry," I whimper in humiliation, sounding almost like a hiccup. I slowly lift my head up to look back at his piercing blue eyes—deep blue, like an angry sea. For a split second there is softness in his perfectly chiseled face, but it disappears as quickly as it emerges.

The stranger looks at me oddly, squinting his eyes, sizing me up, and probably trying to figure out whether I've lost my mind. I move my admiring eyes to his broad shoulders, down to his taut biceps under his tight shirt, and then further down to his narrow hips. I look away immediately, embarrassed, again. I feel my cheeks turning red.

"Watch where you're going next time," he icily replies. I glance up at him. There is a pause, a long agonizing silence while we stare at each other. He squints his eyes again and looks as confused as I feel.

Without saying another word, I hastily gather my things and walk away as fast and as far as I can. I seriously don't need this right now.

I command myself not to turn around to look back at him, and I push on forward, like a woman on a mission hoping to widen the distance between us. It's disconcerting. I'm almost out of breath.

Confident that I've finally escaped, I give in to a sideward glance, and to my surprise, I find him still standing on the spot where I left him, watching me, looking slightly entertained by my awkwardness. A small but distinct smile brightens his face.

I close my eyes, willing my humiliation away and hoping that when I open my eyes, he'll be gone. He's not. He's still there, looking at me curiously. I wish I could will myself to disappear.

"Gabby! Here!" Felicity's familiar, friendly voice is salvation. I give out a heavy, freeing sigh. I turn around, and down the hall I see Felicity giddily waving at me. She's a happy vision in her bright pink top, red bubble skirt, and black kitten heel pumps. And no one—I mean, no one—could ever miss the big black-and-white polka-dot bow in her hair, held by a transparent plastic headband that we got together at the Kate Spade store in Jersey. Yeah, we go to the outlet in Jersey sometimes—Simon used to drive us. The thought of him pierces my heart. I shake the thought away. So, yes, think of Felicity as a Kate Spade model with the entire adorable, ladylike trimmings.

I take a deep breath again, pulling my shoulders back, trying to regain some semblance of confidence as I walk toward my best friend. I take in the old building smell. Musty. The hall is dark, but the ray of sunlight that escapes through slightly cracked windows adds character to the old school feel. There are groups of nervous first-year students walking by. Some upperclassmen are in a hurry and some are simply taking it easy. Here, right now, is my reawakening. New chapter. Rebirth. Independence.

I can sense that someone is observing me. A tingling feeling at the back of my neck gives it away. Or so I thought. I steal another look behind me. He's gone, like a dream. I feel . . . disappointed. Perhaps, I'll see him around.

"Are you okay today?" Felicity chirps jovially—a beautiful welcome after the disconcerting incident. I smile at her with admiration and gratitude. I don't know what I would have done the past six months without her, or the past six years, or the six before that.

"I'm fine," I say, letting my shoulders sag in frustration. Walking a few yards bravely is more difficult than I expected.

"What's wrong?" she asks, looking worried after seeing my uncomfortable expression. I tell her about the stranger, omitting the part about how gorgeous he was and how good he smelled. "Don't mind those douchebags. Unfortunately, there are a lot of them here. They all think that they're God's gift to art."

"I know. This just needs a lot of getting used to."

"Forget about that. So, what's your first class?" She grabs my schedule, printed on a pink sheet visible on top of my obnoxiously red binder, which Felicity gave me as a present when I got my acceptance letter from NYU. "You're in the next building. Not far away. I'll walk you. My class doesn't start for another hour." She instantly links her arm in mine. I can feel a skip coming—and there it is. Felicity skips next to me like a five-year-old on a playdate. I can't help but smile.

The building next door is more serene. Felicity mentioned on the way over that this is where most of the graduate classes are held and where the writing labs are located. My schedule shows that my classroom is on the third floor, which looks like quite a hike up the stairwell. I'm glad I wore my white Adidas sneakers with jeans today. Felicity happily climbs the steps with me. She looks totally at home here at NYU, and I can see that this is where she truly belongs. Although she wouldn't acknowledge it, she is a born teacher, a nurturer, someone young minds can look up to for guidance, for care, for counsel. I look up to her for all three.

I brush my hand along the wooden rail as I climb, observing the dents and scratches, wondering about the stories and circumstances that come with them. I hold onto it, knowing that my story will one day be etched into it too. I smile because the mere touch of my palm on it is already my contribution to the history of this place.

When we land on my floor, I see him. I do a double take in the direction where I thought I saw him. Then he's gone. I shake my head, wondering why I can't stop thinking about that man.

"Are you okay?" asks Felicity. I shake my head again to reset my thoughts. I don't want to worry her or make her feel responsible for me at school. I'm my own woman, and I want to do this. *I got this*, I tell myself.

"I'm fine. Nerves," I say, touching her arm lightly and then making a face, which surprises her. I see Felicity exhale. "Can you please stop treating me like a piece of delicate china," I joke.

"Fine. As long as you're not going to crack on me," she teases.

"I promise." I stand at attention.

Felicity looks at my pink sheet schedule again, walks a few steps forward, and stops further down the hall to the right.

"Your first class is Creative Expressions? I like this. It's freestyle writing. The professor will see where you are in your writing, and the whole class will discuss it." It's the reason why I decided to take the class. I like the notion of its freedom. "Here we are, my child." Felicity abruptly stops, turns around, takes both my arms in her loving hands, and squeezes them in support. She gives me a sad smile, like a mother sending her daughter to kindergarten for the first time, and then pulls me into a tight hug. I let her, rolling my eyes and huffing in fake irritation. She pulls away and we both laugh hysterically.

"Just now you sounded like your old self again," my best friend whispers, "and I'm glad."

How can my situation get any worse? What I'm most afraid of happening has already come to pass this weekend. Simon doesn't want to have anything to do with me anymore. The pain, although numbing, is there, but I know I'll survive.

Felicity blows me a kiss as she walks backward toward the stairwell. I turn around to face my classroom.

I'm twenty minutes early. I push the heavy wooden door, and it produces a loud creaking sound. There's no one in the room yet. I leave the door open. This is probably one of the so-called writing labs. It's a small room with a big rectangular table at the center and twelve chairs around it. The air smells mustier here, like it has not been opened for months, which is probably the case during the summer. I walk toward one of the chairs, set across from the window with a perfect view of today's clear blue New York City sky. I lay my binder and my purse on top of the table and look around. The walls are covered with big oak bookshelves. I saunter to the one closest to me, and I can't help brushing my fingers lightly along the books that it shelters. The books are of various genres, and I am pleasantly surprised to see that romance has earned a spot in this room. In another life I would have been a romance writer. Not in this one though, since my only chance at a happy ever after has already gone up in flames.

This room speaks to me. I can stay in this room all day and write, think, and create. Books are my passion. My escape. It's probably why I neglected to see that my life had become such a mess, because in my books there are adventures and excitement and lots of love—always lots of love—and I guess because of this, I failed to recognize that my real world was falling apart.

I finally take a seat facing the window, crossing my arms over my chest and soaking up the brightness of the morning sun. I stare at it head on without squinting. I breathe it all in. At about ten minutes before eleven, a tall, slender girl in braids walks in and sits next to me. She glances sideways, smiles, and pulls out her MacBook. I look at her digital school supplies laid out right in front of her on the table, and I look at mine. Note to self: *Bring my MacBook to school too.*

"Hi," the chirpy girl says to me at the top of her high-pitched voice. She drags her chair closer to mine. "My name is Heather." She reaches out for a handshake. I didn't think they still did that anymore with the germaphobe generation, but I take her hand anyway.

"Hi," I say, and I smile. "Gabby."

"Aww. That is such a sweet name," she says in a singsong voice with a hint of a California accent.

"Thanks." And just like that, I think, I've made my first friend in school.

"Nice to meet you, Gabby." She then faces the table, pulls open her MacBook, and pushes the power button, which reverberates with a loud, lingering *ding*.

A few more students start arriving.

"This is really exciting, don't you think?" She claps her hands together in a gesture of overexcitement. "Colt James is the best professor in this program. The best!" she squeals.

"I know, right?" The girl with platinum—I mean, almost white—hair across from us joins in our conversation. "I hear he's still really busy doing book tours and talks, even though his last book was published like two years ago," Platinum Girl adds. "Last semester he sent his TA to substitute for him almost half the time. I just hope we get some face time with him to discuss and critique our work before the semester ends."

I look at both of these girls in shame. I should have done my homework. I should have, like the rest of the university, researched my professors. I read a little about him on his photo-free profile on the university faculty page, but I don't know him —not with the kind of background these two girls have. In my defense, I have been busy sorting out my messed-up life.

"And it doesn't hurt that he's extremely hot!" Heather chimes in. So, I guess he's not the old, chubby, balding writing professor I've visualized. Almost as if she's read my mind, Heather adds, "How can someone have written so much at that age? I mean, I think he's only like five years older than I am." *What is he, like twenty-five*? I ask myself sarcastically and silently. I'm mortified to think that I could be older than my professor, and by the sound of these two shrieking girls, I could be at least a decade older.

"Oh, my god, I know," Platinum Girl concurs.

"Really?" I say, trying to contribute to the conversation.

"You really don't know him? So, get this, he published his first book, *Roots*, at twenty-one. Twenty-one!" She lets that info sink in, giving us the I-know-even-more look. "I'm Sophia, by the way," she adds.

"Hi, I'm Heather and she's Gabby." Nods and smiles all around. Heather and Sophia, although their styles are optically contrary—with Heather looking like America's sweetheart in her blonde braids and angelic smile, and Sophia with near-white hair and nose piercings—I feel like they are going to be instant best friends. They're still chatting away after almost all the chairs around the table have been claimed.

I look at my watch, which is an old Cartier Tank Simon gave me. Whoever Colt James is, he is almost half an hour late. I roll my eyes in disgust, and the fact that now I know he is *hot* adds even more to my irritation.

"I hope you don't have very high expectations of this class." The crisp, mild voice comes from behind me, as someone enters the room, dragging the screaking wooden door shut behind him. I turn sideways to get a better view of my new professor, but instead my sight lands on the leather jacket he is tightly clutching with one hand.

Our eyes meet. It's him.

There are no sparks flying, no rainbows or stars over my head, but there are uncomfortable flutters in my stomach. Butterflies.

His soulful eyes bore into mine, and a glint of a smile forms on one side of his mouth. I bend my head, cursing under my breath. I nervously start shaking my leg. Heather looks at me teasingly, as if to tell me that she knows fully well how I feel. But she doesn't, because she wasn't there when I made a fool of my-self in front of this guy, who as fate would have it, is actually my professor. It's official. My first day is a complete disaster of epic proportion.

Then, a realization hits me, and like a crazy person I smile. All these things—the simplicity of being awkward in an un-known place with an unknown guy and a number of unknown people—these are the things that I'd rather face than that thick envelope on top of my kitchen table still waiting to be signed.

I sigh.

I slowly look up, more confident than I was a few seconds ago, and I match his glare. He raises one thick eyebrow slightly, impressed that I'm meeting his challenge. I actually am not. I just want to fake it until I make it.

"My name is Colt James," he says, dropping his jacket at the back of the chair across from me—one of the vacant ones next to Sophia. Sophia cranks her head up to look at him. There's visible awe in her gaze. He then backs up toward the window, leans against it, and crosses both his legs and his arms effortlessly. "People call me Colt. Students call me Mr. James. I don't care how you call me, really, but let me make one thing clear—I don't want to see crap in this class." The room goes silent, dead silent. Like when the air conditioner stops all of a sudden, and every single sound becomes so creepily distinct around you. It's like that. Even the noise from outside seems to have stopped. "You were chosen to attend this class based on the sample pages you sent during registration. This is not a class where you will learn Creative Writing 101. I don't do that. This is a class where I will personally tell you if your writing sucks and if you should just give it up." His voice is not loud or boastful; it's chilly, frightening. Imagine listening to a vampire speak—slowly and long and lingering. The word "sucks" coming out of his mouth even sounds different. He makes the word sound intelligent, and I don't know if that's even possible. I hear sighs all around. "And no. I'm not one to give someone a pep talk. This is not my MO. Understood?"

The door opens widely, breaking the chilly ice that is Mr. James's warning. A young man in his early twenties walks in.

"You. What's your name?" He's obviously annoyed. Sophia turns around to face Heather and me, and widens her eyes in a mix of fear and admiration. Then Heather touches my knee, trying to stop my leg from shaking. I look at her and she smiles at me sympathetically.

"Scott," the young man replies softly, obviously uneasy.

"Speak louder," Mr. James booms.

"Scott!" It sounds more like a scream. I feel terrible for Scott. I look in my professor's direction and squint at him in clear annoyance. He challenges my glare but instantly looks back at Scott.

"Don't be late in my class again, Scott."

"Yes, sir. . . ."

I roll my eyes. I'm too old to endure this kind of crap. He sees it.

"Sit down, Scott." He gets up and starts walking around the tiny room. All heads follow him like starstruck apprentices. I suppose I can't really blame these kids for their ambition. I should celebrate that along with them. I'm here, am I not? And hopefully I'm here because, after almost two decades of complacency, I'm ready to do more. I do hope so; otherwise I'm just wasting a ton of money to get my mind off Simon.

I feel him stop right behind my chair. I don't move or turn around. I stay where I am, looking out the window. I see Sophia give me a glare, but I don't budge.

"As you can see, this is a small class," he says. I can almost feel his breath on top of my head. "We will have intimate discussions about your writings. Let's get personal," he continues, charming all the young ladies in the room but one. Yes, me. Although I wouldn't be too sure, since for a time earlier today, I was so enamored of him that I couldn't shake his image out of my head. "Tell me your names and why you're in my class." I feel his hand resting at the back of my chair and tapping it lightly. Scott, bless his soul, who is sitting on my far left, gives me a knowing glance as if in warning. I don't react or say anything. Colt walks around the table, stops directly behind Sophia, and stares at me. "You." He nods at me.

"Uhm. . . ." Definitely a bad way to begin. "My name is Gabriella Martin . . . oh, Stevens." I shake my head, my bravery and confidence lost in mere seconds. "My friends call me Gabby. You can call me whatever you want."

"So, Ms. Martin . . . oh, Stevens?" he confirms.

"No, just Stevens." I match his glower.

"You forgot which one was your last name?" He's challenging me, and I'm furious that he thinks he has the right to this starkness and sarcasm.

"No," I say more sternly than I intended. "If you really care to know why I got confused about my last name there for a second, it was because I used to be Martin, but since my divorce papers finally came just this Saturday, I'll probably have to start using my maiden name again. Stevens. I hope that answers your question." I see him take a step back, and the softness in his face, which I saw a glimpse of this morning, is apparent again. I can feel my cheeks heating up. Everyone's eyes are on me—some in sympathy, some in shock. The room becomes awkwardly silent.

"Well, Ms. Stevens, divorce is a good place to start," Colt says, his look of surprise vanishing. "I expect good writing out of it." He moves on and calls on Heather next. I clutch both sides of my seat to steady myself. I don't think I've ever been so pissed off, not even at Simon, and he has done a pretty horrible thing to me.

I try to calm myself down as he moves around the room asking everyone the same question. I don't look at him anymore, because if I do, he'll notice how angry I am, and how this is ruining my normally calm aura. I feel like crying in anger, and I don't cry easily. I was just handed my divorce papers over the weekend, and not a single tear dropped. I clutch my seat tighter. If I let go, I'm afraid I might storm out, and then he wins. If his goal is to scare or insult or infuriate his students, I think he's accomplished that.

I sense him moving around the room until he stops right in front of me again. I slowly lift my chin up to meet his gaze. There is weight in his eyes, an unnerving pull. I don't look away.

"Academic writing has no place in this class. In this room I want you all to be yourselves, and to be able to explore the depths of your souls." As he says this, he looks straight into my eyes. "This is not drama. So, if it doesn't need to be dramatic, let's not put it anywhere." He walks to the window and leans, finally letting go of my gaze and resuming his earlier stance, crossed legs and arms. "Look, I had a teacher who was so uptight he wanted me to put two spaces after every period." The class relaxes a little, and some even manage to laugh. "That is not creative writing; that is technical writing. Anybody can learn those things. They're in a book. Remember the rules and you'll be fine. In fact, you can carry the book of rules around if you want." He unfolds his arms and brushes invisible dirt off his sleeve. "That teacher also told me that I should not use the words 'nope' or 'yeah,'" he says without looking up at us. "But, if you think those are the only words that can truly express who you are, use them." And then he looks up and stares at each one of us in his class with such intensity. "Creativity cannot be learned. It is a talent. If you're here, you know you have it. I read your work. Those sentences had so many grammatical flaws, and style guide infractions, but they were all . . . yes, creative. That's why writers have editors. They are pretty much our help—we pay them to clean up our beautiful work. So, in this class, if you're angry, be angry. If you're sad, be sad. If you're happy, don't be cheesy, but show it anyway. Explore that, express that, be that, and creativity will flow. Welcome to Creative Expressions."

I find myself staring at him, entranced. And I hate myself for it.

Chapter Three

My phone rings as I rush to cross Times Square from Seventh Avenue to Broadway.

I've been clutching my phone since I left the apartment, just in case Felicity calls to change her mind about where we'll meet up before the dinner party I was coerced to attend. Felicity and I agreed to grab a drink at John's Bar at six thirty.

It isn't Felicity. Simon's face flashes on the screen. I stare at my phone, battling an inner debate whether or not to take his call. I have to at some point, and I know it. Not right now, I tell myself, and the ringing suddenly stops. I don't have voicemail set up so it's likely he'll call again. I turn off the ringer, drop my phone inside my purse, and continue on toward 48th Street.

New Yorkers hate Times Square. They try to avoid it by all means. But I love Times Square. The vibrant billboards, the colorful electronic advertisements, and the noise of life—they give me energy. I feel like I'm at the center of the world when I'm here. There is no space for sadness or melancholy. There's always just the now, like a time warp. I'm at a standstill as I soak it all in. The swarm of tourists this time of day, especially on a Saturday, is like nothing you've seen before or anywhere else.

I'm early. I have about twenty minutes to kill, and John's is just another five minutes away. I breathe a heavy sigh as I look around me. It never gets old.

This is home.

I never really imagined that I would one day call New York City mine. Simon, Felicity, and I moved here after graduating from Georgetown. Simon received a degree from the McDonough Business School, while Felicity and I graduated with degrees in communications. Simon got a job on Wall Street a few months before we arrived and started his master's at Columbia a few months after we got settled. He was in school during the evenings and worked really hard at his job during the day, which quickly moved him to the top. Felicity jumped straight to a master's program at NYU, started teaching part-time almost immediately, and was later hired by *The New York Times*. I was never as driven as those two. I felt like ever since middle school, I've followed them around. I loved being part of our trio. So it was a surprise to everyone when I ended up valedictorian, with Simon and Felicity tied for second place.

As Simon and Felicity's careers flourished, I floundered. I wanted to have children. That had been my focus for a long time. After years of trying, Simon one night drunkenly confessed that he had never really wanted them. It broke my heart a little, but I trusted that Simon only had the best intentions for us both. I never brought up the topic again and went to the doctor the next day for an IUD.

I was content being Simon's wife. Some people from his office called me "the perfect wife," and I was fine with it. My mother was happy about it too. We were at the very same spot in our respective marriages. She was proud of the daughter I'd become. All I wanted was for Simon to be happy and for us to be happy together. I really thought he was until he met his assistant. Suzanne. I shouldn't be thinking about this tonight. Again, I remind myself, not tonight.

Felicity is already at John's when I walk in, her phone tucked between her shoulder and her ear.

"Bye," she says into her phone and yanks me right out of the bar before I even get the chance to say hi. With her hand firmly clasping my arm, she hails a taxi as soon as we step outside. This is a horrible idea in this part of Manhattan at this time of day.

"What is going on?" I ask, nonplussed.

"I thought dinner was at seven thirty, but it's at seven. With this traffic, we'll probably not make it on time." For all that Felicity is—her brilliant mind, her creative spirit—yes, she can also be a forgetful klutz, and I love her for it.

With the one-way streets and cars on a standstill at every direction, we still manage to make it before seven o'clock. Our driver was a star, dodging every possible road mishap as Felicity coaxed him to hurry.

"Are you sure this is the address?" I inquire, as we stand outside a townhouse that looks like it's worth millions of dollars. Big windows, black metal gates, and massive double oak doors. Felicity was invited by one of her colleagues from NYU, a woman named Tina, for a back-to-school dinner with other professors. "She's a professor like you, right?" I raise one eyebrow skeptically as I ask this.

"Yeah, she teaches undergrad theater." I can see there's confusion in Felicity's face too. Unless you are a big Hollywood celebrity based in New York City, or a big music superstar, or a truly successful banker, this is out of your class. This is a mansion in Manhattan. I don't think a regular NYU professor can afford to live here.

"Call her; we don't want to disturb rich people having some quiet time in there," I say. But it doesn't look quiet. There is light coming out of every window, even on the top floor, and there are shadows of movement inside that are visible through one of the lower windows.

Felicity and I balance on our tiptoes in an attempt to look in. Then I notice that Felicity seems taller tonight. When I look down at her feet, I see that she's wearing higher heeled shoes and a noticeably shorter skirt. Her hair is styled differently too. I brush my palms over my jeans, trying to straighten an invisible crease and feeling a little self-conscious. At this house, with Felicity making an extra effort with her appearance, I can almost guarantee that I'm underdressed for this dinner party.

"Fine, just ring the doorbell," I urge. Felicity pushes the tiny metal button on the side of the door. Even their doorbell fixture is fancy. We hear someone walking toward the door. A tall, skinny, blue-eyed blonde, who looks like the young Cameron Diaz from *There's Something About Mary* with longer hair, opens the door. I stand there staring at one of the most beautiful women I've ever seen up close.

"Felicity! You made it!" She opens the door wider, lets us both in, and gives Felicity a big tight hug. I can hear the chattering further down the hall.

"Thank you for having me," Felicity says, sounding hoarse from the tight embrace. Once out of the blonde's grip, Felicity introduces us. "Tina, this is my plus one, Gabby."

"Nice to meet you, Gabby. Thank you for coming."

"No, thank you," I say, and I pull out a bottle of red wine from my purse and hand it to her.

Tina, an enigmatic presence, leads us down the hall to a big living room that doubles as a library. A beautiful, imposing, old-fashioned brick fireplace is situated at the far end of the room. The house looks even bigger and more expensive inside.

"Colty," Tina turns and calls someone behind her. "Felicity and her friend Gabby made it."

I stop in my tracks and suddenly feel deflated.

Colty, it turns out, is none other than Mr. Colt James.

Colt walks toward us with a slight smirk on his face. He looks infuriatingly attractive and annoyingly breathtaking in his black jeans and white dress shirt with sleeves rolled up to his elbows. At least he's wearing jeans too. His hair is styled like he doesn't give a damn about it, disheveled in an obnoxiously trendy way, but still managing to pull the I'm-so-cool vibe. I suck in my breath loudly, a little disoriented by how this man makes me feel. He stops next to me, and I whiff the scent of wood and cider.

He doesn't look all that surprised to see me, and I can only imagine the look on my face. Stunned.

"Hey," he says to both Felicity and me.

"Hey, Colt. This is my friend, Gabby. I told you about her the other day. She's in your class, right?"

"Yes, hi, Ms. Stevens."

"Hi, and please call me Gabby," I say lowering my head to avoid his gaze.

The doorbell rings. Tina excuses herself and walks right back to the hallway toward the door.

"I'm glad you guys could make it," Colt says. Is this his dinner party too? If that's the case, well, there is no doubt he's with the supermodel. I stop myself as soon as I think this because the malice and sarcasm in my thoughts are palpable. Why do I care anyway?

"Let me get you guys drinks." Felicity and I follow him back to the hallway and walk across to enter a spacious den. There's a fully stocked bar set up next to a massive flat screen TV. Some of the guests are watching sports, but I can't quite figure out what; it's foreign, like cricket, maybe.

"Felicity Adams . . ." A cute guy with black-rimmed glasses comes over and plants a kiss on Felicity's cheek. They move farther away, leaving Colt and me alone. There's a bartender behind the oak bar looking crisp and smart in a tuxedo. If he's wearing this fancy costume here, that definitely means I'm underdressed for this occasion. I find Colt watching me as I indulge in my internal monologue.

"We have red, white, rosé, and sparkling, vodka, gin, tequila, beer, scotch, and whiskey." The bartender recites the list with confidence.

"Red wine, please."

"We have merlot, zinfandel, and malbec."

"Malbec is good, thank you."

"Not my guess, but excellent choice." Colt narrows his eyes and looks at me curiously. "Can I have scotch on the rocks, man?"

"Why?" I ask.

"Huh?" He looks at me, surprised.

"Why was it not your guess?"

"Well, I see you as the sweet kind of wine drinker," he says.

"Well, no. I hate sweet wine. I like them dark, dry, and woody." I sound snappy.

We stand there together in awkward silence while we wait for our drinks. The mirror backing the bar shelves reflects Colt and me side by side, and I, irritatingly, like what I see. Our eyes meet in the mirror. I feel a sudden jolt like the one I experienced the first time I met him. I give him my Gabriella Stevens awkward smile— all teeth and blank eyes. He almost bursts out laughing and covers his mouth with his fist. I can't help rolling my eyes.

"You think you'll ever stop hating me, Gabby?"

"I don't hate you, Mr. James."

"Really, Mr. James? Is that what you're calling me? No offense, but I have a feeling we're the same age, Gabby."

"I doubt that," I reply sarcastically. I've confirmed that I'm actually almost seven years older than him, but I don't offer this information.

The handsome bartender hands over my wine, which Colt accepts and courteously offers to me. Our fingers accidentally touch and send tingles down my spine. I close my eyes in embarrassment because I have never imagined myself feeling this way toward another man. I don't remember even feeling like this with Simon.

I take a sip of my wine and look around for Felicity. She catches my eye and walks toward us. I'm dying to ask her if Colt and Tina are a couple, or are living together, or are married. Why these questions are in my mind is a mystery to me. I'm going through a divorce and shouldn't be crushing on my new professor.

"Red wine for me too, please."

As soon as the cute bartender hands Felicity her drink, and Felicity mouths "Hot" to me, Colt leads us back to the hallway that connects to a large foyer.

The lighting in the foyer is vivid—not bright, but vibrant— and the white walls make it sharper. The space provides contrast to the colorful, well-curated art pieces in the room.

I look around with profound admiration, and I stop at one particular piece in the center. I take a step closer and prop my head up to get a better look.

The piece is an abstract in hues of dark blue, pink, and white. It portrays a moving rhythm, swirling, mixing the colors together and connecting them. That, right there, is talent. My attempt to swirl colors like that would likely turn out like accidental splatters of paint. I arch my head slightly to the left to look at the painting from a different angle and realize that whichever way I look, I get the same feeling. This is how you fall in love with art—it brings out beautiful feelings from within you. Lightness. Peace. Calm.

"You like the piece," Colt whispers from behind me, close enough for me to feel his breath on my ear. He's a foot taller than I am, so he must have bent down as he said this. I refuse to turn around and face him.

"It's powerful," I say, closing my eyes as I speak, and glad that he can't see my face. His nearness is affecting me in ways I can't explain.

"Do you like art?" I feel him taking a step toward me.

"Yes," I whisper, trying to catch my breath.

"I'm very glad that this piece made an impression on you." We stand there motionless, our bodies touching, and I can feel the heat emanating from him. His breathing is slow but heavy.

Maybe it's just my imagination, but I can sense that our closeness affects Colt as well. And why is he standing so close to me, anyway?

I feel my hands tremble a little. Nerves.

We must have lost Felicity along the way to the foyer because she suddenly pops right in front of us.

Colt and I are both startled, like we've been caught doing something inappropriate.

"Is that your phone?" Felicity asks, pointing at my purse. I suddenly feel the vibration.

I break away from Colt's nearness and search for my phone inside my purse. From the looks of concern from Colt and Felicity, I can tell that my expression is giving away the caller's identity.

"Don't answer." Felicity pleads, probably afraid that this will dampen my party mood.

"I've been dodging his calls all week," I say, lowering my voice so Colt can't hear, which is nearly impossible because he's no more than a couple of feet away from me, my phone, and my thudding heart. He doesn't need to know the details of my distress. But as I lift my eyes to steal a look at him, his attention is all on me, and there is kindness in his stare, a certain gentleness that speaks straight to me.

"Do you need some privacy to take that call? You can use the study upstairs. C'mon, let me take you," Colt offers. He looks away as he says this, like he too is embarrassed for knowing what this call means. There is no point hiding this situation after our tense little exchange in class on Monday.

"Why are you taking it now, of all times, Gabs?" Felicity asks with grave concern.

"I think she should take this call tonight. If everything goes south, at least we're here for her. I can't imagine taking this call alone would make it any easier." I look at him with gratitude as I realize he truly understands what this call means to me. He has remembered.

"Do you want me to go with you?" Felicity asks.

The phone stops vibrating.

"No, I'm fine," I reply, and I walk behind Colt up the steps. The big wooden staircase is a majestic vision all by itself that leads to three more floors above us. We stop on the second floor. A few steps away, Colt opens a door that leads to a small study. He moves sideways to let me in. I don't know why I feel this self-conscious around him.

"I'll close the door. You have a few minutes before dinner, so take your time," he says, closing the door quietly behind him. He's definitely a host of this party, and no doubt is an occupant of this expensive home.

What is his relationship to Tina? And why am I so concerned?

There is a desk in the corner of the room facing the window. A couple of big bookcases grace the wall on one side, and a luxurious love seat is positioned next to the desk. This is not a man's space. I can envision Tina in here.

I feel my phone vibrate inside my purse again. I blow out a heavy sigh, preparing for this conversation I'm not ready to have. I haven't spoken to Simon since I received the divorce papers. I don't know what else to say to him. I swipe the green icon on my iPhone to answer.

"Gabby?" I'd like to believe there is concern in his voice. "Are you there? Are you okay?" I try to catch my breath. I still need to get used to the fact that he's no longer a part of me, that our conversations will, from now on, be strained, and that we're not even friends anymore.

"Hello, Simon? Yes, I'm here." I slowly lower myself down on the loveseat.

"I've been calling you since Monday," he says.

I don't answer. I don't know what to say. We're silent for a little while.

"Are you home? Can I drop by?" He sounds hurried, anxious. And my instinct suggests he wants to make sure I sign the papers.

"No. And I haven't signed them yet, if that's the reason you've been calling. I'll call your lawyer on Monday."

"Can we—I—expect them next week?" We. The "we" I'm no longer a part of, and that right there brings pain that pierces my soul.

"Sure."

"Gabby." He says my name like I've heard it a million times before, but now the sound of my name in his voice seems unfamiliar. "I'm sorry. . . ."

"Let's not do this. I'll have the papers signed by Monday, and I'll mail them the same day." I'm so proud of myself for staying composed and collected. This new confidence I have is a welcome surprise. "I have to go. I'm late for dinner." I push the end button, and the line is dead.

I wait for my sadness to return, for the pain I felt minutes ago, but I am empty. I try to reach within for any kind of emotion, because I believe I deserve it—but there is nothing. I am silent.

I can hear the chatter downstairs, faint classical music playing in the background and laughter all around. Downstairs, where everything is fun and free, is where I should be.

I get up and look around the room. There is a big portrait of Tina by the door, which I didn't notice earlier. I stop to stare and appreciate it. She is at the beach, in a white-and-red bikini under a big straw hat. Although her body is facing the photographer, her face is angled backwards looking at the horizon. You can feel the magic of the photograph. She looks like she belongs there.

The portrait is intimate and personal. The photographer has captured her very essence, and you can tell there is great love in the moment.

I think about my place in this world: in New York City, in this tiny room, in me. That is where I belong—with me. That's not something I should be scared of anymore; it's something I should celebrate. I'm stronger today than I was yesterday. I know that I will be stronger tomorrow than I am today. One day at a time.

I look at my reflection in the full-sized mirror hanging at the back of the door. I dust invisible dirt off my jeans, tuck my tank top back in, and pull my chambray blazer tighter around me. I look hideous in these jeans. Tina, on the other hand, who looks gorgeous in this portrait, looks elegant tonight in a floor-length caftan that doubles as an evening gown. Yes, I tell myself again, I am without a doubt underdressed for this party. I bend down to grab my purse on the floor and start searching for my lip gloss inside the black hole that is my purse. I had to use a bigger tote tonight because of the bottle of wine I had to carry. I reach for my lip gloss and dab some on my lips. Not that it will make any difference standing next to Tina. I put some gloss on my finger and blot it into my cheeks as well. A little shimmer doesn't hurt. In fact, I'll probably need a lot of shimmer in my life from here on out.

I find my glass of wine on top of the table across the hall when I step out of Tina's study. Under it is a white mono-grammed CJ napkin with a handwritten note that says:

"Take your time—Mr. James."

It starts like a whirlwind in the pit of my stomach. Then it travels upwards in a slow swirling motion, and when the intensity picks up, it fills my heart with excitement, giddiness, and exhila-ration—a smile, which right now is as true as it's been for quite a while, because it's for no one other than myself.

I reach for the glass, sip the wine, and shove the note inside my purse.

Chapter Four

As I descend the stairs, the foyer is empty except for an elderly couple whispering to each other, inspecting the same painting I admired earlier. I hear distant chatters from the living room, which means dinner hasn't started yet.

I wander into the den and look around for Felicity. She's nowhere to be found. Tina, looking radiant and animated, is engaged in a lively conversation with a woman with pink hair and a septum ring. When I reach the entryway to the living room, Colt immediately sees me. There is no surprise in his stare, but I see anticipation. He excuses himself from his conversation and slowly makes his way toward me.

"Everything fine?" The softness in his gaze relaxes me. All of a sudden my defenses come up. He looks like he's going to hug me, or kiss me, or hold my hand. I jerk away a little. I suddenly feel mortified. I don't quite understand why I react this way around this man.

"Yes. Thanks." I look at him intently as if searching for something in his eyes. I instantly look away hoping he doesn't see how his attention is making me feel a little off, strange—good strange. Considering.

Tina claps her hands together to get everyone's attention.

"Dinner is served. It's buffet style. Find your seat with your name on the table in the dining room," Tina announces.

As we push our way to the dining area, I crank my head

higher to search for Felicity. There in the corner I see her talking to a guy wearing an orange fedora and bright pink suspenders. He's hard to miss. I smile. I'm glad Felicity is having a good time. When I turn around, Colt has disappeared. I feel a little disappointed.

I move with the crowd. There are sixteen of us, if I've counted right. I smile to a few ladies walking next to me. When we reach the dining room, I look around the table for my name, praying under my breath that Tina didn't forget about me. Thankfully, I immediately see it written beautifully with a fountain pen on a gold and glittery place card. I look at the name card next to mine. Colt.

"You again," he says, appearing next to me out of nowhere.

"Yeah, can't shake me off that quickly. . . ." I close my eyes instantly, regretting the second I say it. It sounds like an unsuccessful attempt to flirt. Either Colt is not detecting any of my bloopers, or he's simply giving me a free pass tonight—with my going through divorce and all.

The table has been meticulously set. The details are impeccable with every fork tine in a flawless row, the wine glasses sparkling like diamonds. Three multicolored clusters of peonies serve as centerpieces, equidistant from one another, pulling the entire look altogether. I have been to a lot of formal dinner receptions with Simon, but there's no comparing this table with any of those that I've seen before. This table is fun, creative, and inspiring. It sets the tone for relaxing conversations.

After everyone has found their respective chairs, the lights are dimmed by one of the wait staff, creating a more intimate and tranquil atmosphere. Sets of brightly burning candles scattered around the table provide a perfect cozy glow and make me feel unexposed. I appreciate the anonymity because, aside from Colt and Felicity, these people are strangers to me.

The guy sitting on my left is one of Tina's friends from grad school. Princeton. His name is Ben. Born in the Philippines, raised in North Carolina. We have the same Filipino ancestry in common, so we hit it off right away, and he is an all-round funny guy. I don't remember laughing as much in the past six months. It feels good. Plus, he's cute too.

"So, how about you? How do you know Tina?" he asks.

"Honestly, I just met Tina tonight. I'm someone's plus one."

"Oh." There's a slight shift in his expression: displeasure maybe, or disappointment. I can't quite place it.

"I'm my best friend's plus one," I add, looking around the table and pointing out Felicity.

"Ah," Ben says, and a hint of a smile forms on his lips. What am I doing? It feels weird that I'm actually setting myself up for some flirting opportunities. I've not even signed my divorce papers yet. I sigh. I can't believe I feel guilt. I shouldn't feel this way, I know, because I can guarantee that Simon is with Suzanne right this minute and not thinking about me at all. I roll my eyes in disgust.

"Are you rolling your eyes again?" I jerk a little when Colt suddenly whispers in my other ear. I feel his warm breath and I shiver a little inside.

"What?" In a daze, I am lost. I feel a tingle down my spine, and I hate it. Not that I can help it. I turn around to look at him, our faces inches away. He sucks in his breath and stares straight into my eyes.

Is he flirting with me? We're in Tina's house. This is just all wrong.

"How's it going, Ben?" And just like that, the moment disappears.

"Good. Good. I decided to move to the city, finally."

"Wow. You're giving up your house in Long Island?"

"Yeah. It's time. I really don't need that much space. And I'm in the city all the time anyway."

"Right." Colt inches closer, moving both his legs next to mine. I'm sitting between two good-looking men, but no one is talking to me. I pretend to listen. Nodding my head, smiling some, and making appropriate facial reactions. Then Colt drapes his arm around the back of my chair and leans even closer to me. I look at him, but he doesn't return my gaze. He seems totally absorbed in his conversation with Ben. Then I feel his hand settle on my knee. Before I know it, I'm half in his embrace. Ben looks at us uncomfortably.

"Will you folks excuse me. I need to use the rest room." Ben stands up and leaves.

"Not him."

"Huh?"

"He's a dick."

"He seems really nice."

"I'm actually saving you from a bad night."

"Is that right?" I ask sarcastically, with a hint of playfulness. "What did you think I was planning to do, sleep with him?" I'm feeling bold.

"You're right, it's none of my business. I apologize." His warm breath touches my cheek. I like the closeness. This, right here, is a recipe for disaster. I've not even signed my divorce papers yet, I remind myself again.

When Ben comes back, he and Colt resume their conversation. I learn that Colt recently signed a new book deal, though he jokingly admits he hasn't started writing yet.

"I have to find the time, man. It's tough. Too many distractions." Colt says, looking at me ambiguously. I can feel myself blush. Ben laughs.

Ben is also a writer. He is a regular contributor to *The Atlantic* and *The New Yorker*. I look from one gorgeous man to the other, fascinated that I'm sitting between two brilliant literary minds. I think about my own dreams, which I had to put on hold because I thought being married was more important to me than my ambition. I was brought up in a culture where wives stay at home. My parents have always been happy, and I didn't think it was something I needed to question.

When I check on Felicity, sitting at the other side of the table, she is still talking to the same guy. Even from a distance, I see that her eyes light up every time he speaks. She keeps tucking her hair under her ear, which means she is terribly nervous and self-conscious. Sometimes that feeling is a good thing. It keeps you on your toes.

I excuse myself after dessert. Walking past the buffet table, I see Tina clearing some dishes away. She smiles weakly at me, and I notice a change in her face. She looks exhausted and a little pale. One of the wait staff is carefully replenishing the buffet table with fresh food. I smile back at her. I feel guilty all of a sudden. I hope she doesn't think I'm flirting with Colt. Appallingly, for a moment there during dinner, I actually was.

I make my way to the restroom. Once inside, I take my time.

I splash some cold water on my face and put on a new coat of lip gloss. I look into my eyes through my reflection in the mirror. I look different, like a cloud has been lifted. One party is not going to change how I feel about my circumstances—I'm still getting a divorce and I'm still losing part of my family—but tonight has helped. I lightly brush a stray hair off my face and tuck it behind my ear. My attention shifts to the white pearl earrings I'm wearing, which were a gift from Simon. I used to love them. Now I should probably give them away. It is regrettable that all my prized possessions, some of which I dearly love, are now a constant reminder of our failed marriage. This means I have to dispose of twenty years of my belongings. I involuntary start thinking about all of our shared mementos in the apartment and begin a mental list of things I intend to keep and things I should let go.

I'm about to open the door when a loud knock surprises me. "Someone's in here," I say, a little irritated. More hurried knocking ensues. I swing the door open wide in a hurry.

I see Tina clutching her midsection and looking awfully pale.

"Tina! Are you okay?!" She drops to the bathroom floor holding tightly onto my arms. I grab her and her caftan is wet. Red. Blood.

"Tina?! God, you're bleeding! Let me get some help!" My voice trembles as I say this. I'm about to get up and run for help when Tina's fingernails dig into my skin.

"Don't. Please don't . . . don't leave me." She's so pale it looks like the blood has drained from her face. I'm trapped under her, and I hold on to her tightly, trying to calm her.

"Shh, I'm here. I'm not going anywhere." Her eyes are piercing into mine, pleading for help.

"Help!" I shout through the door. "Anyone! Help us here in the bathroom!" The panic in my voice is apparent. A waiter comes running to check on us. "Call nine-one-one now! And find Colt immediately." Tina presses her body against mine, holding on for dear life. "Tina, talk to me! What are you feeling? Why are you bleeding? Tell me! Oh, my god, please talk to me!" I'm quite sure everyone from the next room can hear me. Colt rushes in, sees Tina, and immediately drops to the floor.

"What's happening?" Colt's face is ashen. He looks at me for an answer, which I don't have. I shake my head to indicate my own confusion. "Tina!" He shakes her for dear life.

"Tina, sweetheart. Please hold on tight, okay. Help is coming. First, tell us what we can do. Is there pain?" I ask. She nods her head violently, and then she screams. I hold her tighter. Colt grabs both her arms, stroking them soothingly. "Should we move her?" I ask, looking to Colt for direction.

"No. We don't know what's going on." There is vulnerability in Colt's posture. Tina means a lot to him; I can tell. His beautiful face is a reflection of horror. He is white as a ghost. I stop myself from reaching out to touch his soft cheek and shake my head to gather my thoughts.

This man belongs to someone else.

"Five minutes. They said they'd be here in five minutes!" Ben rushes into the bathroom, holding the phone to his ear. He's talking to the 911 operator. "Yes, she is bleeding. There's a lot of blood." Ben looks at Tina and brushes his hair with his fingers forcefully in distress. "Yes, yes, there's a lot of blood on the floor too. It looks like she's in pain. Sitting down. Yes, upright, but on the floor. Our friend is supporting her from behind. Cradling her. Yes. Do we need to do anything else? We don't know. How did it happen, Gabby?" Ben looks at me questioningly, brushing his fingers through his hair again in obvious distress.

"She fell on me, and I saw a lot of blood. That was all. She was clutching her stomach the entire time." Ben relays my answer to the operator. The horror in his eyes is no different from Colt's.

These minutes are the longest of my life. The energy that comes with fear makes everything crystal clear. I can see every drop of sweat from Tina's forehead. I can hear the loud beating of Colt's heart. My skin has become totally sensitive to Tina's tight grasp. Every fiber of my being has come alive. This is not a film I'm watching. This is real life, and the dramatic pain I felt when I received my divorce papers pales by comparison. This feels like life and death.

After a few minutes, which seems like hours, we hear distant sirens.

"They're here! Make way!" Felicity's voice reverberates from the hallway.

The paramedics enter the room with expert precision. The tiny space of the bathroom has magically grown to accommodate them and all their equipment. I'm waiting for them to take over when Tina slowly turns to face me, "Please don't let me go." Colt and I look at each other. He motions for me to say yes.

"I won't." One of the paramedics reaches out to take Tina from me. "I'll stay with her, if that's okay. You can put her on the stretcher, but I'll hold her hand until we get to the hospital."

"No problem, miss."

It takes a lot of energy to get up. I can feel my legs going numb. I push myself up with Tina's hands still clutching my arms. Fortunately, the paramedics are supporting us both. As soon as she's positioned safely on the stretcher, she grabs me around the neck. I bend my head to face her. I know this is not death, but looking into her eyes this close sends shivers down my spine. I feel her pain. I feel her fear. I let her hold onto me. Now that help has come, everything starts to be a blur. I don't need to be the strong pillar anymore. I let go somehow, and when we get into the ambulance with Tina still clinging onto me, I feel Colt rest his hand on my back. I let his hand lie there, connecting the three of us in some way, like we belong together, but in truth I am just a bystander in this picture.

Chapter Five

When we arrive at the emergency room, the doctors try to convince Tina to let me go. She pulls me closer and starts to scream. Colt and I look at each other, uncertain what to do. When the doctors eventually promise that they will call me in the waiting room immediately after some tests, Tina—although reluctantly—finally lets go.

Colt and I walk side by side toward the waiting area at a slow pace. Neither one of us speaks. Everything seems foggy. I know where I am, and I know why I'm here, but the rapid events of the past twenty minutes have put me in a very rattled mind space. I look at my hands still drenched in blood. As if by instinct, I wipe them on my equally drenched jeans. They're almost dry now. Colt reaches for my hand in haste and looks at it.

"Do you want to go to the bathroom and clean up?" His eyes are hollow. I can only imagine the storm that must be going on inside his head right now. I want to comfort him, but I don't know how. He lets go of my hand, and I walk away.

The bathroom is eerily quiet except for an electric buzzing from the florescent ceiling lights. I'm alone. I look at the mirror's reflection of the person I am tonight. I look strong. I don't think I've ever been this collected. Perhaps I'm overcompensating for my lack of control in my own life. I shouldn't even try to dissect all this tonight. There is nothing about tonight that is about me.

I turn the faucet on and let the warm water run down my

hands. I splash some on my face and arms, and I try to wash the dried bloodstains away. There are flashbacks, fast segments of my own life in my head, and I close my eyes to chase them away. My own demons are catching up to me. I can't be alone right now, so I wash myself as quickly as I can, wipe myself with rough brown paper towels from the wall dispenser, and rush back out.

The waiting room is surprisingly empty. I always have this vision of an emergency room pulled from the scenes of *Grey's Anatomy* or *Chicago MD*. I see Colt leaning against the wall in the corner, and I let him be. I sit in one of the chairs facing the doorway. I bend my body down, my forehead touching my knees, and I close my eyes. A few minutes have passed, and neither one of us speaks. I start to feel drained. After all the adrenaline rushing through my veins earlier, I feel spent.

A few minutes later, I feel Colt join me. It's a welcome nearness. I pull myself up a little, my elbow planted on my lap to support me. I turn my head toward him, and I smile. There's still terror in his eyes, but he manages to smile back. I see hints of indentations on his cheeks, dimples, which I've not noticed before. It makes his face look younger, defenseless even.

Surprisingly, he puts his hand on the nape of my neck and starts rubbing it. Perhaps he needs to feel another human being. I don't blame him. It doesn't feel sexual. It feels more like kindness. He saw how Tina grabbed onto my neck earlier. I don't know if I want to cry, or collapse in his arms, or both. I'm so tired, and my arms are so sore.

"Do you need a drink or something?" he asks with softness in his voice.

"I'm okay, but feel free to go get something for yourself. I'll be right here."

"I'm fine," he says, drawing a heavy sigh. He pulls his hand from my neck to his lap. There is nervousness and uncertainly in his stance. "Do you know what happened?"

"No." I pull my body up, and when I sit upright, our shoulders touch.

Instinctively, I put my arms around his shoulders for a hug. For a second I see shock on his face, but he welcomes my closeness anyway. We hug for a long time. No one speaks. We simply find solace in each other's arms.

"She's going to be okay, Colt." I have to say something. I don't know if he has any idea what Tina just went through. But I know because I've been there before.

"I hope so," he replies like a small boy. I pull away from our embrace. "My first thought was . . . I didn't know. That she was . . . pregnant," he says uneasily. So he felt it too. I nod slowly, not really knowing what else to say.

"She could be. But we're not sure. Let's wait for the doctors. Or, do you want me to check? I can run back in there." I'm ready to get up, but he pulls me back. I feel his sturdy hand on mine. So I stay.

After a few minutes, the door to the waiting room opens, and one of the doctors walks in. Both of us hurriedly stand up, anticipating the worst.

"She has lost a lot of blood," the doctor begins. "She had a miscarriage. And I'm sorry we can't save the baby." Colt bends his head in despair. I put my hand on his shoulder. This must be crushing him. "We'll try to get her stable, manage her pain, and maybe you can see her in a little while. I'm sorry." The young doctor walks away, leaving us in the empty waiting room.

"I'm sorry. . . ." I whisper. I reach for his hand and pull him to the sofa. He collapses onto it, and I sit next to him.

I didn't get to see what Simon's reaction would have been. He never found out. Would it have been like Colt's right now? I doubt that very much.

"I've been through this before. Tina is lucky she has you." It's not my intention to open up, but I can't help myself. Colt turns to me, puzzled. "I had a miscarriage once before. Nobody knew. Not even Felicity. I kept it from everybody. I was at the hospital by myself. It felt horrible. But it will be fine." I bend my head as I remember the moment I lost a part of myself.

"Gabby . . ."

"It's okay. It's been a long time. My ex-husband didn't . . . doesn't want any children. It was just as well it happened."

"Do you mean that?" He stares at me intently, waiting, genuinely looking at me for an answer. I don't need to tell him my truth—the truth that nobody knows about but me.

No, I say to myself. I'm answering my own doubt. I lean my head on the back of the sofa. I'm too tired to think. I don't want to be reminded of old pain. But it's here, rushing back to me, as if it happened just yesterday.

"Are you okay?"

"I am now. I wasn't six months ago, or a week ago. But I'm better. One day at a time. It's not his fault, I guess he fell in love with someone else. We've been together forever. We met in middle school and started dating in high school. Better it happens now than when we're both in our fifties. This way, I still have a chance. . . ." I laugh a little uncomfortably. "Maybe this time he would like children. I know I do. I'm sorry. That's too insensitive."

"Why?" Colt looks at me, confused.

"With this, and what you're going through. . . ."

"It isn't mine, if that's what you're wondering."

"Oh."

Chapter Six

I finally signed our divorce papers and sent them to Simon's lawyers. The weekend's episode with Tina made me realize that life is too precious to waste on regret. That night, Felicity came to get me at the hospital. We stayed for a couple more hours until the doctors told us that Tina might be out for the night, and that we all should just go home.

Monday morning means I will see Colt, my professor, again.

I'm early. I want to keep my old spot. Heather is already seated on the chair next to where Colt sat last week. Not subtle, but endearing anyway.

This classroom soothes me. It feels eerie and dark—like a lot of sad, raw stories have been told here. These brick walls must have heard it all. There is an atmosphere of the past. I bet Colt chose this room for that reason. I still don't know him, but I know him enough now to appreciate his sensitivity—he is human, and he has a heart that gets hurt and a soul that fears.

"How has your week been?" Heather asks. Today she is wearing her hair down, like a golden glow around her porcelain skin. Her pink lipstick and pink sweater complete her sweet look.

"It's okay. How was yours? How are your other classes?" Small talk and making friends, and I'm back in college all over again. I smile.

"They're amazing!" she says. The sparkle and excitement in

her eyes are apparent. I think about what drove me when I was her age, and all I can think about are Simon and Felicity. I've lived through their dreams. And I was content. But something has shifted in the past week. "How about you?" she asks.

"I have Williams for Storytelling," I say with a new zest about being in school again, making new friends, and slowly recognizing my need to aspire for more.

"Oh, my god, I tried to register for his class and it was already full. How was it?"

"The first day was great. We talked about Cinderella and fairy tales. And well, we also talked about *Gone Girl*." We both laugh.

"I hope to get him next semester, so you have to give me some tips!"

"Sure. Let me know."

She hands me her phone. I look at it like I don't know what it is. She laughs even harder. "Put your name and number on my phone," she says in between snorts. I take her phone and punch in my contacts. She takes it back and calls my phone. "Now you have my number too."

The entire class walks in after a few minutes, and following behind them is Colt. He gives me a sideways glance, which I pretend I don't see. I pull out my notebook, and I avoid his stare.

"The thing about writing . . ." he begins, walking to an empty chair and dropping off his leather jacket. "It defines who you are as a person. It evolves and revolves around you, around how you feel, or around how you perceive life. Some writers try to outsmart their truths. They try to stay away from themselves, so they write the opposite of what lives in their soul." His fire is gone, his face looks tired and weary, and all I can think about is how I want to give him a hug, to comfort him. "Good writers succeed, but new writers fail trying. Write what you know." He continues, "The more you know about your story, the more authentic it will feel to your readers. At this stage of your writing career, I highly recommend you stick with what you feel is your own." He leans back on the window in front of me and crosses his arms. "Don't try to experiment. Don't pretend to be an expert. Be an expert on your truth. Having said that, it doesn't necessarily mean you have to write nonfiction. Meaning, the characters can expose a little of who you are as a person. Or how you feel toward a certain individual in your life. Even great love songs are based on composers' innermost feelings. Whoever says otherwise is a liar. Taylor Swift didn't make money out of another person's heartbreak. She tells her story under the cover of fiction." I look at him with great admiration. I have seen this guy at his weakest, and yet here he is, being strong—or pretending to be.

I could listen to him forever. His lectures are like dance movements. The rhythm, the rhyme, they are all connected—he inspires us to weave our stories from our souls. I do get it. Sometimes our hearts can deceive us, but our souls are our truest forms.

"Heather, tell me about what you want to write about. What are you passionate about?"

"Love," she replies, and dissolves into giggles. The class giggles along with her.

"Have you fallen in love, Heather?" His face is serious. He walks slowly to the corner of the room with his head bent down and his hands clasped behind him. The ray of sunlight that follows him gives him an angelic luminosity, which is in contrast to his arched eyebrows and creased forehead.

He pauses, deep in thought. He then turns around to face us

and crosses his arms again. His taut muscles threaten to burst from the sleeves of his tight white T-shirt.

"In high school, I think. I don't know if that was love." Heather has stopped smiling.

"I don't need to know the details, but did it make you feel something? Anything? Did it make you want to write about it? Do you want it to live forever in your books?"

"I think so."

"Thinking is important in writing. But feeling is key. Authenticity is what makes art your own. Look deeper within you. Is love the central part of your story? Or the lessons you've learned from it? Or, perhaps, the things you've experienced that connect you to another genre?" He looks pensive, distant, unattached, but present. "Gabby? How about you?"

"Life."

"That's quite general. What is it about life that you want to tell?" he asks.

"How unpredictable it can be. How, even at an older age, you are still uncertain of what is. That, though you think you've got it all figured out, you'd still be left dumbfounded and ignorant." I don't look at him while I speak.

"I like that. Write it."

And he moves on. I was just trying to be a smartass. But I think about what I just said and realize it is what I want to tell. It is my story.

When the class ends, I expect Colt to talk to me—not his student, but the person he spent some very deep emotional time with over the weekend. He doesn't look my way, so I leave.

Felicity and I meet for lunch. We walk all the way to midtown and stand in line outside a ramen house.

Felicity gives me an update on Tina's condition. "I heard she's okay. She's back home. Is it Colt's?" she asks, and I shake my head. That much I know. "Well, whose is it? Those two are very tight. I don't understand their relationship, really. I just know they're always together. Colt is covering her classes this week." It makes sense.

"I mailed my divorce papers today," I say nonchalantly, changing the subject.

"Whoa!" Felicity looks at me like I've grown horns. "Good for you! You should be done with him. Forever!"

Although I get to keep Felicity, I know that this divorce is also breaking her. It's the end of the three of us. Our friendship was one both she and I had. We all grew up together. It isn't easy to let go of what we're used to.

"I'm sorry. . . ." I begin.

"For what?"

"I know Simon is your best friend too. And you don't have to lose him, you know, just because you picked a side. I'm grateful for it, but you don't have to."

"I know. I want to," she says, but I see the subtle flicker of sadness in her eyes.

"Thank you."

～✒～

A few days later I get a call from Simon's lawyers, informing me that Simon will no longer pay for our mortgage. I suspected as much, but I didn't think he would take the apartment away from me as soon as the papers were signed. I don't call Felicity or my mother to complain this time; I should give them a little reprieve. Instead, I decide to head to school, to the Student Services building. I see a lot of for-rent flyers there all the time. I should do this on my own.

On my way out of the apartment, I see Simon. We're both startled. I look at him from head to toe, and he does the same to me. We have become strangers. How could I know him so intimately and not know him at all?

"Hey," he says. I see a cloud of doubt and confusion in his eyes. He's probably expecting something different. He probably thought I'd locked myself inside the apartment, wallowing in pain about ready to kill myself.

"Hey," is the only reply I can muster.

"I didn't think you were going to be home. I thought you'd be in school. I'm just here to get a few things," he says. I should demand that he give me his keys. But I don't want to do that.

"I just talked to your lawyer. He said I should be out of the apartment. That's where I'm going," I reply.

"To where?" he asks.

"To look for a place." I am calm. I'm trying. I was never the loud wife.

"You don't need to do that right now." I can tell that he's truly sorry. But the damage has already been done. "The lawyer should have mentioned that you have at least three months. And we sell the house. I'm giving you everything we make after our mortgage is paid."

"He didn't say any of that." I sound stone cold.

"Gabby, I'm not that cruel." He brushes his hair out of his eyes. He doesn't need to redeem himself to me. It has been done.

"I know. It's fine. I'll figure it out." I don't move a muscle. I feel that any movement could break me.

"Can we go inside and talk? Do you have a class?" I shake my head. I don't know what our conversation will accomplish, but I turn around, and he follows me.

I open the door, and we walk into the apartment. This place is starting to feel like the center stage of my pain, where the spotlight always seems to be on me. He looks around and gives a heavy sigh. I can tell he feels as uncomfortable as I do.

We stand a few feet apart. And I look at this man I knew as a boy and loved as a boy. The smartass grin, the boyish smile, and his ambitious nature. I should have seen it coming. What was he doing with someone like me? I didn't do much. I wasn't much. And now I know I was not what he wanted in a partner. I was so wrong to believe he wanted me where I was. He looks different now too. His hair is longer, which is a surprise since he used to hate it when it touched the nape of his neck. I can also tell that he's been in the gym more. He has developed some muscles. He looks like a different person. His hair is still brown, his eyes are still blue, he's still six feet tall, but there is something about him that has been transformed. He's no longer the man I used to love. He has become a stranger to me.

"I've boxed some of your things in the coat closet there, if that's what you're here for." I have to say something to break the ice.

"Thank you."

"Check it out, and if there are others feel free to get them. It's your apartment too." I don't move and neither does he.

"I was actually going to leave you this note." I see him pull out an envelope from his back pocket. He bends his head and looks a little embarrassed.

"Okay. You can just leave it there. I'll read it later, I guess."

"I'm here now. You're here. So, let me just tell you."

"You don't have to. We don't have to do this anymore, you know."

"You don't even say my name anymore." He shakes his head, like he's the one broken. I don't want to be mad. "And I'm so sorry to make you go through this."

"It's done. We're okay. We're moving on. We both are." Why I'm trying to be the calm and collected side of this equation, I really don't understand. Perhaps it's because I'm so tired of the roller coaster ride and the back-and-forth. Perhaps he hasn't really processed the enormity of these changes until now. It makes sense. He's been having the time of his life with his new girlfriend, and probably didn't realize how much everything was going to change us. I have felt the change from the moment he started withdrawing from me. I saw it coming long before he did. But I shouldn't feel bad for him. This was all because he chose to leave me, and because he chose to be with someone else.

"Do you hate me, Gabs?"

"I'm done with hating. I don't hate you."

"Can we still be . . ."

"Please . . . please don't say *friends*. Please. We cannot be friends. Not right now. Not yet. Maybe someday, but not today." I take a few steps backwards, trying desperately not to be angry.

"We grew up together. You were . . . are . . . my family."

"But we also grew apart." My face is stoic. I can see that this frightens him greatly. I'm not the same girl I was two weeks ago. How can one grow up so fast in a span of two weeks, but barely grew up the previous two decades? Experience makes one a better, stronger human being. I didn't have much of that, but I'm ready to have it now.

"But that doesn't mean I never loved you." I know he's not a bad person, but I don't understand where this line of conversation is going.

"I know you did. We were kids. You protected me. You were my hero. You gave me everything that I could have ever imagined in a husband. But don't expect me to be okay right now. I told Felicity that she could still see you. You are her best friend too. And I don't want you guys to break up just because we did. I'm not that selfish. But give me my time . . . to heal, and maybe . . . I can't make any promises right now, but I'm not closing the doors, either."

"I'll take that." He smiles, and I can see that his eyes are starting to get teary. I have never seen him cry. Not once. I don't know why he's crying now. "Also, I have a check here for you. It's half of what I have in my savings account, separate from the account we own together. I just think you have to move out of this apartment. I don't want you to carry all the burden of our past by being here alone. Use this money as a down payment for a smaller apartment if you want, or I don't know, save it. I just don't want you to have to stay here alone." Until the very end, he's still trying to take care of me. This is one of the reasons why I can't hate him as much as I should.

"I'll be fine. You don't have to take care of me anymore. I can handle this on my own now. Thank you." He takes a step toward me, and I take a step back. I'm as surprised as he is. I don't want him to touch me. I don't see a need for a hug. I'm too fragile, or perhaps I've become too strong for that. He bends his head and shakes it. I don't want to ask why. I just want him to go.

He lifts his head up and looks at me. There are tears in his eyes. I'm so nervous I close my eyes and look away.

"Goodbye, Gabby."

"Goodbye . . ."

He turns around, leaves the envelope on the kitchen table, and walks out of the apartment. And I start to shake. And finally, I start to cry. Because somehow he made me feel like this was not all my fault. He blames himself, and he seems as heartbroken as I am. We've been together almost twenty years, and it will not be easy to recover from the pain of losing someone you've known that long. I let a few minutes pass before I run out of the apartment, emboldened by the thought that I'm finally free to take care of myself, to decide on my own, and plan the rest of my life.

Let's start with a place to live.

Chapter Seven

The Student Services building is quiet this afternoon. Classes are in session. I go straight to the bulletin board outside the registration office and scan through all the for-rent and looking-for-roommates flyers. There are a few employment flyers on the board too. I pull the one that is looking for a sales associate for a small independent bookstore near school. The job sounds interesting. It also says they have monthly special events with local authors. And when you say "local authors" in New York City, it's a guarantee that they are award-winning and best-selling writers.

"Are you looking for a job now?" I turn around to see Colt behind me, reading the flyer over my shoulder. I look up at him, startled. His smile turns to worry when he sees my bloodshot eyes. "Hey, are you okay?" He touches my arm lightly, and the dizzying jolt makes its presence known again. But I don't move away.

"I'm fine. Really, I am." I have to give him a reassuring nod. "How's Tina doing? I didn't get a chance to ask you on Monday in class."

"She's doing fine. She's still at home, but I think she'll be back in her classes next week."

"Good. That's good to know."

"I'm actually thinking of going home for lunch to check on her. Do you want to come?" he asks.

"I can't right now." I unconsciously put a finger on my temple and start stroking it. "I need to map out my life." My eyes widen in shock. I have surprised myself by saying it out loud. "You don't need to know that," I add, embarrassed.

"Is everything okay? Is there anything I can help with?" He is so tall I have to crane my neck so I can look at his striking face.

"I'm fine. I just need to sit down, sort myself out, and figure out the rest of my life. Too heavy." I give him a slight smile, trying to make light of the situation.

"You've been crying." He sounds worried and genuinely concerned. He takes a step closer.

"Simon was at the apartment this morning. We talked and . . . I don't know. I signed our divorce papers on Monday. I blame myself for everything. And he blames himself for everything too. We're just really sad." I smile to assure him that I'm fine.

"So, he's not as much of a dick as I thought he was."

"No. He really isn't. It's time I started taking care of myself, you know. He took care of me for almost twenty years."

"Whoa. Twenty years? How could you be with one person for twenty years? Hey, wait. What, you started dating at seven or something?" We both laugh.

"I'm not as young as you think I am, Mr. James. I'm probably almost a decade older than you."

"And yet I feel like you are a lot younger than I am in many ways. Come on, pull out all the flyers you need and let's grab coffee or lunch. It's almost noon anyway." I don't know what and who Tina is in his life, but suddenly his plan to check on her at lunch has changed. Instead he's spending it with me.

≈≈≈

I'm still leafing through the flyers in my hands when Colt stops in front of a small, dilapidated building a few blocks from campus. I abruptly stop behind him. The building looks so rundown that there are metal scaffolds scattered all over the entrance. It appears to be in the middle of a major renovation.

"Are you good with Italian?" I nod and furrow my brows a bit. He reaches for my hand, holds it like it is the most natural thing in the world, and leads me down the stairs that take us to the entrance of the restaurant in the basement.

"Are they even open?" I look at all the construction going on, and I don't think anyone would know where to enter. He laughs at me, still holding my hand, as we stand in front of a wooden door that says *Benvenuto*.

Colt pushes the door open. I'm hyperaware of our hands still clasped together, and the tingling sensation that comes with it. I let him pull me with him. It feels so natural, like I belong here, connected to him—the same connection I felt with him at the hospital a few days ago. I shouldn't be reading too much into this. We were both so vulnerable that night that it was easier to share our inner selves than it would be under normal circumstances. I've only known him a couple of weeks, and already he knows almost everything that's going on in my life.

Inside the restaurant, the atmosphere has completely changed. The heavy door blocks the sunlight, creating a cozy nighttime ambiance. Each booth has a candle burning. It looks awfully romantic. The brick walls are adorned with photos of big happy, laughing Italian families and big plates of Italian food to share.

"Welcome to Rosa's. Do you have a reservation?" A tall Italian receptionist, black hair and amber eyes, greets us with a raspy voice and bright red lipstick. I see how her eyes sparkle at Colt.

"No," Colt replies, somehow managing to make the word flirtatious, "but please tell Rosa that Colt's here."

"I'm sure we can accommodate you and your guest—" the receptionist begins, but she's cut short.

"Did I hear someone say Colt? I know that voice anywhere!" A big Italian woman walks through the swinging, saloon-style wooden door of the kitchen. Rosa looks like she's in her fifties and is wearing a flowing red dress and a flower in her hair. She gives Colt a big hug, and I take a step backward.

"Is she one of your new girlfriends, Colt?" Rosa turns around, looks at me, and winks. She has a loud, heavily accented voice. You can tell from the way she hugs Colt that she holds him dear, like a mother welcoming her long-lost boy.

"She's one of my students, Rosa," he says.

"Aha. Yes, I remember. No students for girlfriends. So, you are safe, young lady." I don't know why, but that statement clearly disappoints me. "Unless of course . . . well, why would you not want to date this gorgeous soul, *bella?*" Her loud, exuberant voice amuses me, and I smile broadly. To my surprise, she pulls me in for a hug too.

"Tara, give Mr. Colt and his student the best table in the house. And Eduardo, take care of these beautiful people, okay? I need to do some stuff in the kitchen and let you kids be. I'll see you in a little bit." She walks back into the kitchen while blowing air kisses our way.

Tara leads us to the farthest booth in the room. Eduardo appears with glasses of cold water and the menus. I grab the menu, and I suddenly feel hungry. I have not had breakfast. I didn't even have coffee today, and it's almost noon.

"Coffee! I want coffee!" I raise both my hands and clasp them together.

"You haven't even had anything to eat yet."

"I know. I got this awful call from the lawyer this morning, and I ran outside and saw Simon, and we had that big talk, and then I ran as fast as I could to school. I didn't have breakfast or coffee. And I can't live without coffee."

"Well, you seem to be alive now, so I'm sure you're fine. But yes, Eduardo, can we get this lady coffee as soon as you can, please? And then we'll order some food."

"But of course, Colt." Eduardo's accent is definitely not Italian. I smile, and when I look at Colt, he too is smiling. I don't think I've seen him like this before. His smiles are always so guarded, even at the dinner on Saturday.

"Do you come here a lot?" I ask.

"Not a lot, but often. I like Rosa and Eduardo. And I love their food. I hope you'll like it."

"I love Italian. And it smells good in here." This feels like a happy place, and I can tell it is Colt's happy place too.

"So, what's the plan, Gabby?" Colt straightens up, puts both elbows on the table, hands on his chin, and looks at me sincerely. His eyes pull me to him. I try to look away but I can't.

"I really don't know. I went to school today to try to sort out my living situation first. We're selling the apartment. I have to leave in three months. And no, it's not because Simon is a bad man. He just doesn't want me to stay there and be reminded every day of our failed marriage." I see Colt nod his head. "It actually makes sense."

"Would he at least help you out? I mean, financially."

"Yeah. I almost wish he wouldn't." I touch the candleholder

and toy with it, looking at the hypnotic flame and thinking about Simon.

"Why?" he asks. I look up at him and smile sadly in defeat.

"Simon has taken care of me since I was sixteen. I'm thirty-six years old. I should learn how to take care of myself, you know. I want to be able to take care of myself. Everyone treats me like a baby, even my parents." I don't know why it's so easy for me to share myself with Colt. There are only two people in my life who know me—Simon and Felicity. Maybe Colt will be the third. I don't even share all my intimate thoughts with my mother. Why am I letting Colt in? Should I? What is there to lose? I'm already at the heart of a big storm, so I can't see how Colt can put me in any more danger.

"Are your parents here in the city too?"

"No. Felicity and I are from Virginia, in the DC Metro area. It's not too far. I can take the bus anytime I want. It's three and a half hours by train, and about four hours by bus. I try to visit them as much as I can."

"When were you home last?"

"Six months ago. When I found out about Simon and his girlfriend."

"Oh, so he cheated on you."

"Yeah. I don't blame him."

"For cheating on you? Are you serious, Gabby? Cheating is not okay. Unless you guys agreed that you are both okay with an open marriage."

"I let myself go. I don't make an effort. I'm a little over-weight." I look up at him, interested to see how he will react.

"No, you're not!" He looks at me dead serious.

"I am too!"

"What, do you want to be as skinny as Tina?"

"Yes! She's gorgeous. Like a supermodel!"

"You're very pretty; you don't need to be skinny to be pretty. . . ." We both let his comment slide. "So, the plan? Don't change the subject, Gabby!" Now, he's teasing. And we both share a light, comforting laugh. This is what I need today.

Eduardo comes back with my steaming hot coffee. The smell is divine, so I dive right in. I add a dash of milk and half a packet of sugar. I take a sip.

"Oh, my god! This is delectable. And I don't use that word very often. Or, ever." I laugh so hard there are tears in my eyes. Colt is smiling and looking at me like I've lost my mind.

"I'm glad you like it. So now, the plan, Gabby. Stop changing the subject."

"I move out. I look for an apartment. I don't know if I want to be alone, so I'll also explore living with someone."

"How about Felicity?"

"She doesn't even know this yet. I stopped myself from calling her this morning. That girl needs a break from my drama."

"Call me." I am taken aback by this comment, and I can tell he is as well. Both of us immediately peruse the menu, not wanting to consider what this means. It feels like a whirlwind, a rushed friendship, probably a result of the tragic circumstances we experienced together a few days ago. For whatever it's worth, I guess Colt means I am branching out. I'm finally making friends outside my comfort zone—outside the confines of Felicity and Simon. I don't think that's a bad thing.

◦◦◦

Rosa's cooking is the best Italian food I've had in my life. The ingredients are fresh, and I can tell that the sauces are made from rich, healthy tomatoes. Rosa serves it herself with pride. Colt and I are having such a great time that the memory of my encounter with Simon seems miles away.

"Thank you, this is the best lasagna I've ever had in my entire life!"

"I know, right! That's what I said the first time I came here." Colt is different too. He's less guarded. He laughs more, smiles more, and I even hear him giggle a bit. Nobody who rides a Harley should giggle, but Colt totally pulls it off. And those dimples, they are like magic. They completely change his face when they appear.

"So, talk to me about you, Colt."

"What do you want to know?"

"I don't know."

"I turned thirty last month."

"Ha! Older than you, see! And a belated Happy Birthday!"

"Not quite ten years though."

"Older, nevertheless. Anyway, go on."

"I'm an only child. My parents are both dead. I'm alone. I don't have family that I know of." I stop and stare. "This shouldn't make you feel sorry for me."

"I'm not. It just makes me feel sad. I'm sorry." I don't know what has gotten into me, but I reach for his hand on the table and I hold it. I pull away a few seconds later. This is not how a teacher and student should conduct themselves.

"You shouldn't be. I've been alone a long time. More than twelve years. I'm okay. Anyway, so, after moving out, what's the next plan? We were interrupted by our sumptuous meal."

"Let's see. I think maybe that I should also look for a job. It doesn't have to be like a life-changing career. I can start with bookstores. I love books."

"There you go."

"Finish school. And take it from there."

"So, to recap, here is your plan. One, to move out and look for an apartment, but you're not sure whether you want to share it with someone. Two, look for a job. We can start with bookstores. And three is finish grad school. Am I still on the right track?"

"Yup. Pretty much." I nod in confidence. I like the sound of that plan.

"Get married. Have children," he continues.

"I just got divorced. I was in a relationship with the same person for more than half my life. I think that part of my plan can wait."

"Fair enough." He brings his coffee cup to his lips, and I stare with heightened anticipation. His lips open to touch the cup, and I immediately look away. I don't even know why I'm staring at his lips. They look soft, supple, and dead attractive. I bite my lips as an unwarranted thought enters my mind—how would those lips feel on mine?

Chapter Eight

It was hard to leave Colt. It was way past three o'clock when we left Rosa's. The other diners had come and gone, but we stayed and drank coffee after coffee. Rosa even joined us for a cup. And when she said it was time to close for the afternoon, Colt and I were pushed out with playful shoves.

Colt had a class at four fifteen, so we went our separate ways outside the restaurant. I needed that. The time I spent with him today made me feel special, different, and free.

I decide to walk in the direction of the bookstore on the flyer. After about a ten-minute hike, I am standing in front of an old-fashioned shop called Gallagher Books. I see the "Help Wanted" sign on the window and feel nervous. I don't even have a résumé with me.

My only experience in retail was when I worked for Target the year I turned sixteen because everyone from school started working that summer.

The bells above the door chime when I push it open. A gust of air brushes my face, releasing the familiar book scent I enjoy. It smells both old and new, with a hint of incense.

I slowly close the door behind me and look around. The center of the store is an open space with tables of books of different genres. On the left are rows and rows of big sturdy wooden shelves. I see that further at the back is the old titles section, where tattered books are displayed haphazardly. It's not a big store, but it is well stocked. It's cozy and quiet and just the way I like it. I walk toward the other side, where a big old leather sofa is positioned close to the window next to the fireplace.

It is crowded this afternoon, mostly students, as far as I can tell. An elderly gentleman, wearing a bow tie, sits behind the counter reading. He looks up over his glasses to watch me, and as soon as he catches my eye, he smiles in welcome. I smile back.

I pretend to browse some more, uncertain how to approach him about the job. He catches me looking at him twice, and after the third time I finally walk up to him.

"Hi," I say. He regards me with genuine eagerness.

"Oh, hello there. What can I help you with today, young lady?" His British accent is enchanting. Dumbledore from *Harry Potter* pops into my mind. If not for his clean-cut white hair, he could pass for the Hogwarts headmaster himself. I smile secretly at the thought. I can tell that this place is magic.

"Well, actually, I'm here for the job vacancy. I saw this at school," I add, handing him the flyer.

"Are you a student at NYU?" he asks, putting his book on the counter and removing his reading glasses.

"Yes, sir."

"Very well. Do you have a curriculum vitae for me?"

"This is embarrassing. I actually don't. I saw this flyer, and I ran here to check if the job is still available. I can come back tomorrow, if that's okay." His face softens, and I feel hopeful.

"You can come back tomorrow if you'd like. But since you're here, how about we have a little chat."

"I would like that. Thank you." I'm both nervous and elated, and I don't remember feeling this independent in the past decade or so. What's more exhilarating is that no one but Colt knows that I'm applying for a job. Nobody told me to do this. I'm doing this on my own.

"Come on over and walk around the counter. You can take a seat right here." He pulls out a tall bar stool for me, and I sit down. The floor is cluttered with more books. I love it. "Pardon the mess." He smiles apologetically. "So, my name is Thomas Gallagher. I prefer to be called Thomas. And your name is?"

"Gabriella Stevens. People call me Gabby."

"Nice to meet you, Gabriella."

"Nice to meet you too, Thomas." I smile at him, not because I have to, but because he's so easy to be around. I should be nervous, but I'm not anymore. His presence calms me. I have not been on a job interview since my undergrad days when I interned for a public relations company in DC that works mostly on book publicity and tours.

"So, tell me, Gabriella, why do you want to work in a bookstore?" He regards me intently. I want to tell him what he wants to hear. But I also want to say what I truly feel.

"Thomas, I started reading at age three. At least, that's what my mom tells me. Instead of toy stores, I loved going to bookstores. Growing up as a teenager and shopping with friends, I would always, always finish my shopping quickly so I could spend the rest of my time waiting for them at Barnes and Noble. I love to read. I also love to write. No, not just write. I love to create stories. I like getting lost in them. So, now that I'm finally in this amazing creative writing program at NYU, I want to surround myself with more books." I am breathless as I say this.

"Splendid. So, what kinds of books do you read?"

"I read everything: young adult, romance, women's fiction, historical drama, fantasy, thriller. You name it, and I'm on it. I'm also into pop culture, so whatever is trending in the books sphere, I'm sure to get my hands on it."

"What are you reading right now?"

"*The Picture of Dorian Gray.*" I sense him taken aback. And then he slowly smiles at me like I've just unlocked some sort of employment vault. A test.

"Interesting choice."

"I am at a very strange time in my life. I want to read more about the kind of man Dorian was."

"Strange time?"

"It's for another conversation, I think." I don't intend to tell my prospective boss that I'm currently an emotional basket case. He peers at me inquisitively.

"Very well. If you care to know, I am also rereading *Dorian Gray* this weekend. It's probably in the New York City air. Such selfish men within our midst." We are kindred spirits, I can tell. He winks at me. Even if I don't get this job, I have a feeling I will come back here again and again. This is now my new favorite bookstore. "How is your schedule in school?"

"I have three classes this semester: Mondays, Wednesdays, and Thursdays. I'm free all day Tuesdays and Fridays, after two thirty on Mondays, and after lunch Wednesdays and Thursdays. I can also work nights and weekends."

"Nights and weekends are for young souls. You should keep them open for fun. Anyway, come back tomorrow with your résumé and some references. Your references don't need to be former employers. It can be a professor or a friend who can vouch that you are who you say you are. But I have a good feeling about you, Gabriella Stevens." I like being called that. I feel a certain spark within.

"Thank you."

"This interview is over. In the meantime, feel free to browse through our books."

"Actually, I'm also here to see if you have *Roots* by Colt James."

"Ah, yes, Mr. James's angst-filled first novel. I have it in the fiction aisle. My books are alphabetical by last name, and J is on the third aisle from the door. I think I have all three novels, plus his compilation of short stories."

"Thanks."

"Is he one of your professors this semester?"

"Yes."

"He is a great teacher. A little rough around the edges, but definitely an amazing artist of his time." Thomas walks over to the cash register to help a customer. I turn around excitedly to look for Colt's books. I should have done this on the first week. I don't know why it took me this long to find out more about my professor.

Instinctively, I pull out my iPhone and Google his name. Just as I expected, thousands of search results pop up. He is an only child to Timothy James and Athena Heart-James. Both were prominent figures in the New York literary scene and both died in 2006. It was also the year his mother won the Nobel Prize for Literature. No details on their deaths. There is a news article from three days ago, a review of his new exhibit at a gallery in Soho. *He also paints?* A photo of his painting is quite similar to the big piece of art in Tina's house. It makes sense now why he was very proud of it. There are some photos of him, including some with girls on his arms. Tina is in most of them.

Colt's books are not on aisle three but in the store's bestseller section—*Roots, Listening,* and *A Grave Sunshine on the Horizon.* I read *Roots'* back cover. It's a story of a young boy who lost his parents at age fifteen. It talks about the boy's struggle to find his place in the world, and his journey in search of the human connection he has lost because of his parents' death. "Write what you know. As a new writer you should tell your truth under the cover of fiction." I remember Colt said that in class. If I want to know him, I should read his first book.

I grab all three books and proceed to pay Thomas. He is pleased to see my haul.

"Excellent. Colt's first book is his most powerful, in my opinion. It's raw and it's honest. I think that was when he was most real. So if you want to get into your professor's head, this is the way to do it."

"I'm excited to start reading it."

"He comes here to read sometimes, you know. Not often, but he comes when I host other local authors. He's a great supporter of the writing and independent bookstore communities. I usually put his name on the flyers so we can draw more people to come to other authors' book signings."

"He seems like a nice guy. I've only been in his class a few times this semester."

"Oh, he is a great teacher, but not an easy one. So, good luck. And, see you tomorrow?"

"For sure! I will be here the same time tomorrow."

"Excellent. See you then, Gabriella."

"See you, Thomas."

Felicity is waiting for me by the steps of my apartment when I get home. She has her hands on her hips, which looks like I'm in big trouble. Her eyebrows are prominently furrowed. I shake my head in wonder. I honestly don't know why I deserve that look. I start laughing because she looks seriously deranged, and her Mickey Mouse sweater doesn't help me take her seriously.

"For someone who gets kicked out of your house, you look very happy to me. Where were you? I've been texting you." Simon must have called her.

"I went to school," I say defensively.

"But you don't have a class today. Do you?" I shake my head. "Then why were you in school?"

"I was looking at apartments for rent in the area."

"You did that without calling me?" And there it is. That, right there, is the reason why I am helpless. People think I'm too weak to take care of myself. I appreciate what Simon and Felicity have done for me through the years, but I think it's time to do things on my own. One of these days, Felicity will fall in love, and she too will have to leave me. If I want to be truly independent, I have to learn to take care of myself.

"Felicity, stop! You are not my mother. You are not my husband. Please stop treating me like a child. Please, all of you stop treating me like I can't take care of myself. Don't make me any weaker than I already am." Felicity takes a step backward, and I see hurt in her eyes. Neither of us speaks for a few minutes. We let the sound of a backing truck, the loud construction man joking with his buddy, and the barking of dogs fill our silence.

"I'm sorry, Felicity. I just need to learn not to depend on anyone anymore. Because it's really painful when I fall and no one is there to catch me." My voice is soft but stern. For once, I actually believe that I can do this.

"You're right. I just thought you needed my help." She still looks awfully hurt.

"I know. I'm sorry. I thought, perhaps, you too just needed a break from my drama. Lord knows how much *I* need a break from my drama." I pull her in for a tight hug, but I can feel her hesitation. I pull away and look at her closely.

"Felicity, I need to learn to be an adult, and I want you to support me now more than ever. I'll be forty in four years, and I feel like I've wasted so much time already." I sit down on the steps and Felicity joins me.

"I also looked for a job, and had an interview for a sales associate at a bookstore near campus." She looks at me in disbelief, so I skip the part about having lunch with Colt. I don't mean to keep it a secret, but I don't want to be bombarded with questions about it. If she finds out from someone else, I know I will be in bigger trouble. But right this minute, I want it to be just mine, my secret, our secret—Colt's and mine.

"Fine. I should stop worrying too much."

"Thank you."

"I just want to make sure you're okay."

"I know, and I love you for it," I say, reaching for her hand and squeezing it.

"I love you," Felicity replies.

"I got this," I say confidently.

Chapter Nine

I arrive back at Gallagher Books at exactly three o'clock with my résumé in hand. I stayed up late last night trying to remember everything I've done with my life in the past twenty years. There was the Target job, the internship at Rochers Public Relations in DC, and some articles I published in *Darling Daily*, the *Fairfax Weekly*, our local paper in Virginia, and a small piece in *Washingtonian*. They were not big feats, but I'm proud of them all.

Thomas examines my one-page résumé with curiosity. Then he looks at me over his reading glasses, not really saying anything. I don't want to get ahead of myself, or of him, so I say nothing as well. I decide to just wait until he asks me questions.

"So, how did you manage to support yourself the past few years, if you don't mind my asking?" he finally asks.

I regard him with fear of judgment. I'm not proud of it, but it has to be said.

"I was a housewife." I shrug my shoulders to show him that this is not something I'm pleased to disclose. "I was married for sixteen years. And we were together for four years in high school before that." It feels like I've been telling this story to people on a daily basis as an excuse for why I have not done anything with my life.

"All right. And you are not married anymore, I gather?"

"I'm in the process of getting divorced right now." And that look, there it is again. The look of pity everyone gives me. My jaws harden.

"Well, all right then. By the way, I got your reference from Colt James. He dropped by last night, and I asked if you were his student. Interestingly enough, he has a lot of good things to say. Welcome to Gallagher Books, Ms. Stevens. It pays seventeen dollars an hour, and the schedule is flexible. You should own your weekends. You can take the Tuesday after-lunch shift, and Mondays, Wednesdays, and Thursdays from three o'clock to closing. We close at nine, unless we have an event going on. Also, I might need to ask you to help me with the events we do here every month.

"I would like that very, very much, Thomas!"

"You start Monday. Is that acceptable?"

I want to run around the counter and give him a hug.

My first instinct is to call Colt, but I don't have his number, which is just as well. I don't need to be dependent on anyone else, especially not on him—my professor—and besides, I barely know him. I will drop him a thank you note in class on Monday. What he did, vouching for me with Thomas, is something I'm truly grateful for.

As soon as I'm ten feet away from the store, I pull my phone from my back jeans pocket and call my mom instead.

"Gabby!" She answers on the first ring. I stop walking and move out of the way of pedestrians, mostly NYU students with their school logo hoodies and backpacks.

"Mom . . ." It's nice to hear her voice. We've always been close, with me being an only child, and so I know my silence must have affected her greatly. It was very selfish of me to do that.

"I've been trying to call you for weeks." There is desperation in her voice, punctuated by a heavy sigh.

"I know. I'm sorry. I've been really busy." And I am. Sorry. I can only imagine the anxiety she must have gone through the past few weeks.

"I don't like hearing about you from other people. I've spoken to Felicity more, but well, she told me . . . not to worry." She doesn't sound convinced.

"I'm fine. I'm officially going through the divorce process, if that's what you're asking. And, well . . . I'm looking for an apartment right now."

"Felicity told me." Felicity is like a daughter to my parents. She is one of five kids in her family, and she has always been comfortable with mine. I should have expected this.

I feel a light chill in the air. I back away further to the corner where I can shield myself from the wind. I pin my phone between my ear and shoulder, and I hug myself tight. I think it's too early, but autumn has definitely arrived in New York—my favorite time of the year.

"I'm fine. I actually just got hired at a bookstore. I wanted to share the good news with you."

"Baby . . ." It sounds like pity.

"Mom, I'm fine."

"How are you for money?" Money has never been my issue. My parents are well off, and Simon earned enough for both of us. This is my new reality, and everyone is worried for me. But I'm not worried. I wonder if it's because I know that someone is always going to bail me out. I want to prove them all wrong. I can do this.

"Simon gave me some money from our savings. I'm doing fine. I got a job because I want to do something more. It's in this small bookstore close to the school and owned by an old British gentleman who wears cute bow ties." I laugh a little.

There is a pause. My mother is never at a loss for words, so this is a first.

"I have to say . . ." she begins, then pauses a few seconds before speaking again. "I am surprised to hear your voice this . . . chirpy."

"I am chirpy," I say truthfully.

Another pause. I want to give her time to process this.

"I'm glad," she finally says. My mom doesn't concede easily, and yet here we are.

"Tell Dad not to worry, okay? I'm fine. I'm starting to do the things that I actually like." This is not pretend. I'm not saying this just to save face.

"Do you think you can come home sometime soon? For a visit, I mean." I haven't seen my parents in six months. They've offered to come up to visit, but I outright refused because I wasn't ready to face them yet. I became a failure to them, more so to my mom, when my marriage ended. I'm not ready to see it in their eyes.

"Maybe I can jump on a bus tonight, and be there around ten?" I'm not sure why I say this, but my parents deserve it.

"That would be great, sweetheart! Your dad will be thrilled. Let us know and we'll pick you up in Rosslyn."

"Okay. I'll get my tickets now and call you from the road."

"I'm so excited to see you, baby. I can't wait." My mother has probably been holding her breath since I told them about my divorce. I just wish she would stop talking to Simon. They, too, need to accept that he's no longer part of our lives.

"Mom, please don't tell Simon anything about me anymore." There is silence at the other end.

"I have not heard from you for a while, and I need to know what's going on."

"I'll try to call more often. I promise." I have to offer her this.

～

The bus is surprisingly empty tonight, and I have the entire row to myself. I pull out Colt's book, put it on my lap, and stare at the cover. It is shiny and black with a white root-like font that says *ROOTS* in bold. There is nothing spectacular about the cover. At the bottom of the book, it says: "For those who seek what they do not know."

I am both excited and somewhat embarrassed that I am about to invade his privacy.

"It started with a goodbye to people I barely know. The waves of black clothing pass me by in blur and darkness. These humans deem they are part of me, of who I am, and they attempt to console my broken soul. But why, I ask. They are nothing. They mean nothing."

I'm in tears by the time I finish the first two chapters. We've already passed New Jersey. I look out the window, seeing movements of still life. I am part of that, and yet I feel strangely disconnected from anything other than Simon, Felicity, or my parents. While Colt's book speaks of detachment from those closest to him, I feel that mine have sheltered me so much that I'm unable to take a step without them holding my hand. I'm trying to change that. My divorce is not my death sentence. I can tell that's how people see it. They are frightened for my lack of independence. But I'm stronger than that. I need them to know that I'm capable of being my own person, alone.

I continue reading. The boy of fifteen grew up to be a man of twenty in the next few chapters. With enough money and connections, he was able to navigate the world easily and without working very hard. He was expected to be great. But that wasn't what he wanted.

This is fiction, I remind myself, but how much of this is Colt's reality? I pull out my phone and send a text to Felicity.

"On the way to Fairfax"

She rings back immediately.

"What! Without me?" Sometimes I wonder if my dependence on them feeds their dependence on me.

"It was last minute, sorry." I pin my phone between my shoulder and my ear. I pull both my legs up on the seat and wrap my arms around my knees. Now that I think about it, I don't remember ever traveling back to Virginia on my own. Have I been that powerless?

"It's okay," Felicity huffs. "Have fun in VA. Tell Mom and Dad I miss them." She's talking about my parents.

"I will. I know they miss you too, terribly."

I'm not heading back to Virginia because I'm a failure. This is just a visit. I'm coming back home. New York is home now, and for the first time, I'm excited about the prospect of exploring the city on my own, without Simon telling me what to do or where to go.

"I love you, Felicity. I hope you know that."

"I know. And I love you too."

⌒⌒⌒

I continue reading Colt's book. The next four chapters are dark and heavy—sex, drugs, and violence. I wonder if any of those were true. I remind myself again that this is fiction. But what catches my attention is how the character, Sonny, doesn't seem to know what love is, and how much he struggles with it. There's a character named Kyla, a woman who has been in love with Sonny since they were kids. Although he has kept her close, he never really lets her into his life. Is that person Tina? The similarities are obvious—a tall blonde girl with blue eyes who can pass for a supermodel.

I send Felicity a text. "Have you read Colt's first book?"

"Yes. *Roots*. It's his most popular book. Why?"

"Nothing. I'm reading it. Is it his life story?"

"Yes and no. Don't read too much into it. It's not him, but it's his book. They are different people."

"How do you know that?"

"The violence is just too much for someone to get over. It's not real; it's fiction."

"I get that."

"Ha-ha! Again, don't read too much into it. He's actually with me right now. We're having drinks at Tina's. She's better. She's asking for you, BTW."

"Oh." This news unsettles me. Has Colt asked about me, I wonder? "Tell her I say hi, and that I'm glad she's better." Before I can send my text, my phone rings again.

"Hey."

"Here, talk to Tina yourself. She's been asking about you." I hear classical music in the background.

"Gabby?" Tina's voice is still a little weak.

"Tina, how are you doing? I'm sorry I wasn't able to check on you this week."

"It's fine. I totally understand. I just want to thank you for everything."

"Of course. Are you feeling better?"

"Yes. And I don't know how I would have survived that night without you. You saved me."

"No. We all did. All your friends were there for you." I face the window and watch the weekend traffic pass by. The sky is orange and red, like an angry ember raging in fury. If I were an artist, this would provide inspiration because it displays the inner workings of my heart. My colors are getting brighter within, and like dusk I now welcome darkness. I'm ready to take it on because I'm already there.

"I know. I hope you enjoy your visit with your parents. And maybe we can go to lunch when you get back?"

"Yes, I would love that." She is Kyla. I can tell. I know.

"Here, let me get Felicity back for you." I hear Tina passing the phone to Felicity.

"Okay, so see you Sunday night? Dinner? My house? Or Monday at lunch?"

"I can go straight to your apartment Sunday night. I don't want to go back to the apartment just yet." I hear Felicity sigh, not in frustration but relief.

"I'll order Indian from Heritage, just like old times," she promises.

I wonder if Colt told them about lunch at Rosa's. I'm sure it's not a big deal for him—but it's kind of a big deal for me—a huge deal. In truth, it was the first meal I've ever had with a man alone other than Simon or my dad.

We both hang up, and I continue reading.

My parents are already waiting for me when I get to Rosslyn, a river hop from DC. A trivia tidbit, it's where the Marvel movies' fake S.H.I.E.L.D. headquarters is located. My mom gets out of the car as soon as she sees me and immediately tackles me for a hug. My dad does the same. I understand their fear, but sometimes I wish they would turn it down a notch.

I love their love. I know that deep down, my courage comes from them, a testament to the safe and loving childhood they both provided me. I didn't lose myself in their embrace, I lost myself out there in the wild, in the real world—and I used Felicity and Simon as my shield and protector. I shouldn't have.

Mom pulls away from me, holds me at arm's length, and examines me from head to toe. There is nothing much to see, really. I'm wearing denim cut-offs, a navy blue peasant blouse, a big black cardigan, and black flip-flops to complete my vacation mode look. My hair is in a disheveled bun and my face is makeup free. I'm not one to wear makeup. I should have changed into jeans on the bus, because the nights are beginning to get chilly.

"You look good." She seems surprised. They probably expected to see someone who has lost a lot of weight, someone who is wasting away. It's actually the opposite. I've gained more pounds in the last six months than I ever have in my entire life. "You actually look . . . healthier." There it is. You see, my mother, at age fifty-eight, is nowhere near 120 lbs. She is svelte and slim and outrageously youthful. It's the Filipino genes at work right there.

"I think that's another word for chubby." I laugh. And this surprises them even more. My worst days are over.

"I am glad you're fine, baby." My dad plants a kiss on my forehead. I feel sorry for him because I know how much Simon means to him. He was the son he never had.

"Felicity sends her love, of course."

"We just talked to her. She said she wanted to come with you but has a lot of things on her plate this weekend," my mom says.

"You should send her a text message that you've made it home," Dad says.

"I will."

~✒~

I miss home more than I realized. I can smell dinner. Roast beef, my dad's specialty.

It's eleven o'clock at night and ice cream on the deck time.

"Something sweet, everyone?" My dad opens the freezer and pulls out two buckets of ice cream—rocky road and black cherry, both my favorites.

I drop my bag on the floor in the kitchen and fetch some bowls and spoons. My mom is still looking at me strangely. Like I am an alien from another planet who will transform at any second.

"What?" I tease her.

"Nothing," she replies.

"Were you expecting a skeleton version of my chubby self? I hate to break this to you, Mother, but this is how I'm going to be —heartbroken or not." I laugh again.

"I'm glad you're laughing." I see the love grow in her eyes, and the fear dissipate. In a lot of ways this trip is good for all of us—they need to see that I'm fine. I need to let them know that I'm doing okay, that I'm not wasting away. I hug her tight.

"Divorce is not the death of me." My dad turns and looks at me. Both my parents are staring as if I'd grown horns. I start laughing again. They start laughing along with me.

"Who are you, and what have you done to our daughter?" my dad asks.

Dad and I move to the deck with our bowls of ice cream. I grab one of the buckets with me, just in case. My mom usually takes a shower before bed and has left us alone. The deck is my favorite part of home. We sit next to each other on my favorite matching pink Adirondack chairs, facing the beautiful Zen backyard that my dad has poured himself into creating. My mom is no green thumb. I remember thousands of barbeque dinners we've had here, with Simon and Felicity. I can't rewrite history and make Simon not a part of that. He was, and there is really nothing much I can do about it, but I'm looking forward to making new memories.

I think of Colt.

I shake my head. I try to snap out of it. If his book is a reflection of who he is, there is no way he will find beauty in the simplicity of a backyard barbeque.

"Your mom and I are extremely happy that you're okay," Dad says. I take a slurp of my melted ice cream and smile at him. "How are you, though? Really?" He still thinks it's an act. He stretches his long legs in front of him, something he does when he's tense.

"I'd be lying if I told you that losing Simon didn't devastate me. It did. Especially when I confirmed that she exists." I greedily devour a hefty spoonful of rocky road ice cream and chomp on chocolate-coated almonds. "But I see the positive in this life now." I feel Dad tense a little. I can only guess that he still doesn't believe Simon left me for another woman. "I'm back in school, and I've never been more excited. Today, I just got hired as a sales associate at an amazing independent bookstore near the school." I let this sink in for a bit.

My mother has never worked. She has been the anchor that holds this small family together. She used to dance. She used to perform in college. She gave it all up because she said it was a childish dream. But, had she pursued it, maybe she could have performed on Broadway. Does she regret anything? Me? I was a surprise baby. They were in college when they had me. My dad, who is a heart surgeon, went to medical school while Mom lived with her parents. They got married eventually, but I can only image how hard that must have been for my mom—being a single parent. I suppose that's why they think it's okay to meddle in my life some. Their parents took care of them for a while after I was born.

"I'm a little surprised, I have to admit." I see pride. This makes me happy.

"I loved Simon, but I'm also grateful for this chance." I turn to look at him and give him a soulful smile. At this very moment, I feel the need to console him, to let him know that everything is going to be all right.

"Grateful?"

"Yeah. I was in my own prison." I stop and think about these words. I feel the early autumn breeze on my face and close my eyes. When I open them, Dad is staring at me looking guilty, as if he had failed me.

"You weren't happy with Simon?" There is hurt in his voice.

"I didn't think I was unhappy until now." I reach out to him and squeeze his hand.

"I should give you more credit, baby. . . ."

"I learned about being tough from you."

"I hope your mom and I didn't make you weak. I thought marrying Simon was what you wanted."

"It was. Not anymore. I really can't explain it. Do I wish that we hadn't ended the way we did? Yes. Do I wish I were still married? No. I've never really been alone, and I need to learn to live on my own terms."

"How are you for money?"

"Simon isn't a bad person. He made enough the past ten years to give me some. We're selling the house. In the beginning, I thought it was the worst he could do to me. I don't think that anymore."

"You are surprising the hell out of me, sweetheart. Your mom and I were expecting a teary-eyed baby girl. You're a lot stronger than we give you credit for."

"Thanks, Dad . . . this isn't over. There will be tough moments as I learn to do this on my own. And I'm so glad I have you and Mom with me when it happens."

"We're always going to be here for you, babycakes. . . ."

"I know," I say, and I don't even feel guilty scooping more rocky road ice cream from the bucket straight to my mouth.

Chapter Ten

There are many differences between New York City and Washington, DC. It's a sin to even try to compare the two. They are both home to me. New York is a world of creativity, of the arts and theater, and DC is the world of politics and power. Growing up, my dad would take Mom and me to the Kennedy Center when there was a good musical in town. In New York, you can go anytime you want. But the sound of sirens in DC that tells you that a world leader is in town, driving on the same road you walk on, or a cabinet secretary who lives a few blocks away from you and shops at the same stores—these people make a difference in people's lives, not just in the United States, but all over the world—that too is just mind blowing.

"Good morning. What are we going to do today, baby?" Dad walks into the kitchen in his plaid pajamas, kissing me on top of my head and messing up my hair like I'm still five years old.

"I don't know. Any good exhibits in town?" I flip open the new *Washingtonian* magazine. Aside from the *Washington Post*, the *Washingtonian* is the only other constant in the Stevenses' subscription pile.

"We can see a ballet at the Kennedy Center. I'm pretty sure we can get tickets at the last minute. I can try. I know this isn't New York, but . . ." My dad is a patron of the Kennedy Center only because my mother is fascinated with ballet. She says when she was a teenager in the Philippines, Grandma used to take her.

They didn't have very much money growing up, but her parents taught her everything she could soak up.

"I was just thinking about that, Dad."

"No, Gabby and I are going shopping at Tyson's Galleria today, Chris," my mom says, her tiny Filipina frame waltzing into the room on a mission. If there is one thing I know very well about my Filipino ancestry, it's that we love shopping. My dad steps away with both his hands raised in surrender. This, right here, is love. My parents' love knows no bounds. They probably thought I had found that in Simon.

"Shopping it is!" I say. I need a few new things anyway. New York is better known for shopping, for sure, but I can also get the best in Virginia without paying New York City prices.

"She deserves a new purse, Chris." My mom and her purses—it's legendary. As kids, Felicity and I would rummage through her closet and secretly borrow her Chanels and Guccis. "And shoes! She needs a nice new pair of fancy shoes."

"Of course, the shoes, how can I forget the shoes," my dad teases.

My mom is a shopaholic, the very embodiment of that word. It's what she does. She meets her sisters, who all live in the Northern Virginia area, for lunches and to go on shopping extravaganzas almost every weekend. She scopes out the sales, buys things in bulk, and sells them on eBay—for fun. I ask her if she actually makes money from it, and she just shrugs off my questions. Without a doubt, I will be going back to New York with loads of new clothes, not just from today's haul, but I'm pretty sure she's already bought me a ton over the past six months. Most of the time, that's what our phone conversations are about. My dad indulges her.

"Are you getting hungry?" Mom asks.

"I can eat."

"I know you can. But are you hungry?" She surveys me from head to toe, implying that she doesn't think I need any more food. I've always been on the heavy side, but that has never bothered me, even when I was a teenager. Simon shielded me from that grief too, always assuring me that he liked me just the way I was. I just didn't really care what people thought of me. I had everything I needed back them—a best friend and a boyfriend who constantly told me how great I was.

"I'm hungry. I only had coffee and toast this morning, and it's almost two o'clock," I complain.

"Okay. We can share a sandwich at Paul's or something."

"That'll work." I grab some of her Neiman Marcus shopping bags. I don't know how my dad will react to the bill on his credit card, but my goodness, our purchases are not cheap.

On the way to Paul's, I feel Mom tense up. She grabs my hand without warning and leads me in the other direction. I look at her in confusion. She doesn't give me an explanation, but I can tell her anger is building up. I give her a look that's partly questioning and partly irritated.

"Gabby?" I hear someone call my name from a distance. I turn around and find myself face to face with Simon's parents. I should have anticipated this. Northern Virginia is not that big. I should have known that it's likely that I'd bump into them this weekend. My mother, pretending not to notice, keeps on walking. "Gabby, Maria." My mother freezes. She knows she can't escape. The Martins rush toward us, and Simon's mother, Patricia, pulls me into a hug. I hug her back.

"Hi, Pat," I say casually. Now is not the time for drama. There is no reason to act differently toward them. I've known them since I was a teenager.

"Gabby. How are you? We've not seen you in over a year. We tried to call you a few times, but . . ." Pat is nothing like Simon. She is petite, no taller than my mother. Her emerald green eyes sparkle brilliantly under her brown hair. When you look at her oval face, you are immediately drawn to her eyes. Pat's eyes always give her away. They have a soul of their own. As I look at her, I notice something different. I expect sadness, but it isn't that. I can't seem to put my finger on it.

"I've been busy. I'm sorry," I reason.

I've had numerous talks with the Martins since Simon walked out on me. Pat has been a mother to me all these years, so I welcome her calls like I do Mom's. Nothing has changed between us. But I shut her out too, like my parents, when I received the divorce papers. I just didn't have the energy to explain my feelings over and over and over. I started to sound like a broken record, and I just hated it. I felt like a masochist reliving my pain.

"No, no, don't worry. I'm so glad to see you. Hello, Maria." Pat faces my mother stiffly, which is odd. These two are like two peas in a pod. They can chat the night away and talk about anything and everything under the sun. They are the perfect in-laws. They get along so well, it was a built-in family from the start.

"Pat, Robert." I give her a puzzled look. I don't understand how my mother is acting indifferently toward the Martins, and yet still talks to Simon. It's not their fault. It was Simon who left me. Mom looks away from me with a scowl, rolling her eyes. There. Now I know where I got it.

"Are you home . . . for good? Or are you just visiting? I thought you just started school?" Pat is talking too fast, and I can tell she's feeling a little anxious. She doesn't look at my mom at all.

"I'm just here visiting Mom and Dad for the weekend. I'm heading back to New York tomorrow. Just doing a little bit of shopping with Mom here."

"Yes, of course. Maria is known for her shopping prowess." I can see my mother's eyes narrow in annoyance. "But, can you have dinner with us tonight?"

"We have plans," my mother interjects. I don't know what happened. They used to get along so well.

"I can meet you for coffee, if you'd like," I offer.

"I would love that," Pat says sincerely. "There's a new place close to where we all live. At the Mosaic District along Gallows Road. Do you know it?"

"Yeah, Dad and I drove there this morning to get coffee. Is it the Moms and Pops place?"

"Yes. That's the one. I'm looking forward to it, Gabby."

"I'll call later," I say.

⸙

When the Martins walk away, I look at my mother questioningly. I need an explanation. They just nodded at each other like they were strangers.

"I don't want you getting attached to those people, Gabriella." She is dead serious.

"Mom, what's going on? What happened? You acted like you wanted to claw both their eyes out." Just because their son and I are over, I don't want my parents to fall out too.

"I didn't want to say anything," Mom says softly, looking away from me. "They're still Simon's parents, and I know that for decades he's been a son to me and Dad." We walk toward Paul's and drop all our shopping bags in a booth. Mom takes a seat, pulls out her wallet, and hands me a twenty-dollar bill. "Get us a sandwich to share and iced tea or soda. You decide."

"I'm not going anywhere until you tell me what happened." I remain standing, hand on my hip, waiting for her answer.

"They blame you for the divorce! And I hate them for it!" I look at my mother in disbelief. "Now you know." I slowly slide into the booth across from her, feeling like I've been punched in the face.

"Why?" I ask, hurt.

"They told me and Dad that you should have been a better partner to Simon. You should have given him children." I close my eyes when I hear this. "You should have worked, and not pressured Simon to be the breadwinner of the family. They asked us what you did all day, and said that it isn't a surprise that Simon got tired of it." I want to crawl under the table. No wonder my mother acted the way she did. "They are Simon's parents, I know. But they are not yours. So even if you think that at one point or another they were your parents too, I don't think they ever really were."

"It's okay, Mom."

"Are you still going to see her?"

"Well, I have to now. I made a promise."

"So did Simon, but look where we are now. You don't have

to. I can call Pat and tell her you changed your mind." Mom is
really mad.

⌒ₗₗₗ⌒

Dinner is a big deal in my family. Instead of going out, my mom
calls the Filipino restaurant by Springfield, and I can hear her
ordering everything on the menu.

"I want two orders of *kare-kare*. Of course, one bottle of
bagoong too." My mother has not lost her Filipino accent. It's
interesting that she still has it, considering she moved to the
United States when she was only fourteen. It actually sounds
very endearing.

Kare-kare is one of my Filipino favorites. It's ox tripe and
beef chunks stewed in thick peanut sauce. It is paired with
shrimp paste, which Filipinos call *bagoong*. It's not very popular
among Americans, as it's not very pleasant to the nose. Simon
didn't want it anywhere near our house.

"Mom, get me some *turon* please. Like ten of them!" *Turon*
is banana in egg roll wrappers, fried in vegetable oil with brown
sugar. It's the best dessert ever invented. You can top it with ice
cream or chocolate syrup like my dad does.

"*Oo*, some *turon* also, *sampu*," she says. *Oo* means yes in
Tagalog, and *sampu* is ten. That is the most I know about the
Filipino language. I never learned it growing up. It was not
something my mom was passionate about. I remember her
telling me that I couldn't use it anywhere else, so why bother.

I look at my mom, commanding someone on the phone,
such a strong woman, passionate about things she believes in,
and yet she decided to stay at home to raise me. And when I left,

why didn't she do something else with her life? My aunts were the same way. I thought it was what Simon wanted too, so I did what I knew. Could there be some truth to what Simon's parents are saying? That I let Simon live our lives for the both of us, that I stayed at home and didn't dream of more, that I wasn't a strong partner to their son? It doesn't matter now. It's over. There is no point dwelling on what might have been. These are the things I should take notes on for the next time. Next time? How can I think of that right now? I roll my eyes. Being in another relationship should be the last thing on my mind right now—or ever.

I can hear Dad mowing in the backyard. He loves doing stuff around the house, which I appreciated as a child. I still do. My parents are good partners who know their roles. They complement each other. My parents, although they enjoy an occasional trip in Europe, are both homebodies. Simon is the total opposite. He loves to go out. He loves to eat out. Sometimes I was simply too tired to be bothered so I let him go out with his friends from work.

I walk outside. My dad sees me, turns off the mower, and takes off his ear protectors.

"Hey, babycakes."

"Hey, Dad. You should pay someone to do that. You're allergic to grass."

"This relaxes me. I love doing this. I didn't buy a house with a big yard just so some other dude could take care of it." Growing up in the Midwest, my dad loves the outdoors, as long as the outdoors is next to his kitchen where he can grab a beer anytime he wants. This makes me smile.

"I know." I walk across the deck, and as soon as I reach the last step, I sit down. "I saw the Martins today," I say softly. I see that he is uncomfortable with this information. I've never seen my dad mad. He is a happy, funny kind of man—like Santa Claus, only slimmer and taller and more handsome.

"Oh," he says and pauses. "How was your Mom with that?"

"Not very happy."

"I bet." Dad wipes the sweat off his forehead and pulls off his gloves. He gestures for me to join him at the picnic table. "Beer?" he asks. I don't remember Dad ever asking me if I wanted an alcoholic beverage with him. This is a first for us.

"Sure, why not," I say. I want to surprise him. I want to show him I can be bold. He nods and walks to the small fridge he keeps next to the grill. He grabs two Coors Light bottles, twists both open, and offers one to me.

"I've got you; you know that, right?" He sits down next to me. My dad is not an emotional man, but he is devoted, and he knows how to show his love. My parents are a corny couple. They still hold hands, they kiss on the lips even when people are watching, and they have private jokes that are downright cheesy but infinitely romantic. They are my inspiration. I must admit that Simon and I lost each other along the way. Maybe we became disconnected long before he met his new girlfriend.

"Yeah. I know," I say, without really understanding what he's getting at.

"I'll set up a bank account for you so you can have access to money anytime you want." He takes a swig of his beer. "Nobody can treat my baby like this." He doesn't show anger much, but I can see it right now. The glint in his eyes tells me he is affected more than he is letting on.

"I'm fine, Dad."

"I know you are. You're stronger than you think. It's that

feisty Filipina blood in you." We both laugh a little. I can tell that we're both thinking about Mom.

"I'm tired of talking about my divorce, believe it or not. It's starting to get old. I'm just ready to be with people who don't know anything about it. Does that make sense?"

"That's my girl," he says and kisses me on the forehead. And for the first time, I drink a beer in front of my dad. Yes, at thirty-six years old.

Chapter Eleven

It's almost eight thirty, and Felicity has gone to work. I can tell this by the silence in the apartment. No buzzing hair dryer, no Lady Gaga playing in the background, and no CNN blaring in the living room. She has an eight thirty class on Mondays.

Last night, I arrived at Felicity's apartment around seven. And just as she promised, my Indian food had been ordered, reheated, and served by the time I walked in. I, obviously, filled her in on my encounter with the Martins. She was not too pleased either.

Drawing a big yawn, I walk into the kitchen to get some water. I look around the room in fascination, as I often do when I'm here. Felicity's two-bedroom apartment is totally her, exuding her character down to the tiniest detail. It's colorful. The walls are painted pink and blush, like the colors of peonies in the summer. Photos of every shape and size are framed in white shadow boxes, which make them look like they're floating. And my absolute favorite is her bright pink tweed sofa, decorated with bright blue, green, and yellow pillows. If Felicity were not a writer, she would be an amazing interior decorator. A lot of our photos are spread around in the living room. I notice that she has already hidden all of Simon's. This must have been hard for her to do because all the best memories we have as kids included him.

There is a fresh pot of coffee on the kitchen counter, and on the coffeemaker is a Post-it note that says: "We can do this every day if we become roommates, you know—Love, Felicity." I smile hesitantly. As I look around, I see it would be hard for me to insert myself into her space. My apartment now is all Simon. I want to find an apartment where I also show myself, decorate it without feeling like I'm invading someone's space, and live in it because it's all mine.

I'm conflicted about moving in with Felicity. If I really want to be independent, I should take risks instead of taking the easy way out. Moving in with her would be the most convenient option, but it doesn't serve my goal. I can see myself waiting for her before I do anything for myself. I would be constantly asking for her advice, and I know I would wind up in the very same spot I was in with Simon.

But I can't think about that right now. To say that I'm looking forward to today is an understatement. And it has nothing to do with my living situation. I stayed up late last night reading Colt's book. I couldn't put it down, and by the time I reached the last page, it was almost two in the morning. A lot has happened since we had lunch, and that was only three days ago.

I open the cupboard and reach out for the coffee mug with my name on it. Felicity's apartment is an extension of my own home. Whatever she has, you can count on there being one for me too. I reach for the pot of coffee and pour half a mug.

I miss him.

I'm taken aback by this admission.

I stare at my coffee for a few seconds, gauging the enormity of this revelation. How can I miss someone I barely know?

Colt's book has answered some of my many questions about him. As I was reading it, it triggered memories of him—how his face looks when he's sad, like when we were at the hospital waiting for Tina, or how he effortlessly flirts and dismisses it immediately, or the way his dimples light up his face when he smiles. Colt is not the character Sonny in *Roots*. Colt is *everyone* in *Roots*. He sprinkled a little bit of himself into each character, which if you don't know him well enough, will elude you. I want to know him better.

It's ten o'clock by the time I reach the subway, two blocks away from Felicity's apartment. I love to walk around the city, and I don't ordinarily mind the hassle, but today I do. I rush to catch the ten fifteen train. I slump into an empty spot, and my legs begin to shake anxiously. What do I say to him? I haven't even thanked him for talking to Thomas Gallagher for me. I make a mental note that it should be the first thing I tell him today.

By the time I reach the MFA building, it's nearly eleven, and I'm eager for class to begin. A wave of students pushes me in, and I allow myself to be swept along. My earlier confidence seems to have fizzled. Every door in the hallway is shut closed now. Classes have already started. Colt will not be happy if I'm late. I shake my head to pull myself out of the fog, and I run up the two flights of stairs to where my classroom is. When I reach it, the door is still open. I sigh in relief as I try to catch my breath.

Colt is already in the room.

"Please close the door behind you so we can start," Colt says without looking up at me.

I immediately take the seat next to Heather. She gives me her signature sunny smile, and I smile back. I put my backpack on the floor as quietly as possible. It's the new Marc Jacobs backpack Mom bought me over the weekend. When I look up, I see Colt in his favorite spot by the window, leaning backwards, hands clasped together under his chin in deep thought. He's wearing black denim jeans today and a black T-shirt. His leather jacket is draped on the back of the chair right across from him. I try to look away, but I can't. Our eyes meet. A slight movement of his eyebrow says it all—that he acknowledges my presence, that he sees me.

There is a scene in *Roots* where one of the characters—Andy, a drug abuser who has killed another critical character in the story—begs his sister for help. In the book, Andy has an outburst where he weeps and pleads. The prose is so powerful that Colt is able to flip the readers' hatred of Andy into empathy. Is that redemption? Is Colt trying to redeem himself from something? And that is where I've seen that slight movement of his eyebrow before—in his book, where Andy acknowledges someone's presence the same way Colt just acknowledged mine now. I don't know what to make of it, and perhaps I'm imagining it all. I have become a Colt James fan. And I'm well on my way to becoming a stalker. A stalking divorcée is a good premise for a *Law and Order* episode. I roll my eyes for the first time today, because I now see how ridiculous this is. I seem to be having a silly little crush.

"Let's start with an exercise this morning," Colt begins. "I'll think of a word. A trigger. And you guys write something about it. I don't care if what you write is personal or real, if it's something that happened to you, a friend, or a loved one. But I want to feel the authenticity in your writing. Unless of course you're already James Patterson or Nicholas Sparks, you can never fool me." He walks around the room, still in deep thought. He stops right behind me. "I'll be here if you have any questions. I want you to ask them." I freeze. I can feel the hairs at the back of my neck rising. "The word is *sunshine.*" I suddenly feel a light touch on my shoulder. I look around the room. No one is paying attention to Colt anymore. Everyone is already writing. I want to turn around and look at him, but I don't. He starts walking again, and this time he stops behind Rasheeda, who is right across from me. And then he smiles . . . at me. And I feel my insides soar. I smile back.

I'm not just imagining things.

❦

I think of sunshine and I think of him. But I can't say that in my exercise. How about I say that someone I recently met brought sunshine into my darkness? *Geez, that's cheesy,* I say under my breath. But is he? Sunshine? He is far from sunny, but he has brought back some light into my bleak little life. I don't think I've ever been this excited to see anyone before.

I bend my head and try to concentrate on *sunshine.* Simon isn't my sunshine anymore. Felicity. My mom. My dad. Does it have to be someone else? Can't it be me? I look up and stare into space. I need to gather my thoughts and decide. I don't notice that I have been tapping my pen on the table insistently.

"Gabby." Heather reaches over my hand and stops it from shaking. I see everyone's eyes on me, and I mouth an apology. Scott gives me a mean look. I don't look at Colt for fear of censure.

I turn my attention back to my blank page. I am my sunshine. The sooner I realize that I am the light of my life, the quicker I can appreciate who I am.

I write one line. Nothing else follows. That's all I've got. Colt doesn't give us further instructions. I raise my hand.

"Gabby?" Colt is at the teacher's desk in the corner of the room, reading a book.

"What should we write—a short story, a poem, or an essay?"

"That is your decision too."

"All I have is a line."

"If that's all you feel like writing, and if that is your truth right this moment, then a line will suffice."

"Do we read it in front of the class?"

"Yes. But write like no one will read it. Let go of your fears." Colt gets up, walks around the table and sits on it facing us. "Class. Listen up. Don't overthink this. Just write the first thing that comes to mind. It doesn't have to be *The Great Gatsby*. It can be a page or two. It can even be half a page. It can be a story inspired by sunshine, and you don't even need to mention the word in your piece. All I'm asking is that it should be an expression of your present truth." He looks at each of us inside the tiny room. He is a natural teacher. He is good at it, and I'm breathless just looking at him. I am certain that every woman in this room feels exactly the same way.

An hour later, I'm still on the same one line. I look around the table, and I'm envious of my classmates who have been writing nonstop for a solid hour. Heather is on a roll, writing with such passion and intensity. I am a fraud. I am not a writer. I cannot even think of words that can best describe the word sunshine.

Colt has been looking at me sporadically the past hour. I can tell that he can sense my anxiety. My palms are starting to sweat.

"How are you all doing?" Colt asks the class. My frustration is quite obvious. Everyone says, "Fine." I don't say anything.

"Who wants to go first?" Scott raises his hand, and Colt calls on him.

Scott's short story blows me away. It speaks of death as the protagonist's sunshine. The creativity flowing in this classroom is phenomenal. I am, without a doubt, among the best creative writers in this program. It is not about the topic but how the prose inspires feelings that separate it from mere script.

Heather wrote an essay about life in Africa, about illnesses, poverty, and death, and about how sunshine is the only constant and how it motivates people to wake up each morning to go on fighting. I'm almost in tears by the time she's done.

And then it's my turn. I don't stand up. I rub the nape of my neck. And I begin: "There is no darkness if sunshine is I." I sit down as everyone looks at me in anticipation.

"What does that mean, Gabby?" Scott asks. I don't know if he is being sarcastic, or truly interested in what I have to say.

"Umm, control," I reply, looking up coyly under my eyelashes.

"What about control?"

"If I become light, then darkness can't overpower me. You can't extinguish the light from the sun." And I believe that. I am my own light. But I know too, that because of this line, I may have just failed my first test.

❀

I get out of the classroom as soon as I hear Colt say, "See you next Monday." I have enough time to grab lunch and freshen up before I head to my first day on the job. After today's embarrassing moment, I'd rather not face Colt, no matter how much I want to see his blue eyes up close.

"Good luck on your first day on the job!" Felicity texts me. I don't have the time to reply in length so I send her a smile emoji, to which she replies with a kiss emoji. I stop myself before I send her a heart emoji. Instead, I giggle.

I go to the coffee shop a few blocks from campus and order a chicken sandwich. I see an empty booth in the far corner. I dump all my stuff on the table and head back to the counter to get my order, and when I turn around, I bump into Tina.

"Gabby!" She beams with enthusiasm as soon as she sees me and grabs me for an uncomfortable hug. "I haven't thanked you properly, and you deserve that. You truly, literally saved my life."

"I don't think so," I say, shaking my head.

Tina is about five foot eleven, which makes hugging her a bit of an effort with my five-foot-four-inch frame. Her eyes are a shade of gray sand, luminous but deep. Today, she is wearing denim bootleg jeans, a navy bandana top, and red wedge sandals that show her bright red toenails.

"But you did," she continues.

"So, how are you?"

"I'm getting better. What happened was more . . . I don't know, emotional, than physical." I nod at her because I understand. "I need to get going, but how about that meal we talked about last week?"

"Yes. I'm busy during the day and most nights this week, but we can meet up on a Friday, maybe?"

"Friday is good. We can also do dinner again at my apartment. But wait, I don't want Colt to interrupt us, so let's just go out to eat." My ears perk up. How could Colt interrupt us? Are they living together, as I deduced? This is not making sense.

Is Friday lunch at Upland good?" Tina snaps me out of my internal musing.

"Yes," I reply. I have been to Upland before.

"Perfect. I'll make reservations for noon and call you to confirm."

"That's great. See you Friday." I head back to my booth with my mind swirling in confusion over Colt's relationship with Tina.

⚬⚬⚬

Seeing Thomas is like showing up to a party. He's wearing a khaki suit, pink shirt, and a purple bow tie, and there is always lots of conversation and laughter. I can't quite tell how old Thomas is, but he looks like he's well into his seventies.

"Let's get the formal stuff out of the way, Ms. Stevens. How about you sign all these nuisances?" He hands me the paperwork with disgust on his face, which actually looks quite funny. And a realization hits him, "Actually, these documents are quite crucial to your getting paid, so I would suggest you take your time," he says. "And as soon as you get that done, our magical literary adventure begins."

After I've signed all the forms, Thomas gives me a tour.

"You would think this is a tiny store, but it isn't. In every corner and every space, there lies a story that is bigger than any of us, bigger than the world can ever hold. It takes us into space, a walk on the moon, explores someone's pain in Rwanda, and shows a perfect love story in the Netherlands. When you have a book, you have been everywhere." He says this as he paces around the room. I am mesmerized as I stand across from him, soaking it all up. "If you talk about books this way to children, I can guarantee you that you've already done your good deed. We should not only promote art, we should promote literacy." I am in my happiest place on earth.

Thomas shows me every section of the shop. Our biggest inventory is in fiction, as expected, as well as children's books. The Young Adult section, Thomas says, has evolved over the past few years. "It's a good thing. It means we're inspiring young minds to read early, and because there are a lot of YA writers today, these kids have bigger and better titles to choose from." I don't tell him that at thirty-six I also read YA.

Next, Thomas teaches me how to work the cash register. It's pretty straightforward. He also teaches me to use the credit card machine. And by the time we are done, Thomas says he will walk around the block for a few hours before closing.

It's already eight forty-five. This is proof that there is absolute truth to the saying, "Time flies when you're having fun." I explore the shop some more, checking out the new titles section. Thomas said before the beginning of our tour that I could read any book I like while I'm in the store as long as I'm careful not to damage them. I brush my fingertips along the rows of books, not really caring what they are about. I just love the feel of books around me. It ignites my soul. Sure, I dream of writing a novel someday, maybe when I finish school, but right now enjoying other people's prose is like vitamins to me, and always has been. It was all I did when I was married—I read and read. I sometimes forget where I am or what I need to do when a book is really good. When I think back, that might have been a bit frustrating for Simon. It's probably why his parents feel that way about me.

I hear the doorbells chime and I leave the aisle, which

doesn't have a clear line of sight to the door, to welcome the new customer.

It's Colt.

"Hey," he says.

"Hi."

"It's so quiet here today," he adds. "Where is Thomas? He usually welcomes his customers as soon as they step in."

"He's taking a walk."

"A walk. Wow. He never takes walks."

"What do you mean, never?"

"Well, not while his store is still open. That must mean he really likes you, trusts you."

"That's good to know."

Colt and I stand in the middle of the shop awkwardly. When he takes a step forward, I unconsciously take a step back. He's wearing his leather jacket tonight. I peek behind him, and I see that the New York sun has set.

"What time is your class tomorrow?"

"I don't have a class, but I work here at one tomorrow."

"Well, if you're interested, I'm going to the Back Room tonight for a poetry reading at ten." I stare at Colt, wondering why I'm so captivated by him. I've met hot guys before, and though I appreciate them, I don't think about them after-hours.

"Sure. I would love to. I guess I close in ten minutes. I can meet you there, or if you'd like to wait . . . I don't know if Thomas plans to come back or not."

"I can wait around for ten minutes. And maybe we can grab something to eat before the reading. We have an hour."

The door opens and it is Thomas, whose smile widens when he sees Colt.

"My favorite author is in my shop again. How do you do, Mr. James?"

"I'm great, Thomas. I'm taking Gabby to the Back Room tonight."

"Splendid. Have you never been, Gabriella?"

I shake my head.

"Well, go on, it's nine o'clock, don't waste your time, you creative young souls."

I walk around the counter to gather my bag. "Thanks, Thomas. Thank you so much for today."

"No, thank you Gabriella. See you tomorrow at one?"

"Definitely."

There is a glint in Thomas's eye as he waves us goodbye, as if he knows a secret Colt and I will never fathom.

Chapter Twelve

It is an unexpectedly chilly night.

"Do you mind if we walk? It's about twenty minutes. We can grab a bite on the way," Colt says, looking surprisingly uncertain.

"Sure," I say. My heart is going pitter-patter. This is ridiculous. For all I know, he has had lunches with Heather too, and Sophia. And we're probably meeting a bunch of people at this reading tonight. I need to stop overthinking this.

Colt and I walk side by side. I like our height together. I have to crane my neck to face him, but I like that he towers over me. We're walking so close that when our hands accidentally touch, we both feel a static shock, and we laugh. I like the sound our laughter makes. It blends.

"How was your trip home?"

"It was good and bad. But good, for the most part." And then I remember what he did for me to get the job. So, I abruptly stop to hold his hand and face him. Then I drop it immediately. "Hey, I totally forgot to thank you for talking to Thomas about the job and vouching for me. You didn't need to do that, but you did. Thank you. You're the reason why I got the job."

"You're welcome. And please don't sell yourself short. Never. If Thomas didn't like you, even if you used the entire NYU MFA faculty as your reference, he wouldn't have taken you on." We continue on. It's a good night for a stroll. The noise is subdued;

you hear only faint sirens at a distance, and the soft chattering of passersby.

The pace is calm. I am calm.

"Thank you anyway. I love being there."

"That's good news." We are silent for a few minutes, enjoying the quiet. "So, why was your trip home bad? Unless you don't want to talk about it." He turns his body slightly toward me when he says this, and I can see that he's really interested.

"I bumped into Simon's parents, and they used to be second parents to me. Then my mom told me they blame me for the divorce." I steal a look at Colt, trying to gauge his reaction.

"Didn't you say your ex-husband cheated on you?" He furrows his brows in confusion, and I can tell he's not pleased.

"Yeah. They kind of said that Simon wouldn't have cheated on me if I'd been a better wife."

"Whoa! Ridiculous. How do you feel about that?"

"It hurt me at first. They were like parents to me for twenty years. But then, you know, I just didn't care after. That's what made me sad, the part that I don't care anymore."

"Do you still care about your ex?"

"Yes. No. I don't know. I'm just in a hurry to be done with all this."

"What this?"

"The phase where I'm going through a divorce and everyone knows about it. I just don't want to talk about it anymore, you know. Finally, I can own my life. Plan it the way I want it."

"I'm sorry I brought it up."

"Don't be . . . I don't mean it that way."

"I get it, you just want to be your own light." I turn to look at him again. And this time he is staring right back at me.

"Yes," I whisper, a bit embarrassed that I'm reminded of my disaster in class earlier. I can feel my face turning red.

Colt stops walking, and I stop mid-step to check what he's doing. I move my head sideways. He gently puts both his hands on my arms, and turns me to face him. He bends down. Our lips touch. It starts gentle and unsure. He pulls me closer to him, puts his arms around my waist, while his lips own mine with slowly building intensity. I open my mouth lightly in welcome. Our kiss deepens. I close my eyes. I put my arms around his neck, and I pull him closer. I kiss him like I've never kissed anyone before. I let go of myself and he lets me.

He pulls away and looks at me with eyes reflecting fear and astonishment. I'm too drunk in his kiss to try to question what this means.

The leaves have not fully turned yet this season, but the old leaves have started to fall. I, too, am at the autumn season of my life—getting rid of the old, and hoping something beautiful and new will come my way before long.

Colt holds my hand and I welcome it.

I have heard of the Back Room before, but I've never been there. It's not the kind of place Simon would have taken me to. If you don't know where you're going, you could easily miss it. But Colt knows the place well. It's only a twenty-minute walk from the shop, but it took us more than a half hour to get here because of the few stops we made along the way. Those stops are like dreams to me. I steal a look at him and, still holding my hand, he guides me to the obscure entrance.

The bouncer directs us to a rusty iron stairwell down to the basement. Colt walks in front of me, leading me down a dark alley. At the end, an unremarkable door opens to a dimly lit room with a lot of sparkle. Loud jazz is playing at the far end. A roaring twenties mirrored bar is at the center of attention on this level. Carpeted steps take us to another floor, a mezzanine of sorts, a period-inspired setting with cocktail tables and velvet settees that look more vibrant in the glow of a fireplace.

Colt takes my hand and pulls me closer to him. My eyes are wide in amazement. I can't even take my eyes off those racy photos that grace the walls. Playfully, Colt turns to face me, covers my eyes with his hands and kisses the tip of my nose. I giggle. I stand on tiptoe so I can wrap my arms around his neck, and ready myself for a kiss. The room is so crowded nobody will notice. And he bends his head, still laughing at me, and kisses me like we've been doing this for a long time. Then he spins me around and hugs me from behind, placing tiny kisses on my neck. I hold onto his muscular arms.

"I thought we were hungry," he whispers in my ear, his lips so close that I feel tingly inside.

I turn around and look him in the eye. "What are you hungry for, Colt?" I don't know where my confidence is coming from. I was never this forward with Simon, even when we were married.

"Don't do this to me, Gabby." He grins and pulls me closer to him. I wet my lower lip with my tongue. I can tell that this excites him.

"Why not?" I lower my eyelids and flutter my lashes.

"Now, you're going to have to walk in front of me to cover what you have just woken." He pulls me to a dark corner by a velvet curtain and pins me gently against the wall. I let my backpack slide down to the floor. He caresses me, working his way down the side of my breasts. I look around to see who's watching. People are dancing, drinking, and not caring. It's a crowded room. I reach up to get closer to him. He lifts me up a little, and I gaze into his eyes. They look serene, as if the darkness in the room has somehow softened his face. He looks deeply into my eyes—as if searching, questioning, wanting. I feel my heart flutter, as if right here is where I truly belong.

⁓

The jazz band stops playing, and we agree to behave. I retrieve my backpack. "We will have to do something about this later," he teases. He reaches for my hand and leads me to the bar at the lower level. The bar is packed, but there is an open spot I am able to squeeze into. Colt is right behind me.

"Two scotches, please," he tells the bartender, handing him a twenty-dollar bill.

"I've never had scotch in my life," I tell him.

"You've never kissed me before, but that didn't stop you." He gently pokes me on the side of my waist, where some of my extra bulges are. This ease with another human being is new to me. I've only been with one man before, Simon, and I don't remember ever being this comfortable in my own skin with him.

The bartender hands us two teacups of scotch, a historic recreation of how things were during Prohibition in the 1920s.

The two men at the bar give us their stools as they close their tab. I pull one out for Colt and climb up on the other, and settle in.

"This is a good spot. They're already setting up for the reading right in that corner," Colt says, sipping his drink. I try mine, and I almost choke as I gulp solid heat. He laughs and bends down to kiss me full on the lips.

"Gabby?" I know that voice from anywhere. When Colt lifts his head from the kiss, I see Simon's concerned face right in front of me. I notice a petite girl next to him, looking at me and Colt in confusion. Simon's gaze is penetrating. I see his jaw harden. Colt moves sideways and takes a seat, holding on to my hand as if protecting me from a predator. I am dumbfounded.

I don't bump into Simon. Never. From the moment we separated, I hoped and prayed every single day to accidentally see him somewhere, anywhere, because I missed him so much. But here, right now, is just so farfetched I don't know what to make of it.

The four of us freeze like statues.

Colt finally breaks the ice with, "Hi, I'm Colt." He reaches out to Simon for a handshake, which Simon reluctantly accepts. Colt also shakes Suzanne's outstretched hand.

"I'm Simon."

"Suzanne." Suzanne looks at me, then at Colt, then at Simon. She looks at me again, then at Colt, and her gaze lingers on Colt's biceps for a few seconds. She's probably wondering what a hot guy like Colt is doing with a flabby old divorcée like me.

"What are you doing out?" Simon asks. He's trying to intimidate me with his piercing stare.

"What do you mean?" I hear my voice grow louder, and I jerk my body upwards a little, letting him know that his question is inappropriate.

"On a date with me," Colt explains.

Everyone is silent for a full minute.

"I can see that," Simon says. We all stare at each other. "Well, you take care, Gabby. I'll leave you guys to it." I nod my head, not sure what else to say. Simon walks away, Suzanne following behind him. She gives me a small smile. I can stop holding my breath.

"You okay?" Colt gently takes my chin and moves it to face him. And then I lift my face further, waiting for his kiss. He bends down to take my lips softly. I can get lost in his kiss, I know. But I stop myself and stare into his eyes to let him know seeing Simon didn't faze me. I want to be here with him. When I face the crowd again, I see Simon looking at us from across the room. "Do you want to leave?" Colt asks, seeing that Simon is giving us angry glares. I shake my head, and I pull his hand to my lap. He leaves it there in a gesture that is protective of me.

We stay for the entire reading. It's almost midnight by the time the last reader exits the stage. I didn't notice Simon leave, but he must have because I don't see him anywhere.

If this had happened a few months ago, I would have tried to talk to Simon some more—perhaps even begged him to talk to me. But tonight was perfect, and I wouldn't want it any other way. I don't know what this thing with Colt is, and I can almost guarantee that another heartbreak is looming, but I'm truly happy right this minute. I feel elated, alive. Yes, I've never felt more alive.

Chapter Thirteen

It's raining hard by the time we leave the Back Room. I press my backpack close to my chest and wipe the water off my face. There is a flash of lighting at a distance. Colt looks at me with a glint in his eye, curiously. He takes off his leather jacket and wraps it around my shoulders, for which I am grateful. I don't want this night to end.

"Do you want to get a cab here?" I don't know what to say. I don't want to go home just yet. "Or do you want to take a cab with me?" I don't think; instead I nod shyly. "Are you sure?" he asks again. I can tell that he's searching my face for reluctance.

I've never been more certain.

"Yes." My voice is sturdy.

⟶⟵

To my surprise the cab stops outside Tina's townhouse.

"You live here?" I ask, confused.

"Yes." He doesn't offer any explanation. He gets out of the cab into the pouring rain, runs around to my side, and helps me out. He grabs my backpack with one hand and reaches for my hand with the other.

It's quiet when we walk in. He closes the door gently behind us and leads me upstairs to the master bedroom at the far end of the hall. I glance over the private study where I took Simon's call during Tina's dinner party a few weeks ago. The door is ajar, and I can see the glow inside from the streetlamp coming through the window.

When Colt shuts the door of the master bedroom behind us, I stand there looking at him, not really knowing what to do. I've never done this before. The closest I've come was prom night.

"Let's get you out of those wet clothes," he says casually. He opens one of the drawers and pulls out a white T-shirt. "Use the bathroom in here, and I'll use the one down the hall."

I walk into the enormous bathroom, afraid that Tina will suddenly burst in and confront us. I shut the door gently and consider my reflection in the mirror. I'm drenched, but I look happy. I may feel a little nervous, but I see excitement written all over my face. I try to reach for a memory of a time when I was this joyful, and I can't think of one.

I turn the shower on, remove my soaking clothes, and jump into the soothing warm water. I let it sprinkle on my face to wipe the day away, and I relax. I surprised myself by not freaking out seeing Simon and Suzanne together. I've met her before, but she didn't affect me tonight. I always thought that when I saw them together, it would destroy me. Remarkably, I'm still standing strong. I'm actually okay. Colt helped me through that. I don't know what my reaction would have been if he'd not been there to hold my hand. I see a shower gel on the rack, and I lather some onto my body. I let the fresh scent envelop my senses. I close my eyes, and anticipation starts to bubble up inside. I'm in Colt James's shower, getting ready for something that is entirely new to me.

He's already freshly showered by the time I step out of the bathroom. He's naked from the waist up with a dark blue towel modestly covering his lower parts. His body, as I imagined it would be, is flawless. His abs look hard. His arms are perfect, and his gorgeous shoulders show off taut muscles. I can't help staring.

"Come on over here," he says. I walk timidly toward him. I'm ready for this, I know. But my legs are shaky. My body is a long way from perfect. I instinctively pull down the hem of the shirt he lent me to hide my flabby thighs. He opens his arms to welcome me in, and I melt in his embrace. I lean into his chest, touching it with my fingertips. He lifts me by the waist and carries me onto the bed. His scent is intoxicating, and his arms are strong.

I sink into his bed facing him, my wet hair spread out on his soft pillow. He stretches out on his side next to me, putting his arm under my head, and pressing against me. He stares straight into my eyes, and I lazily gaze into his with newfound readiness. I want him. He softly touches my back and inches me closer to him. He pulls his towel away, letting it slide down on the side of the bed. I can't take my eyes off his face. I reach out to touch his cheeks with my fingertips, and slowly start caressing the outline of his jaw. In one swift motion, he pulls my T-shirt off me. And although my body is nothing compared to his, I don't give a damn now. I don't mind being naked next to him.

I close my eyes for a second, etching this moment in my memory. He searches for my lips and kisses me with impatience. I kiss him back, opening my mouth to welcome him. His hand moves slowly from my hip to the side of my breast, and I arch willingly in pleasure.

"You have seen nothing yet," he whispers as he nibbles on my lower lip playfully. Boldly, I move my hands to his center and I touch it. It's angry and throbbing and ready to be owned. I stroke it gently, and he lets me. His breathing quickens. I move to kiss him on the side of his lips, licking them softly, enjoying the sound of his quiet moan.

"Don't. What are you doing to me, Gabby?" he asks. He pulls away and stares into my eyes again. There are questions in them. I don't know how to respond.

"Don't you like it?" I ask. He takes my hand, pulls it up where we both can see it. I laugh a little.

"You don't want me finished yet," he warns, smiling. He pulls his arm out from under me, turns me on my back, and kneels between my thighs. I don't cover myself, and I leave my breasts —my entire body—exposed to him. I see him in full view. I'm ready to take him. I can feel myself swelling with need. He bends down to touch my neck with his tongue. He expertly moves downwards, from my shoulders, down my chest to my nipples. He pulls me up, closer to him, and I arch my back to give in.

"Colt . . ." I say, moaning his name in pleasure. "I want you. I want you now."

"Patience, Gabby." He moves his tongue to my navel, licking around it, brushing my love handles with delight. Then he moves further down. I run my fingers through his hair, willing him to come up to me. But he doesn't. He continues, playfully kissing my pelvic bone. I feel his finger touch me there, and I whimper. He pushes right in, and slowly pulls out. His finger moves steadily in an enchanting rhythm. "Are you enjoying this?" He looks up at me, and I cover my eyes with my hand. And then to my surprise he owns me down there while his finger continues its motion. I muffle a scream. I dig my nails deep into the bed, and clutch the sheet tight to contain myself. He doesn't stop but moves with skilled precision, taking me where I need to be, where I want to be. I scream at the top of my lungs. And he lets me, rocking me, pushing me harder to my very peak. He reduces his pace, but he doesn't stop. He lets ecstasy linger some more.

"Colt . . ." I try to catch my breath as I say his name. When he finally stops, I pull him to me. He moves effortlessly to reach a condom on his nightstand, rips the package with his mouth, slips it on, and dives into me with impatience. Pushing into me deeper, harder, outraged. His motions are fast, pulsing, pounding. I find myself back in that moment of pleasure. I move my legs out of his way, and I let him pound into me like I've never experienced before.

"Gabby, what are you doing to me," he says almost harshly as he looks into my eyes, in and out of me, our bodies moving in rhythmic waves.

I come again. My body trembles under him, holding on to anything that I can grab onto. I arch my body upwards to submit further to him. And then I feel him inside me. Colt moves with freedom and abandon, and together we scream to the unknown.

We don't stop at one or two or three. There's already light outside when we scream together for the fifth time. I finally fall asleep in his arms.

～✒～

Colt is gone by the time I wake up. I linger in bed for a few minutes thinking about what happened last night and well into this morning. I put my hand over my mouth to soften a cry. I'm still on top of the world. I don't want to think about what this means. Today, I will simply bask in the pleasure I never knew possible with another human being.

I crawl out of bed and reach for my backpack to get my phone. It's almost nine o'clock. I immediately get out of bed and jump into the shower. My clothes are no longer on the floor in the bathroom where I left them last night. This poses a problem. How do I get out of this apartment without my clothes? I don't plan to call Felicity.

I'm drying my hair with a towel when I hear a light knock on the door. I don't answer. I don't know the rules. Colt didn't tell me anything. Should I tiptoe out of the house? Should I leave without being seen by anyone? The neighbors? Tina? I've seen one too many movies. I sigh at this.

"Gabby?" I hear my name. I pull the towel tighter around me and walk to the door. I open it a little, unsure who would be on the other side. It's Tina. I want to disappear right this instant. She notices my discomfort and laughs.

"Hi." I look away immediately. She laughs some more.

"Here are your clothes. Colt loaded them in the wash this morning, and asked me to move them to the dryer when they were done."

"Thank you," I say, embarrassed.

"How about you get dressed and we'll have some breakfast? Unless, of course, you need to rush to class or work or something?"

"I don't need to be at work until one today, and I don't have a class."

"Perfect. Let me scramble some eggs."

I can just dive into a sinkhole right now. I've never been more embarrassed. I always make fun of Felicity when she tells me about her walks of shame, but this is not something I can willingly reveal. I close my eyes as memories of last night come into my mind, and I shiver. I can still feel him on me, in me, everywhere me. I shiver again. I want him again. Gosh, yesterday I was just a Colt James fan. Twenty-four hours later, I have become a Colt James addict.

Tina is singing cheerfully when I enter the kitchen. I smell freshly brewed coffee. Tina turns around and sees me, clasps her hands together, and pulls a chair for me.

"Scrambled eggs and toast?" she asks. I nod. "Don't lift a finger; just stay put. This is my thank you breakfast."

"You don't have to," I say.

"But I want to. I don't know if Colt said anything about what happened, or if the doctors told you while I was out that night. But I didn't realize I was pregnant then. And now, I'm not." I try to look for sadness, remorse, any pain in Tina's face, but there seems to be none.

"Let me be clear, right here, right now. It wasn't Colt's. Just in case you wonder how screwed up this is that we're having breakfast together in a man's apartment. Colt is my best friend since childhood." I knew as much, but I don't tell her this. "I got pregnant by this guy I met in Paris two months ago. He doesn't know, and never will." I nod my head in understanding. "So, you and Colt, huh?"

I don't know what to say to that. But I feel I need to say something without looking stupid. "I know. I just don't know what to say."

"Yeah, I understand. Colt is weird like that. Just don't take things too seriously, you know. Just be cool about it. Most importantly, don't fall in love." And with this, she laughs again.

This is not reassuring—at all. But . . . well, I kind of knew that.

Chapter Fourteen

I run to my apartment to change before heading to the shop. Something feels odd as soon as I walk in. Instead of the usual cold welcome, the apartment seems to be occupied.

"Hello?" There are no sounds except for the constant humming of the fridge. I hold my backpack at arm's length, ready for an attack. It's not a very large apartment, and every movement can be heard from all corners. There is silence. I tiptoe to the bedroom, not really knowing what to expect. I push the door gently. It's empty. The bed is as I left it Friday afternoon. I do notice, though, that my dresser has been rearranged. I can only think of one person who does that.

Realizing that I'm actually alone, I head back out to the kitchen. Monday's mail is on the counter, and to my surprise, there is a used coffee cup, which I'm pretty sure wasn't there when I left. It can only mean one thing: Simon was at the apartment.

I feel somehow violated.

P!nk starts wailing inside my backpack to alert me of a phone call. I make a mental note to change this ringtone. It's really starting to get on my nerves. I still like P!nk, but she has always been a part of Simon and me, and now she's got to go. I reach for my phone and swipe to answer.

"Where were you last night?" It's Felicity, sounding anxious. I can only guess that Simon has already talked to her.

"Did you talk to Simon?" I couldn't hide my irritation.

"Yes. Are you seeing someone I don't know about? Gabby, what's going on? Is everything okay? Is there something you need to tell me? Are you in trouble?"

"Felicity, what are you talking about? I'm not in any trouble. I saw Simon last night at a bar with Suzanne."

"He told me. He also said you were with some guy and you were all over each other. You've never kept a secret from me before."

"I'm not keeping any secrets. I just didn't tell you because it was sudden. And I don't know how. I was going to tell you tonight."

"Who is the guy? Is he someone I know?" I look at the clock on top of the fridge. It says it's quarter after twelve. I have forty-five minutes to get to work.

"Look, I need to change and head out to work in a few minutes. Am I still welcome to stay at your apartment? Can I crash there tonight? I promise I'll tell you everything. I just don't want to be late for work."

"You promise?"

"Yes. I'll be there around seven."

I run to the subway with my backpack dangling from my arm. I pull my hair up into a tight bun as I take the stairs two at a time. I made the mistake of putting on my old jeans instead of the ones I just bought over the weekend. They're grabbing my ass the wrong way and pushing my excess fat into a muffin top. It also doesn't help that my shirt is slightly short and was buttoned up unevenly as I rushed out the door. Sweat trickles into my eyes, and I wipe it with the back of my hand. I can only imagine how I look right this minute. I should be glowing. People should notice the difference in me today. I just had sex after almost a year. Instead, I'm running like a headless chicken. How did my life get so hectic? I suddenly find myself laughing all by myself in the middle of a subway platform, surrounded by other people. I don't care about their glances.

The train finally arrives, and I clamber aboard. I find an empty seat at the back of the car and as soon as I get settled, I reach for the red headphones inside my bag. I need some Yo-Yo Ma today to clear my head. I close my eyes as I relax into Bach's Cello Suite Number 1 in G Major, Prelude. I breathe in the music. I need the tunes to weave me together. And then it happens again. I see Colt's face as he kisses me in places that send tingles down my spine. I can still smell him on my skin even after that shower. I stroke my own arm as I remember the feel of his hands, and I imagine him whispering into my ear right now, here in the train, not caring about the people around us. The music floats me, taking me into a very calm space, letting me daydream of my night with Colt.

Tina said I shouldn't overthink this, and I won't. For the first time I actually feel myself waking up. I'm invigorated.

I get out at my stop near the store with plenty of time. It's only twelve forty-five, and I hear a buzz on my phone.

"Are you on the way to Thomas's now?" It's a text message from Colt. I involuntarily yelp for joy. Yo-Yo Ma is still playing in my ear.

"Yes."

"Sorry I had to rush out this morning. Tina told me you got your clothes dry just in time."

"Thanks. How has your morning been so far?"

"Meeting at eight thirty, and I'm back in the house. I need some sleep. Someone kept me up all night." I giggle softly. And I fly, like a princess, swirling in woozy delight.

"Well, go get some rest, you might need energy sometime soon."

"How soon?"

"Very soon?" I add a smile emoji.

"Like, tonight?" I didn't know it was ever possible to be this happy.

"Dinner at Felicity's for me tonight."

"Boo! Tomorrow night?"

"Yes." I skip again.

"Dinner. This time, we should go to dinner. Where do you want to go?"

"Surprise me."

"If it's my decision, we'll head straight to my room."

"Ha-ha! Talk to you later. Am at Thomas's now."

"Later."

I push the shop door open. The soothing chime welcomes me. Thomas looks up and beams excitedly.

"Ah, you are back, Gabriella. I'm glad." He stands up from where he's reading, and opens his arms wide in theatrical welcome. Thomas is such a fine and funny old gentleman.

"What made you think I wouldn't come back, Thomas? I love it here. The first time I stepped into your shop, I knew that even if you didn't hire me, I'd still be back here every week. So, you really can't get rid of me, you know." I walk to the back and dump my backpack on the desk in the office, where more books are stacked. I promised Thomas yesterday that I would schedule an inventory day to get our office organized. He was pleased. He said the room had not been touched for years. I step back out to join him at the counter.

"So how was our date with the young Mr. James last night?" He shakes his head as he speaks, teasing me. I look over where some students are browsing the new releases section and put my finger to my lips, shushing him.

"I don't know if that was a date, Thomas. Mr. James took me to the Back Room because there was a reading there last night." I speak louder, staring at him, warning against the eavesdroppers. He booms into laughter, holding his stomach as if trying to stop himself. I walk over to the new releases section and glare at him.

"Right." He finally stops laughing. "I forgot about that. Did you hear Thelma Pillar?"

"I did! Is she Filipina?" I busy myself rearranging books and trying to hide the smile on my face, which Thomas doesn't seem to notice.

The table is looking thin, so I bend down to get some more titles from the drawer underneath. I scan through the back cover of a new one that was not here yesterday.

"She is, actually. Do you have Filipino ancestry? Your hair and eyes are brown, but your lips are fuller than most Filipinos I know."

"My mom is Filipina and my dad is of Irish and Scottish descent."

"Aha, a beautiful mix. I knew there was something special about you, Gabriella." I charm him further with a smile.

"So, how was your walk yesterday?"

"It was pleasant, relaxing, and most important, lazy. New York has been my home the past fifty years, Gabriella. Fifty years. But only yesterday did I explore it without a plan, and I loved every minute of it."

"That's good. I'm glad. Where did you go?" I ask as I restock the books on the desk and organize them by titles.

"Here, there, everywhere. I retraced my steps from when I was a young lad. Looking back on those times I loved. Ha, such a beautiful word, and yet such a painful fact." There is tenderness in his eyes as he speaks of love. I haven't known him long enough to ask if he's married, was married. If he has any kids. And where they are now.

Two of the customers come up to the counter to pay. Thomas helps them, making small talk, complimenting them on their remarkable choices of literary stimulation. I can't help but smile as I move to the next table and rearrange more books. The customers thank Thomas and walk out of the shop.

"Have you been in love, Gabriella?" I stop what I'm doing, holding a stack of books that needs to be moved to another shelf and look at Thomas in deep thought.

"As I mentioned, I am in the process of divorcing. I just signed the papers about a week ago." Thomas puts his hand on his heart in a display of shock. Although it looks like he's joking, there is real surprise written on his face.

"Poor Gabriella. Oh, poor, poor baby. Are you okay, love?"

"I am okay, Thomas. Thanks for asking. But to answer your question about love, that I'm not a hundred percent sure. I've known my husband since I was a kid. We were classmates in middle school. So, I really don't know if what we had was love. I mean the kind that moves mountains, you know. The kind people write books about."

"All great love stories end in tragedy. So, maybe it was love?"

"Or maybe it wasn't love at all. We were young, and we didn't know any better. Plus, there were no defining moments in our relationship. We did everything that was expected of us. How about you, Thomas?"

"My love is real and everlasting, Gabriella." He walks around the counter, joining me on the floor. The shop is empty. In his posh pinstripe suit, just like yesterday, complete with a pocket square and a bow tie, Thomas glides into the room like a dancer in *Mary Poppins*. "There was once a boy I loved, Arthur. We were lovers for a long time. But then his family found out, and he was forced to marry the lovely Irish girl next door. It broke my heart. It still does." I fall quiet and stare at Thomas with such sorrow in my heart. I can only imagine the pain he must have to endure. "But that is in the past. We are friends now. We still meet up every once in a while, as friends." His eyes cloud over.

Everyone has a story. Thomas is such a cheerful man. You wouldn't think that his story is of tragedy. But here he is, soldiering on, one brave day at a time.

"I'm glad you remain friends. I hope that Simon and I will someday find it in our hearts to be friends again." I walk to the farthest corner of the shop and stop to stare out the window, not because I'm sad, but because I want to be able to tell my story one day without hurt in my heart. But that's not something I should contemplate now. Not today. Today is a good day.

"Gabriella, I'm old enough to know that we are but puppets of our own making. It's such a cliché to say that we reap what we sow, but it's the truth. Listen to me because I'm old enough to be your great-grandfather." He laughs again with such freedom that it sounds like magic. I can't help but laugh along with him. "Do I regret loving as much as I did, and finding myself in such great despair that, at one point, I wanted to take my own life? Absolutely not. Oh, those moments kept me alive. They happened. And they happened to me. How rare it is to be able to say you have loved with all of your heart, and with more than your soul. I say that with pride because not everyone is given that chance."

I turn around and see Thomas leaning back on the counter, crossing one leg over the other. Behind him is the shop logo, Gallagher. I want to take his photo right now and freeze this moment forever. It is a vision—I imagine it in black and white—of the old times that warrants a good place on someone's wall.

"So, dear Gabriella, do not be afraid to love. Seek it. Conquer it. Live it. And when it is done, just be, and the memories will be far more than your lifetime can ever hold."

All I can think about is how lucky I am to experience the wisdom of this man. How lucky I am to be here at all.

Chapter Fifteen

The shock on Felicity's face is indescribable. After I tell her what happened last night, she slowly sits on her sofa and stares at me like an intruder in her apartment.

Her doorbell rings, which means our dinner has arrived. Still, she doesn't say anything. I open the door, pay the guy, and grab our Chinese food. I'm still waiting. I walk to her kitchen and pull out some tableware. I purposely make loud noises, clicking the silverware together, the glasses, the plates—and still nothing.

She sits frozen on the sofa.

I don't know whether to laugh or be alarmed.

I move to her dining table and lay out our meal. She has been sitting on the sofa, considering this new information without movement for quite some time.

I let her be.

After a few more minutes have passed, I sit down across from her on the floor.

"You do know that Tina is in love with him, right?" she finally says. She looks troubled. This is news to me. I didn't get that from my conversation with Tina this morning. "You don't know Colt, Gabby. He's different." She buries her face in her hands. I don't say anything. In my heart, I guess I knew this, but I don't care. He makes me happy.

"You don't need to worry about me, Felicity."

"When did this happen?"

"I really don't know. It was sudden."

"He's your professor."

"I know."

"He's going to break your heart too."

"I know."

"Then why?" I shrug. I don't have an answer. "He's different, Gabby. He loves the attention. Most of the students I know in his class have fallen head over heels for him. I've heard rumors. What if he breaks your heart too?"

"Like Simon did?" I don't feel vindictive. Or defensive.

"Yes!" She stands up and starts pacing. "He will break you, probably more than Simon did. I can't let this happen."

"But it did. Happen." I stand up to face her. I want to ease her mind. Tell her not to worry. I am a grown woman. "I don't care what happens next. Right now, I'm happy. And I don't think I've ever been this free."

"Because of the good sex?" she asks me, wide-eyed in disbelief.

"Yes, yes, the sex, and everything else." I reach out to her, and take her hand gently. "Look, I'm not a young girl. I've read *Fifty Shades of Grey,* remember?"

"But that ended up like a fairy tale. Don't even think that will happen with Colt." I knew that too.

"Why can't you just be excited for me? Why can't you just be a girlfriend? Giggle with me. Teach me more about this world that I know nothing about. I want to live it. Experience it. And be a woman. I like the feeling of being wanted." She shakes off my hand.

"I don't want to see you miserable after what you've just

been through with Simon." She sits back down. We are both quiet for a while.

"Is the sex really that good?" she finally asks. I can tell she's softening up.

"Yes, and more." And I can't help but chuckle. I have to show my best friend that I'm ready for something like this. "You said it yourself, I should meet guys. Have fun with them. I don't expect anything from Colt. I don't expect . . . love." I whisper the last bit.

"As long as you know what you're doing. And that you're being safe."

"My god, Felicity. I've been married before, you remember?" I roll my eyes.

"How good?" Now, I see a twinkle in her eyes.

"Goddamn good! Five times last night."

"Holy shit, you're in big fucking trouble, my friend. . . ."

❧

Felicity jumps into the shower after dinner. I tell her I'll clean up. As I'm washing the dishes, I hear a ding from my phone. I wipe my hands on my jeans and reach for it on the sofa.

"Done with dinner yet?" It's Colt, and I smile.

"Washing the dishes."

"Naked? With ruffled apron?" I can't help but laugh.

"That would be really inappropriate. But sure, if it tickles your fancy."

"I want to see you right now." I look up, checking if Felicity is done with her shower.

"I can't go anywhere right now. I also have an assignment I need to finish for my class tomorrow with Williams."

"Screw him," he texts a few minutes later.

I send him a laughing emoji, and I add a kiss emoji to sweeten the deal.

"Does Felicity still live at 43rd and 6th?"

"Yes. Why?"

"Look out the window." I rush to the window. And there he is across the street on his Harley. I run to the door as Felicity is coming out of the bathroom.

"I'll be back," I tell her.

"Why?"

"Colt is outside."

"What the fuck!" Felicity screams. But she's not as angry as she was earlier. In fact, because I know her well, I can tell that she is as excited as I feel.

"I'll be right back."

"For fuck's sake, invite him up if you want. Just don't scream in the bedroom, I'll march right in."

"I'm not going to do that to you. I'm not letting him in."

"Aha. I like that. The hard to get tactic." She pulls the towel off her head and starts drying her hair with it.

I look horrendous, but I don't care.

I dash out of the apartment and down the steps, and then saunter out to meet Colt.

He's still sitting on his bike, more handsome than I remember. I stop myself and look at him, breathless as I admire him from a few steps away.

"Don't stand there, come here to me." And I do. The moment I reach him, he grabs my waist with one arm and buries his face in my neck. "I miss your scent. I miss you." His lips are cold and warm at the same time, sending me into shivers. I wrap my arms around his neck and bury my face in his hair. He smells of pine and dew. We don't say a word. We are frozen in our embrace.

"Get up here, you screwups!" We both look up and see Felicity at the window, waving at us to come up. We both laugh. He lets me go and gets off his bike. Then he grabs me around the waist again and bends his forehead to mine.

"How was your day?" I ask.

"I needed to see you. What have you done to me?" And then we kiss. It's beautiful. It's like I've always dreamed it should be. What does it mean? I still need to figure that out.

⌒⌒⌒

Felicity is all dressed in pajamas by the time we get up to her apartment. We couldn't keep our hands off each other on the way up, and by the time we see Felicity, we're both flushed.

"Well, hello, Colt," Felicity says with her arms resting upwards on the side of the door to greet us.

"Hello, Felicity." Colt shyly bends his head in response.

"This is quite a surprise."

"Believe me, I'm as surprised as you are," Colt says. I take his hand and lead him in. Felicity skips in excitement and secretly grins at me. I don't know what changed her mind about all this, but I can tell that she is excited too, all of a sudden.

In the month that I've known Colt, I have never seen him this uncomfortable. He drops his helmet on the side table, looks around, and wipes both his palms on his jeans. He looks good. He looks really, really good. I wrap my arms around his shoulders and give him a quick kiss on the lips.

"Holy shit, this is happening," Felicity murmurs under her breath. "Before you kids get too frisky, do you need a drink, Colt?"

"I can probably do one beer," he says.

"One beer it is." Felicity walks to the kitchen, opens her fridge, and, still looking at us, grabs a bottle of Flat Tire. She pulls a drawer to look for the bottle opener, removes the cap, walks around the counter and offers it to Colt—still curiously staring at him. "Does Tina know where you are?" I really don't understand why she needs to ask that. Colt looks up at her, surprised.

"I don't feel the need to tell her where I am, or my every move. But yes. She was actually the one who told me where you live." *Yay, Tina,* I think. In a lot of ways, I knew about Tina's feelings for Colt. It was written in *Roots*.

"Very well. I'm going to my room now. I don't mind the noise as long as the neighbors don't complain." She's teasing us, and I am grateful for it. I do know she's still not sold on the idea, but as my best friend, she has my back. I smile at her, letting her know how grateful I am. "Goodnight, kids," she says, walking to her room and shutting the door behind her.

The moment Colt hears the door click, he reaches out to me and pulls me to him. I move as swiftly as I can into his arms again. I reach up to kiss him. I kiss him softly, but he won't have it. He grips me forcefully and kisses me like his life depends on it. I kiss him back with the same intensity, forgetting where we are, not caring that my best friend is in the next room. I need him to be as close to me as possible, to feel his lips on mine, to have his hands all over me. The lust I feel for this man is something I've never experienced before with anyone. It's so overwhelmingly physical. It's both frightening and exhilarating.

He pulls away and looks deep into my eyes, questioning. I'm in a daze, an intoxicated high.

"What have you done to me, Gabriella?" he asks me again. I like the sound of my name on his lips. I touch it and trace my finger around his mouth, teasing him. I flutter my eyelashes at him. I'm such a minx, a seductress. I want to get out of my dress, pull him onto the bed, and own him again like I did five times last night.

"What have you done to *me*?" I reply with confidence. "You have made me into a woman in lust."

"But I want much more . . ."

"More than my lust?"

"Yes, even more than your soul . . ." He stares into my eyes with such passion that I know I'm in big trouble. Big, big trouble.

—⁓⁓—

It's almost midnight when I lock the door behind Colt. I invited him to stay but he declined, and I appreciate him more for it. There was a lot of kissing and touching, and we almost did the deed, but we stopped ourselves. This is uncharted territory for me. I lean on the door, daydreaming about him next to me.

I hear Felicity's door creak open. She sees me and makes a face—one eyebrow raised and lips twitched on the side, like that gymnast who lost in the Olympics.

"Hi," I say dreamily.

"I don't know what to say, Gabs." She laughs a little, then a lot. And I can't help but join in. "Holy shit, this is hot!" We laugh some more.

"I know. I mean, he just left and I want to call him back. Oh, his kisses! I don't think I've been kissed that way before. I mean it was different with Simon. We were kids. We really didn't have any experience beyond what we learned together. But with Colt . . ."

"I get it, I get it. I can't believe you're finally getting some." I turn the light off in the foyer and move to the kitchen to clear up the bottles of beer Colt and I had. Felicity is studying me. I can tell by her fixed stare. "Gabby?"

"Huh?" I drop the beer bottles in the recycling bin.

"I love you. I hope you know that."

"I do. And I love you back."

We tell each other this as a reassurance, when we're both uncertain of the other. We've been saying it quite a lot lately.

She's still not okay with this.

Chapter Sixteen

I *lived!*

This morning, I received the letter from Simon's lawyers that the court clerk of Manhattan had dutifully entered the judgment of our divorce into the court record making it final.

Official.

Closed out.

Complete.

I'm a single woman again.

I'm processing. I still don't know how I feel about this.

When Thomas found out when I walked into work this afternoon, he closed the shop early and dragged me to Lips on 56th Street. He believes that I deserve a sprinkle of joy in my life today, and there is no better place to get that than at the house of the fabulous drag queens.

Lips is more than I imagined it would be. It's sparkly, glitzy, and just downright loud. It's bright, and it's colorful, and so . . . happy. I'm like a little kid, wide-eyed, walking into a chocolate factory for the first time, discovering a whole new world with my purple feather boa courtesy of Thomas. My palms are sweaty from excitement, and I can feel my heart beating double time. This is totally contrary to how society tends to perceive a middle-aged woman should be handling a divorce. I think, in ways I'll never truly comprehend, this is what happiness should feel like. Free.

Thomas and I settle at the bar, giving us the perfect view of the stage. As Thomas talks to the beefy bartender, I continue to observe. I clap my hands together in merry wonder. I gaze around some more and, after a few minutes, I come to the realization that this place is just like Barbie's Dream House. Everything is pink. Lights are bouncing off mirror balls that surround the big elegant chandelier at the center of the ceiling, giving the place a dreamy, enchanted vibe. One can live here forever, shut out from the harshness of the outside world, from the pain of heartbreak and the agony of loneliness. In here, one can never be lonely.

Suddenly, I feel a light but alarming tug. I jolt backwards in surprise. A tall, gorgeous queen walks right in front of me, pulling her long-tailed silver gown and unintentionally hitting me with it. She turns around immediately and looks at me with horror in her eyes.

"I'm sorry, princess. . . ." she says. There is no denying the deep tenor of her voice. Her eyelashes are long and embellished with diamond-like sparkles. Her lips are as red as apples, and she has the highest cheekbones I've ever seen. Her hair is as black as night and styled like a big ball of cotton candy with tiny silver and gold barrettes. I want to reach out and touch her, but I don't. Instead, I smile—the giddy kind—and she returns it by lightly touching my cheek. She radiates kindness. She glides toward the stage, leaving me starstruck.

The queen takes center stage. Loud music reverberates from all corners of the darkened room. I didn't notice earlier that she was—is —Barbra Streisand.

She belts out the opening of the song "Memory" with a booming voice. She owns the moment as she owns the stage. I stare at her in awe. She is larger than life. I can tell as she stands there in front of the crowd that she knows who she is, that she finds freedom in what she's doing, and the courage that surrounds her is because of everything that she embodies. I'm envious of her bravery.

I feel Thomas's hand reaching out to mine. He squeezes it lightly—a simple but powerful form of encouragement, letting me know that everything is going to be all right. And I know that.

I'm not lonely. I'm relieved. And with this, I feel guilty. I shake off the feeling. I remind myself that it wasn't I who left the marriage.

At the end of the song, the crowd roars in applause. Barbra takes a bow and the crowd roars some more. Thomas puts his hands up in thundering claps, and I join in. The energy in this place is contagious. This, right here, is living.

"We need some happy cocktails, Gabriella. Come, let's join the others." I follow Thomas to the other side of the bar closer to the stage where a dozen more queens are gathered. I stare at them in amazement. There is Cher in a white jumpsuit with black flowing hair and purple lipstick. She is taller than Barbra, for sure. I look at her shoes. They are white with silver studs and clunky platform heels that could possibly be seven inches tall.

"You like them, sweetheart?" Cher asks, catching me staring at her feet like a doofus.

"I love them!" I don't feel embarrassed squealing like a five-year-old. "Come as you are and as you please" the sign outside says, and I'm enjoying every minute of it.

Thomas hands me a pink cocktail in a martini glass. Thomas's favorite, of course, a cosmopolitan. I take it with pleasure. Thomas's smiles are the brightest. They provide me with solace. It is not just Thomas's smiles, really. Everything about Thomas is comforting. Working for him the past few weeks has been one of the greatest honors of my life. Not only have I gained employment and financial independence of sorts, I have also gained an invaluable friend. Our conversations, no matter how mundane at times, are what I look forward to each day. The wisdom he imparts and the experiences he unselfishly shares are like anchors to my soul. They enrich my perception about the true meaning of prosperity. It's never about money or anything material for Thomas; it's always been about the journey and the many lessons we learn along the way. He is teaching me to accept fate, to embrace the challenges, and to grow along with whatever life throws at me. I give Thomas a tight hug. The tightest my chubby little frame can manage.

"You are so much fun, Thomas!" I say as I pull away from him.

"Oh, I know. Life should be like this place, Gabriella. A dream."

I sip a little of my cosmopolitan to gather courage and shyly move closer to where the queens are. One of the ladies slowly pushes a chair toward me, and unexpectedly lifts me up and sits me down. Our faces are inches from each other, and I can't help staring. Because, well, what do you do when faced with this bizarre situation? She returns my gaze and, probably realizing how idiotic I look, starts to laugh. I hesitate for a little but then join her. In the end, we look like two old friends sharing a private joke. Eventually, all the other queens crowd around me, finding me as fascinating as I find them.

"She's with me, ladies," Thomas says in an attempt to rescue me. And in unison, upon hearing Thomas's voice, they all scream in excitement. There are lots of cheers and hugs and air kisses—as if a long-lost friend has finally been found. I sit there in the middle of it all, and although I'm an outsider, I feel so welcomed.

I let Thomas have his time with the ladies. There is so much to see to entertain myself in this place. The queens may be the stars of Lips, but the entire venue is a spectacle in itself. Every table is occupied. There are small groups and there are larger groups; some have champagne buckets, and some even have big balloons decorating their booth. There are no divides—young and old, all genders, orientations, and races gather in this place without borders or hesitation. It's such a welcoming atmosphere that anyone—even those who recently went through a taxing divorce—can enjoy themselves.

"We love Thomas," Katy Perry, who appears from nowhere, whispers into my ear. I give her a nod of acknowledgment, letting her know I understand perfectly because I probably love Thomas as much or even more. "He is the granddaddy of us ladies here." Katy has short platinum blond hair, a nose ring, full on pink and purple makeup, and a gorgeous metallic gold evening gown. She also has a purple feather boa like mine, but obviously bigger and brighter—and as I touch it, I realize it's also a lot heavier.

"He looks really happy here," I say to Katy as we observe Thomas, who seems to be having a magnificent time with the queens.

"Yeah," Katy agrees. "Thomas has been coming here for as long as I can remember, and then he stopped when his son died. This is the first time since. You must be special to him. I'm glad."

I put my hand over my heart as I listen to this painful tale. "If you didn't know, please don't mention anything to him. I'm just glad he's back, and I'm sure so are the other girls." I sit frozen in shock. There are so many layers to Thomas, and I hope that one day we'll have the kind of friendship where he can open up to me—to share with me not just his joys, but also his sorrows. I want to be able to return the favor—to be his friend if he needs one.

Suddenly, the entire place goes dark.

"That's my cue," Katy says, squeezing my hand and heading toward the stage.

"Good luck," I whisper.

A big bright spotlight focuses on Katy, whose back is toward us. Then the song "Firework" starts with a big bang, and Katy turns around and begins to sing. She is the spitting image of the real Katy in the smoke and mirrors here at Lips. And just like the song, I start thinking about my situation—the lyrics are a true reflection of my life. And then the chorus comes. I stand up, and I start jumping toward Thomas. I reach for his hand and together we dance.

I am a goddamn firework!

I scream at the top of my lungs.

I've never screamed so loudly, or twirled so vivaciously, and I jump up and down like no one is watching. Thomas is dancing next to me with such poise, doing what looks like a John Travolta move from the old movie *Staying Alive*. It's hilarious, and I love him even more for it. I can see a twinkle in his eye, which makes me very happy I came here with him. I hold both his hands, and we dance together. He starts jumping up and down like a seventy-year-old yoyo, and then he lets go of my hand and turns around and around in his spot, toasting everyone with his fresh cosmopolitan before drinking it down. The queens around him are just as happy. I look up at Katy onstage, and she smiles at me intimately.

◦⁀◦

It's almost midnight by the time my Uber delivers me to Colt's townhouse. He's sleepily waiting for me on the steps, shirtless and barefoot and wearing low-hanging jeans. He gets up as soon as he sees my car. I watch him walk toward me, and I'm blown away. He opens the door and bends down to give me a kiss before helping me out of the car. He notices my feather boa and gives me a questioning look—with his brows furrowed and eyes squinting, I think he's the hottest guy on the planet. Masculine but not ostentatiously beefy, beautiful but not soft, tall and dark without looking like a villain, and most of all, his eyes are a calm river of blue. Looking at him makes me question the extent of my luck—who am I kidding? Whatever this is, it must have an expiration date. In the meantime, I jump into his arms again tonight because things might be different when I wake up tomorrow.

"You're super lit," he teases, and I let him, because I love being in his arms.

"Let's go to sleep. I'm sooo tired." I walk behind him, my finger holding one of his belt loops. He turns around with a sleepy smile and wraps his arms around my shoulder.

"Feather boa, huh? Do I want to know where you've been?" he finally asks and kisses the top of my head.

It's still dark when I open my eyes. Colt and I went straight to bed last night. He was already asleep by the time I got out of the shower. I've been staying at his townhouse the past three nights. And in the past three weeks since our first night together, there was not a day that we were not in touch. Felicity tells me that we're moving way too fast. Of course, we don't tell anyone at school, and when we see each other in the hallway or in class, we behave exactly like a professor and his student.

To my surprise, Colt is already up, lying on his side facing me with one arm under his head, and the other caressing my waist.

"Hi," he whispers.

"Hey," I sleepily reply. "Have you been up a while? Are you okay?"

"Just looking at you."

"Why?" I reach for his face, barely visible in the light coming in through the window.

"I like it," he says thoughtfully.

"You like looking at me?" I cover my face with both hands, feeling self-conscious.

"Yes . . ." He pulls my hands gently off my face and brings me closer to him. I put my arms around his neck. This has been my perfect happy place the past three weeks.

"I like looking at your face too. It makes me happy." I kiss him on the nose. He wiggles it lightly and smiles. Something stirs inside me.

"You make me happy." He brushes some stray hair off my face, and I feel like my heart is going to explode. I'm too afraid to understand what we have. I'm not ready to put too much attention into how I feel about him right now.

"How do you feel about your divorce?" He shifts, raising his head and shoulders, and leans on his arm.

"I'm fine. I thought it'd be harder. It was a piece of paper. My marriage ended a year ago."

"Did you talk to him today? Simon?" He never speaks his name, so this here is a surprise.

"He sent me a text. I know this isn't easy for him either."

"Why are you making excuses for him?" His jaw hardens.

"I'm not. I just don't want to blame him. In some weird way, I'm actually happy that I'm free." I look away from him and stare at the ceiling in deep thought.

No one speaks for a few minutes; we just enjoy the silence of dawn in each other's arms.

"My dad killed my mom when I was seventeen years old. He was such a jealous, insecure man." He lowers his head. I gasp and, wanting to protect him, I bring him closer to me, and kiss his forehead.

"Oh, baby . . ." I say, as I feel my emotions welling up inside me. "Colt . . ." I pull him even closer, not wanting him to let go.

"Nobody knew about it, but I heard the lawyers and the police talking after they found them together dead." I hold him tighter. "I'm complicated, confused. I have so much shit to work through."

"Colt, it's over now. You're safe. You're great. You've turned out just fine."

"I don't know how things like this work, and I'm so screwed up. I don't want to screw *this* up." He heaves a heavy sigh.

I don't know what else to say, so I kiss him. I kiss him with all my heart, baring my soul, stripping away my veil of self-preservation. He makes me brave.

"You've been doing an awesome job so far. You make me happy and proud and giddy." I smile at him, demonstrating how he makes my eyes sparkle.

He moves his head to kiss me on the temple, moving his mouth to my cheeks, then to my nose, and finally to my lips. There is no hunger in his caress. The lightness of the moment makes the emotions seem raw and more powerful. This feeling is dizzying. I want to stay in this bubble forever.

"You'll have to be tough for me, Gabby . . . fight me, fight *for* me." He's staring deep into my eyes now, and slowly moves on top of me. His arms are like rock, his body a gorgeous temple, and his eyes are deep in worry, but his heart—although I can't see or touch it, I know it's real. He cups my face and gazes into my eyes. I hold his stare. "Gabby. What have you done to me?" I lift my head and reach for his lips and I kiss him like there is no tomorrow. "Don't leave me, no matter what." Those words are the key to my heart, and I know I should be afraid, and I know I should run as fast and as far as I can. Instead, I surprisingly admit to myself that there is a very good chance that I'm in love with this man.

"I'm right here, Colt . . . right here," I say like a prayer.

Chapter Seventeen

Felicity is already at Lovely Day, one of my favorite coffee shops on Elizabeth Street, working on her laptop, when I walk in all excited to share my news. She looks up and kicks the red synthetic upholstered chair next to her out from under the table without saying a word. Then she lifts her index finger and gestures for me to wait until she's done with whatever she's working on. This is classic Felicity. When she's in one of her creative spells, she is not one to multitask, and I tease her heavily about it. I pull out the chair, sit down, and wait obediently.

I pull my phone from my backpack and start scrolling through my Instagram feed. I'm not a big Instagram poster, but I like seeing how old friends are living their lives. Sometimes, I regret not being part of it—being in their pictures, living alongside them, and creating memories I can take with me. I love witnessing how they celebrate new jobs, marriages, babies—and I also mourn with them over heartbreak and loss. Growing up, my world was all Felicity and Simon—and I'll forever be grateful for it, but I sometimes wonder if life would have been different if I'd explored outside my comfort zone.

"Done!" Felicity shouts. She pushes her computer away and throws her hands in the air in triumph. I shake off my thoughts and look around to see the people at the next table staring at us. I give them an apologetic smile. "What's up?" Felicity adds.

"I found an apartment!" I pretend scream in a whisper so as not to further disturb the others around us.

"Where? How? When?" Felicity is way too enthusiastic. I can tell that she's only pretending to be excited. Her eyes say otherwise. When I told her a few days ago that I intend to live on my own for a while, she was disappointed. She didn't push it, which I truly appreciated, but I knew that she always wanted us to live together. In college, we both lived at home, commuted via the metro to Rosslyn station, and took the Georgetown shuttle from there. By the time we moved to New York, I was already married to Simon, so we never really got the chance to be roommates.

"I was looking online last night and found this tiny one-bedroom flat, so I called the realtor this morning. That's where I was. And, get this! It's only a ten-minute walk from here!" It's my turn to gesture in victory, spreading both my arms wide with pride. "Isn't that great!" I smile to find myself tooting my own horn. I'm never like this in public.

"That's a long way from my apartment," she says, pouting, but I can also sense pride. Because that's what best friends do.

Since my divorce with Simon was finalized last month, I've been looking at apartments constantly. It's time I moved out and cut the cord. The money I received from the divorce is more than enough to start over, and I haven't even touched the check Simon gave me when he came to the apartment that one emotional day.

"Where is it?"

"Noho!"

"Yeah, that's a great neighborhood. Lots of students live there too. It makes sense. You work here and study here, so really this is your neighborhood. But that's like literally on the other side of the city from Colt's," Felicity says, the practical side of her making the calculations in her head.

I shrug. I haven't even said anything to Colt about this. We've talked about my apartment hunting a few times, but since I've been staying at his townhouse a lot lately, we always seem to forget my urgent need to move.

"Hey, Gabby. Can I ask you something?" She suddenly looks serious, and Felicity is rarely serious, so this must be important.

"Shoot." I jerk my head sideways at her, puzzled.

"I got a call from Simon the other day. . . ." she begins nervously.

"Okay?"

"Well, he's inviting me to his new apartment for dinner . . . and she will be there."

"Oh." I wait to feel something, but there's nothing. Slowly, a smile forms on my face.

"I won't go if you don't want me to." But I can tell that she wants to. Her begging eyes say it all. Who am I to deprive other people of friendships just because I don't think it's fair to me? This, whatever Simon and I are going through, is not about fairness. This is about moving on and deciding to live different lives. I get it. I was the victim when all this started—but not anymore.

"Do you remember how we met for the first time in middle school, Felicity? Simon and I carried you to the nurse's office after you got into a huge fight with a girl named Hannah because she was making fun of Simon. You called Simon your brother, and for a while, because I didn't know you guys, I thought he was. I only figured out the truth in high school, when the three of us started hanging out together. You guys were already friends before I came into your lives. I'm not going to get in the way of that friendship. I'm not that shallow, and I hope you guys know it."

"I do." Felicity pauses, unsure what to say next. "Gabs, you've been moving so quickly the past few months, meeting new people, going out with other people, dating the hottest guy in New York City—sometimes I feel like I'm losing you too. And I don't want that." She bends her head as she speaks.

"I sometimes wish Simon and I hadn't gotten married. I wish we'd all stayed friends like we were in high school. Life would have been easier. We'd all still be together, as friends, right now. I'd like that. But know you'll never lose me. Never."

"It's not too late for that, is it?" I can see hope in her face—a hope I'm not quite sure I am able to offer just yet.

"I don't know. In time, maybe."

"You have Colt." I sense desperation.

"You warned me about Colt once, remember? We both know he's different. He's not the kind of man I can hold onto forever." I put my hands on my lap nervously. I can feel Felicity staring at me, looking worried. Her eyebrows are drawn together.

"Then why are you with him?" She's almost whining, so I give her a small reassuring smile—meant for both of us.

"You and I thought Simon was going to be with me forever. We were sure he was never going to do anything to break my heart. Simon was reliable and steady, someone you could easily trust. But he broke my heart anyway. With Colt, I know what I'm getting into."

"That's very brave." She grabs her half-empty cup of coffee and takes a sip.

"Hey, don't expect me to be all tough when it happens. Losing Colt will probably hurt more than my divorce." I know this. There is no point trying to sugarcoat it.

"You've only known him a couple of months."

"I know. Isn't that crazy? Just a few months, and I can't imagine my life without him."

"Are you serious?"

"Yes."

"Why?"

"Because . . . I love him." Felicity gasps and puts her hand over her mouth. This revelation catches me off guard too, but there is no fear in my heart as I admit it—only serenity.

"Have you told him?"

"No. But I will."

"Has he said anything to you? About love?"

"No." He doesn't need to, I tell myself. Loving someone shouldn't have preconditions.

"Do you think he at least cares about you?" I know these questions are not easy for Felicity. Her eyes are as wide as head-lights as she watches me closely.

"Yes. He makes me happy . . . in everything that he does. But every day, I'm also waiting for the other shoe to drop."

"That's not how a relationship should be."

"Keeps me on my toes. Keeps me alive. Every time I wake up next to him, there is this steady smile on my face, not because of sex or because of, my god, yes, he is so hot, but because he treats me like a woman. Like I deserve to be seen. He sees me like Si-mon never did."

"Was it like this with Simon before too? This feeling, I mean?"

"I loved Simon differently. I love Colt with all of me."

I may not know much about navigating my new life, but one thing I know for sure—I am in love with Colt James.

❋

I have a few weeks to finish two big projects for school. Colt didn't require us to do midterm work in his class, which is a great relief because my other two classes have me bogged down with research.

I don't go to the library when I'm facing a deadline. I don't want to be surrounded by people who are as stressed out as I am. Instead I go to Washington Square Park. I don't mind the noise on the street, or the laughter of children running around, or the old men bantering while they play chess. When I'm deep in thought, contemplating the words I need to put on paper, I raise my head from time to time because I love to look at life, to stare at the colors that make up our existence. I want to be where the action is. There is a certain kind of glory in learning to appreciate the simplicity of being alive.

I usually sit on one particular bench when I'm in the park, with my computer on my lap, a backpack next to me filled with snacks, and a jug of ice-cold water. Sometimes, I have my headphones on with Yo-Yo Ma playing in the background while motions of life dance beautifully in front of me with every cello stroke. I think of it as my own film, in my mind, where I try to speculate what people are feeling that day—looking at their expressions, pondering why some have sadness in their eyes and celebrating those who are noticeably happy and carefree.

I take a break from work, close my computer, and pull my legs up crisscross on the bench. I tug my bag of sweet-and-salty trail mix from my backpack, and I pick out the M&Ms one by one. I should have just bought an entire packet of M&Ms. I reach for my phone next to me on the bench, and I see one missed call from Colt and two unread text messages—one from Colt and the other from Felicity.

I check Felicity's message first.

"Are you all packed to move on Friday?" it says. After weeks of deliberating, talking to the realtor, opening a checking account, and getting my parents to guarantee for me (which is really embarrassing at my age), I finally signed my lease last week. I don't have much to move. Simon and I agreed to sell our shared belongings, and last weekend was busy with people coming in and out of our apartment to pick up their purchases. I put it all on Craigslist, and everything sold within two days. I'm not keeping much except my books, a few of my clothes and shoes, the purses that Mom gave me, and some other personal belongings. Even the paintings Simon and I collected together the last ten years were sold, and some pulled in a few thousand bucks a piece. I kept some smaller pieces for myself, which Simon agreed to and even encouraged.

"Yes," I reply.

"I'll be there first thing Friday with the car." I didn't want Felicity to skip work for my move, but she insisted. I didn't have the energy to argue, and I also know that since I'm making new memories on my own, she wants to be a part of it. Thomas gave me the day off and offered to close the shop to help, which I straightaway declined. "Are you staying there tonight?" she asks.

"Yes, I have to. I still need to look over some stuff."

"Do you want me to come over? I can bring dinner and a bottle of wine."

"Sure! We'll end up in sleeping bags on the floor though."

"Slumber party!"

I'm about to open Colt's message when my phone rings. I've finally changed my ringtone to the *Harry Potter* theme song, exposing the nerdy side of me.

"Hey," I answer softly. It's Colt. The feeling of excitement doesn't get old, even after nearly three months.

"Hey, you. Where are you?"

"Hangman's tree."

"You're creepy. Why do you like hanging out there?" He asks. I laugh a little.

"It's beautiful here. Plus, it's daytime, so it's not really creepy. So many kids playing." My eyes follow a group of toddlers running around with moms behind them, ready to catch them when they fall.

"I just got out of my class, I'll walk over to you."

"Okay, but let me remind you that I'm here because I'm trying to get some work done, because you see I've been busy with other things at night." I like how our relationship has evolved into something comfortable and easy, and I'm not afraid to tease him.

"Well, I don't have anything to do with that. That's all your fault," he teases back.

"Ha-ha!" I say sarcastically. Colt starts laughing at the other end. His progress had been slow, but he's more relaxed around me now, around us. We've not been out much with other people, but we've been around close friends—Felicity and Tina, and some others I met at the dinner at his townhouse that first evening. I've mentioned him to my mom briefly once, during one of our daily phone calls. Colt and I were going to watch a movie that night, and I accidentally told her. Of course, I've been badgered about it nonstop and have to keep trying to convince her that he's just a friend. Our relationship, or whatever this is that we have, is still too new and fragile, and I don't want to jinx it.

"I'm on my way. Where are you, exactly?"

"My favorite study bench."

"I'll be there in two minutes. I'm very close. Do you need lunch or a drink or something?"

"I've got that covered. I have an entire bag here filled with goodies."

"Please eat healthy, Gabby."

"I have trail mix!"

"Yeah, I know. And I'm pretty sure all the M&Ms have gone missing." I laugh. I love to hear the sound of my laughter. It sounds new, real, true. And I can't believe that after only a few months, he already knows me so well. "You look crazy laughing there by yourself, silly." I lift my head up, and I look around, scoping out the place, searching for him. And then I see him across the park, in his plain white T-shirt under his leather jacket and black denim jeans, aviator Ray-Ban sunglasses covering his beautiful face and making him look incredibly hot. I feel a breeze on my face, and I've never been more inspired. In his hands is a bouquet of lush peonies wrapped in manila paper. Peonies are my favorite. He remembered, and I only told him this once. And how did he find them this time of the year? His other hand is holding the phone to his ear.

I feel my spirit soar, more in love than I was just a few minutes ago.

His strides are slow, unsure. I want to burst with joy. But I stay seated with a giddy smile on my face. When he stops in

front of me, I raise my head, and then I jump up on the bench
and hug him. I kiss him forcefully on the mouth, and he enfolds
me in his arms. We pull apart. He hands me the flowers. I take
them, cradle them in my arms, and I look at the man who gave
them to me, and I know that it's time.

"I love you, Colt." There is no fear, no surprise, only calm.

Right this moment, as the hangman's tree bends its head to
shade us from the blinding sunlight, we have now become one of
the many stories it has witnessed in its 310 years of existence.

*

He sits next to me on the bench. I don't need him to say anything. I don't want him to feel under any obligation to return my
gesture or how I feel. Only just recently I've realized that the less
I expect, the less frustrated I get. I'm just happy that he's in my
life, and that he's pushing his boundaries for me. I inhale the
scent of peonies, and I'm transported back in time to my mom's
garden. Peonies smell like roses, but sweeter and less intense, and
that's what makes them less imposing.

"There is one other thing, actually, that I need to give you,"
Colt says shyly, which is very unlike him. Colt speaks with purpose at all times. It's one of the reasons why he's a great teacher.

"More gifts?" I squeal excitedly.

"Don't get too excited," he says, and I can tell from the grin on
his face that he's both happy and unsure of himself. The flowers
are a brave step for him. I've never really imagined him holding
them in public, wearing his heart on his sleeve like that, especially
somewhere close to school.

"Okay, I won't get excited." I put my arm around his shoulders and wait patiently for said gift. He hands me a key—one single key, without a chain or any charm to hold it. "It's the key to the townhouse." Although he's staring at me, expecting a reaction, his head is bent down. "You get off work late some nights, and you stay out with Thomas or Felicity other nights, and I always end up waiting for you until midnight. You know how I like to be in bed by ten thirty." Finding out that he's a morning person shocked me at first, as I'd always assumed he was a night owl. He opens my hand and puts the key in it. "Here, the key to my privacy."

I stare at the key in my palm. I don't know what to say. Instead, I pull him to me and kiss him on the cheek.

"You surprise me every day," is all I can say, because he does.

"I'm trying," he says, stroking the back of my hand.

"I know, but you don't have to if you don't want to."

"That's the thing; with you, I want to."

Chapter Eighteen

I stare at Felicity like she's grown horns after she confesses that she's been sleeping with Tinder Dude—a guy she spoke about in passing a few weeks ago—for over four weeks now. Over four weeks!

"Four weeks!?" With my eyes wide and beaming like headlights, I scream in surprise. Livid. She nods her head as best she can while sprawled drunk on the living room floor with only a thin comforter, which I decided to keep from my shared belongings with Simon, to cushion us. We've not moved for twenty minutes—not a muscle—and are both starting to look like crime scene human chalk traces.

"He's amazing. . . ." Felicity says after finally supplying me with the intimate details of their romantic interlude last night, and I can feel the dreamy tone in her voice, emphasizing on the Z. "I think he's my best yet." I know I should be happy for her, and I am. But . . .

"You should have told me the minute it happened." I'm hurt that she hadn't bothered to share this information with me sooner.

Probably trying to escape the hot seat, Felicity finally gets up. My eyes follow her movements, but I still don't have the energy to move. She looks for her purse, which is tucked on the side of the lone arm chair left in my apartment, pulls out her phone, seriously starts scrolling through it, smiles, stops, and finally hits a button that prompts "Let's Get Loud" by Jennifer Lopez.

"Get up, you lazy witch!" Felicity cajoles, kicking me playfully on my foot. In her pink bunny print pajamas and bunny ears headwear, Felicity is a sight to behold.

JLo is our jam, and this is our song—just ours, Simon not included. She pulls me from my comfortable spot on the floor, drags me up, and lures me to dance. I start to jump up and down —it's my default dance setting.

Felicity is a hilarious drunk—with her eyes closed, she puts both her arms up as if trying to reach something high in the air and starts shaking her hips left and right to the rhythm of Jennifer Lopez screaming. The bunny ears add a lot to this image. I burst out laughing, and then I jump up and down some more around her while waving my arms desperately, trying to mimic some form of dancing. I'm such a loser in this department. Simon is the suave one on the dance floor. Felicity and I don't have that talent. Felicity then starts belting out the song with JLo, an invisible microphone in her hand, simulating a catwalk on my bare living room stage. I follow her with my invisible pom-poms and twirls with no grace. Felicity sees me almost stumble and we both start laughing.

Oh, the freedom of the laughter we both once shared. I remember vividly, in high school, when the only thing we were both scared of was failing P.E. But our happiness was innocent, and painless. There's no going back to that blissful time, and although I regret not doing much in those days, I'm more than ready now—I'm ready to face all my experiences to come.

Finally, after four minutes of screaming at the top of our lungs and hoping the neighbors won't call the police, we both collapse on the floor in hysterical laughter.

"I miss you, Gabs."

"I miss you too."

No one speaks for a few minutes, and only the heaving of our breath occupies the silent space.

"I'm sorry for not telling you about Phil sooner." I hear regret in Felicity's voice, but I don't say anything. I turn to my side and face her, and she does the same. Her face seems so tiny it would fit in my palm, and I smile at this thought. Her cute and stubborn antics are what I love most about her, so this sadness is unexpected.

"Felicity, I've known you more than half my life. I know that if it's something I need to know, you'd tell me. I'm not going to lie that it didn't sting a little, but I trust you have your reasons." I smile at her weakly.

She gets up, which is quite a challenge, and opens the window. I feel the light breeze entering the room. It's refreshing after our workout with JLo. She sits on the open window ledge with her butt sticking out on the railing.

"I think I really like him." The sparkle in her eyes is obvious, and I don't think I've ever seen Felicity so besotted. Felicity is normally a well of sarcasm, and from the few minutes she's talked about Phil, there is not even a trace of that. She then starts blushing.

"Sex is that great, huh?" I tease. She blushes some more, and Felicity is not the blushing type.

"Yeah, I can't even explain it. We've seen each other about ten times before last night, so it's been pretty consistent." I get up and join her on the window ledge, wiggling my butt in to fit next to hers.

"I'm glad. And I can't wait to meet this guy!"

"I can't wait for you to meet him. I'm sorry I didn't let you know sooner. You've been busy a lot lately."

"I'm sorry. . . ." I bow my head as I say this, because she speaks the truth. I'm so wrapped up in Colt that I almost always forget that there is life outside him, apart from us. Now I feel guilty—for feeling stupidly hurt not knowing about Phil, when in fact I'm the one who's been incommunicado. I think about the past few weeks, and had it not been for Felicity constantly texting, calling, and emailing me, I probably wouldn't have been in touch. I should be ashamed of myself. No guy should ever come between us like this. I bury my face in my hands. "I'm so sorry, Felicity. . . ."

"But you shouldn't be, though. That's my point." She pulls my hands away from my face. "You shouldn't apologize just because your life is moving in a different direction, and I'm stuck where I was before all this happened to you."

"But you're not," I say. "You have Phil now."

"I miss you, and I miss Simon, and I miss the three of us together. I know it's selfish, but sometimes I feel like a kid in the middle of a nasty divorce, and I don't know who to pick. I feel like I was part of the breakup too."

"I know . . . I'll try to be a better friend."

"Gabs, you're a great friend. This is me. This is all me."

"We should try to do things like this more often. Not just the rushed lunches after class, or sporadic text messages that I can barely reply to. Let's do our weekly movie nights, and our every other Friday drinks, and go to dinners at leisure. We should make more effort, especially now that I'm moving farther away from you."

"I don't want to lose you, Gabs."

"And you won't. Why don't you join Thomas and me on our nights at Lips?"

"I would love that. It's insane that I'm jealous of a seventy-year-old man." We both laugh at this.

"Are you crazy? Thomas is in love with you!" I say to Felicity.

"I guess you're right, and I love him too." I steal a quick sideway glance at Felicity and finally see a trace of a smile on her face. She turns to look at me too.

"Felicity, you're so much like a sister to me, and my very best friend in the world. Please don't ever doubt that."

We're silent for a few minutes.

"This thing with Colt, I think it's getting more and more serious, huh?"

"Yeah, I guess. He just gave me a key to his apartment, and I know that's a big deal for him."

"Whoa!" The shock on Felicity's face is not comforting.

"I love fairy tales just as much as the next girl, but I've been hurt before by someone I trusted all my life. I don't expect whatever this is to last a lifetime. No one can tame Colt James."

"But he's tamed now."

"Until when?" I ask as I contemplate the news articles that I've read about him online. The nightly parties, the many blonde babes in his arms, and the drunken bar fights. You can't change overnight. No one can change anyone overnight. "Colt is a very complicated man, and I knew that from the start, so . . . I shouldn't really expect much. In fact, all this is much more than I can ask for."

"Geez, Gabs, that's deep shit."

"I can't own that beautiful man forever, you know." I try to make light of the moment. I'd be lying if I said that I'm looking forward to the day Colt gets tired of me.

"You've grown up the past year, Gabs, and it's frightening." Felicity grabs my hand and holds onto it tight.

"Divorce will do that to you, that's for sure, but enough about me. Tell me more about Phil. When will I meet him? Wait . . ." I suddenly remember. "Wasn't last night your dinner with Simon?" Still holding my hand, Felicity looks away and stares at the only light fixture left in the apartment, the chandelier in the dining area.

"Phil and I went." I feel another pinch of pain in my heart, but I let it go. This is her time. It's her story to tell. I'm just a friend, ready to listen.

"So, how was it?" I'm trying to keep it light.

"It was okay. Quiet."

"Dinner was quiet? C'mon!" I nudge her shoulder. "Tell me more."

"Actually, it was pretty uncomfortable. It was just the three of us. She wasn't there." I sigh with relief. I can tell that there is much more story to tell, but I don't push it. It's not a story I'm particularly eager to hear.

"How was Phil, though?"

"Gabs, are you interested in knowing what's going on with Simon?" Felicity asks slowly, with difficulty, uncertain of my response.

"Not really." I bow my head because I know I should care. More than anything else, Simon was also part of my youth, my life, my family—how can I throw that away just because there is a Colt now who's making it easier for me? But at the same time, why shouldn't I be callous? Don't I deserve to be carefree too, and not be concerned about what he feels? He didn't worry about my feelings when he left me. Anger bubbles inside me again, and I'm done with recrimination.

"He's very interested in you."

"Tell him to stop. I'm fine."

"He knows that. It's just weird. I think the tables have turned."

"There are no tables, Felicity. I don't think of it that way. Is he okay, though?" I have to ask.

"He's not. You were all he talked about. It was frustrating. I felt so bad for Phil that he had to sit through it all." Felicity lets go of my hand and jumps off the window ledge to face me. "It was just sad, and it pissed me off a little. He knew I was bringing someone. He could have warned me." I don't say anything more. I just let her pace back and forth in annoyance. I cross my arms over my chest because I don't know what else to do. "They've been having problems. Suzanne assumed that as soon as your divorce became final, he would propose to her. Well, obviously he didn't." I close my eyes as I hear this. "He's still in love with you, Gabs."

"I probably understand how he feels. It wasn't easy for me either, when I got the final papers in the mail—but I'm pretty sure it wasn't love."

"You need to talk to him, Gabby."

"I don't have anything to say to him."

"Maybe you can tell him that what he feels is understandable, expected even. . . ."

"Felicity . . ."

"I know, I know . . . he did this to himself. But if he reaches out, please don't shut him out. I'm asking as a friend. He was really in bad shape last night. He finished two bottles of wine all by himself. Phil and I had to help him to bed." The crease of worry on Felicity's forehead is obvious.

"I can't promise anything. . . ."

Chapter Nineteen

Ding. I swear if I hear that door chime again, I will lose it. That front door chime has rung three times in the past ten minutes. If it were another day, I'd be ecstatic. It means the store is having a good day. But, please, not today.

Carrying two big boxes filled with books, I give the new arrivals my usual big smile despite my pounding headache and bloodshot eyes.

"Welcome to Gallagher Books!" I say with extra chirp, hoping no one will notice that I'm probably still drunk from the night before.

Another set of customers walk in. I prevent myself from rolling my eyes in frustration and instead plaster a fake smile on my face. If Thomas were here, I wouldn't hear the end of it. He would tell me that customers can feel when they're not welcome. I make my smile even bigger. The guy in a denim jacket—whom I remember as Todd—looks at me curiously as he walks toward the old books pile. I don't blame him.

"You okay, Gabs?" Todd asks. I give him an even wider smile and nod. At least he's a regular and has seen me on my better days.

I drop the boxes on the floor with a loud thud. I push my hips forward with both my hands and then bend backwards in an attempt to do some mild stretching. I've been lifting box after box from the middle of the shop to the counter for the past hour, checking the contents, and storing them back in the stock room/office. I promised Thomas a while back that I would do the store inventory, but I should have chosen a better time—like, perhaps, when I'm not hungover and when Thomas is not out of commission with his own hangover. I gently massage my temples. It also doesn't help that today, of all days, the New York City sun is at its brightest. I just want to crawl back in bed, pull the covers over me, and sleep the day away. I think I'll be fine as soon as the sun sets—like a vampire.

I'm on my own today, and for some reason book lovers are in the store in throngs this morning. We're not even having a sale. I can't stop the inventory now because I pulled out all the old books last night and piled them out in the middle of the store, certain that I'd have it done before Thomas and I decided to go to Lips. That didn't happen. I should have begged off going since I'd gotten drunk with Felicity the night before. But Thomas insisted that celebrations are inevitable this week as we welcome a new chapter of my life—living on my own.

I barely had a drink when I was with Simon, but I guess now I'm making up for lost time. So, here I am, carting heavy boxes of old books with a pounding headache, my eyes bloodshot, and missing Colt. I should have just stayed in his arms this morning—but as a responsible adult, he pushed me out of bed, made me breakfast and super strong coffee, and called an Uber to take me to work. It was not a cheap ride, but he said he'd paid for it so I could get here on time.

I pick up one of the boxes blocking the door and make my way to the counter. I drop the load with another loud thud, startling the costumer in front of me. I think that hurt my head more than it hurt hers.

"Sorry," I say apologetically, putting two fingers on my right temple again. My customer, probably in her early twenties, gives me a knowing smile. I think I'm too old for this, but so is Thomas. The memory of Thomas onstage last night singing with Cher makes me giggle a little.

"Great night, huh?" Todd asks as he walks up to the counter for assistance.

"Yeah, Thomas took me partying last night."

"No idea that Thomas is such a party animal." We both laugh at this. Well, everybody knows Thomas. Everybody who loves books and loves Gallagher Books loves Thomas.

I ring up his purchases.

"Here," I say, handing him his haul and receipt. And a line magically appears behind him, putting my store inventory on hold.

It's one of my most successful mornings alone, and I'm so proud that in the past three months, I've learned to manage the store by myself. Thomas has discovered some freedom since I started working at the shop, and now takes hours for walks and lunches. I don't mind, really, because after almost fifty years, I think he deserves it.

It's almost four o'clock when the store finally slows down. There are a few customers milling about, but I can tell they'll be here for a while browsing and killing time. It's one of my favorite pastimes too, so I get it. We are soul siblings.

My phone vibrates in my jeans back pocket. I pull it out and see Mom calling.

"Hi, Mom," I say. I have a feeling she'll be asking why I'm not chirpy enough this afternoon.

"Why is your voice like that?" And there it is. I smile despite my headache.

I move to the fireplace, which I finally learned to operate this morning, and I sit on the sofa to regard the sunny, albeit chilly day outside.

"I'm hung over," I admit. There is no use keeping anything from her. She'll find out eventually. She's good like that.

"Are things okay? Why were you drinking?"

"Oh, it's my night with Thomas. Remember, we go to Lips once a week when we can."

"Right. Okay, good. Is Thomas hungover too?"

"Yes, but he's at home recuperating, and I'm here working."

"Well, babycakes, you don't need to work if it's about money," my dad says from a different phone. If they're on the call together, this must be really important.

"Dad! Hey!"

"Hi, sweetie, sorry to jump in . . . you know that if it's about money, we're here to help."

"Dad, I love what I do. So, no, it's not for money. I love it here."

"I know," he says.

"I don't understand that," my mom chimes in.

"But you were the one who took me to all those bookstores when I was a kid. You taught me to read early, Mom," I say.

"It was because Starbucks was new in the neighborhood back then, and they were next to Barnes and Noble." I laugh at this—never mind the pain it triggers in my hungover head. This is so much like my mother. Dad laughs along with me.

"Gosh, I miss you guys," I say mid chuckle.

"Good, that's why we're calling!" I hear an undeniable excitement in Mom's voice, which makes me a little nervous. "Are you moving to your new apartment soon? Dad and I want to help." Mom sounds like she's already packing. I don't answer for a few seconds, trying to come up with a careful answer.

"I move Friday, actually. Felicity is going to help me, and I think we're fine. You don't need to come for that."

"Okay, but do you think we can visit next weekend? Dad and I are really excited to see your new place."

"Mom, there's nothing to see, really. It's a one-bedroom apartment and not much to it."

"We don't care. We want to visit you anyway, even if we stay in a hotel nearby."

"Okay, I guess. You can probably stay at Felicity's. Let me ask her first."

"I already did, but she told me to check in with you first." I knew it.

"When did you call her? I was with her the other night."

"I called her before I called you." I roll my eyes.

"Fine."

"Do we get to meet your new boyfriend as well?"

"Mom!"

"I know, I know, it's probably too early. You kids these days."

"It's not that. I don't want him to think I'm plotting to get him to meet my parents or something. We haven't been dating for that long."

"A few months is an eternity these days," Mom says, defensively. "We just want to meet the man our daughter spends her time with. Is that too much to ask?" And there it is, the guilt trip. My mother is also an expert at this.

"Fine, I'll ask him. But I'm not making any promises."

"We're fine with that!" She almost screams my eardrums off. "Did you hear that, Chris? She'll ask him. Okay, so next weekend. Dad and I will be there." I sigh, because there is really nothing I can do to stop her. Not that I don't miss them. I do. I just feel I need to straighten out my life first before I can show them what I've made of myself. Moving to a tiny flat, after living in a million-dollar apartment for almost a decade, doesn't look like progress.

"And we're taking everyone to dinner. I've always wanted to try that Per Se place that people are talking about."

"Mom, that's like three hundred dollars apiece!" Yes, my parents are well off, but that's ridiculous.

"Dad and I insist. Ask your boss, Thomas, too."

"Mom, that would be, like, thousands of dollars!"

"I don't care. It's how much I spend on a pair of shoes. We'll live."

And that's that. My parents are coming to visit.

The subway traffic is light tonight. My head is better. Just as I suspected, as soon as the sun dropped, I was a new person. Not that I'm ready to party again. In fact, I'm looking forward to bed. Colt's bed.

The subway is quiet, except for Mr. Beard here across from me singing along with whatever's playing on his AirPods. I don't mind. At least it's not some awful rap piece. He winks at me, and I smile back before reaching for the book in my purse and starting to read. It's another of Colt's books, *Grave Sunshine*. It's different from *Roots*, that's for sure. The theme is still quite dark, but less so than *Roots*. For some reason, I can imagine that there had been changes in his life when he started writing this. It has some positive tones to it. It is about a young man who falls in love with a lake house and starts restoring it, and every stage of improvement is a reflection of a phase of his, the hero's, life. I've just come to the part where he meets a gorgeous neighbor. They've developed a carnal relationship, and it is quite obvious that the gorgeous neighbor is starting to fall in love. In some ways, I'm very anxious to see where this relationship is heading. It is apparent that our hero doesn't seem to feel the same way.

When I raise my head for a break, I see Mr. Beard looking at me and pointing at Colt's book. He removes his AirPods. "I've read that one. It's not a fairy tale. Dark shit, that one." I nod at him in agreement. "Where you at?"

"The neighbor looks like she's falling in love."

"Don't want to spoil it for you, but there's no love anywhere in that book. I hear the author is as screwed up as his characters." Alarm bells go off in my brain. But I already know that.

I smile in reply, thankful that I'm finally at my stop. I put my book back in my purse and head out of the subway. Everywhere I go, someone seems to be reminding me that I'm headed for total heartbreak—even complete strangers. And yet here I am, on my way to that looming pain.

I receive a text message as I climb out of the station.

"Close?" Colt. Dread is replaced with sudden joy and optimism. I turn around to see if anyone is watching, and I surrender to a jolt of excitement. The youngish lady in a gray suit behind me gives me a scowl, and the older bohemian woman next to me smiles like both of us share a secret the rest of the world doesn't know.

I move out of the way at the top of the stairs and reply, "Fifteen minutes." This conversation could be about anything, and could belong to anyone. There is nothing special about it. It does not hold any meaning. But it is ours—Colt's and mine—and that makes it everything. For now, it is my happiness.

I shove the phone back in my pocket and hoist my big camouflage tote onto my shoulder. I'm about to join the herd of people going about their New York City business, but I stop again and look up. New York City dusk is hypnotic. But it's not something that you stumble upon. You have to remember to experience it—the smog and noise, the whirlwind of shifts and flows, the movements of people in a kaleidoscope of sparkle and colors. I close my eyes to deaden the noise around me. This is worth interrupting a minute or two of your New York City existence; it makes you appreciate your fight for survival in this big urban jungle.

≈≈≈

I arrive at Colt's fifteen minutes later, but I don't walk in immediately. Last night, he waited for me to get home from my night out with Thomas, so I didn't let myself in. He was waiting for me on the steps like usual. Today, I get to use my permission to invade his privacy. I climb the five steps as slowly as possible, nervous, savoring this moment as a rite of passage in our relationship.

I stop at the top of the steps and look at the imposing door. I heave a nervous sigh before I pull out the key from my jacket pocket. I insert it inside the hole, turn it slowly, and the clicking sound signals my acceptance into the small circle that is Colt James's life.

I'm in.

"Babe? Kitchen." I hear his voice echo inside the big apartment as soon as I step in.

When I enter the big bright kitchen, I see Colt with a pastel apron over his black T-shirt, deep in food preparation. I smile at the sight. The room, all white with sparkly stainless-steel appliances, is an immediate contradiction to Colt's personality.

This man is a dream I don't want to wake up from. He is my perfection. Amid all the warnings, even from that dude on the subway, Colt has not made me feel uncertain about anything. In fact, during the past months, he has been a steady and sturdy rock as I lived through and let go of my crumbling past. He is patient. He is kind. He is love.

He stops what he's doing and walks toward me. He anchors his hands on my arms and bends his head to touch my forehead with his. His eyes sparkle. I reach up to plant a kiss on his lips. We stand there in each other's arms for a few minutes, savoring this new stage of our relationship. Words are left unspoken. We don't need them to understand where and what we are now.

"Ahem," Colt and I hear and pull away from each other. I look where the noise comes from. "Ahem. . . hmm. . ." Tina, smiling mischievously, is at the breakfast table, tapping away on her computer.

"Hi, Tina," I say. I drop my stuff on the floor by the counter and settle into the chair next to her.

"Hi, Gabs." I have grown fond of Tina the past three months. She's like a ray of sunshine in Colt's occasional dark atmosphere. Her smile brightens up any room she walks into. It is, perhaps, the reason why Colt keeps her close by. They balance each other out.

She stops what she's doing and gives me a hug. Her hugs are

always so personal, never for show like the ones you give and endure at formal gatherings.

"How's your apartment hunting going?" Tina asks, pushing her chair backwards and putting both her feet up on it. She's so skinny that she can bend her entire body without difficulty.

"I move on Friday. It's tiny, but I like it." I look at Colt, busy chopping cilantro. I bet he's making lamb chops with his famous mint sauce.

"Is it close by?" Tina asks.

"Noho."

"I guess it's good that it's close to school, but it sucks that it's on the other side of town from here."

"Has Felicity seen it?" Colt, still chopping herbs, joins the conversation.

"No, but she's helping me move."

"I can cancel my class that day," Colt says.

"Nah, it's fine. I think it's also a good time for Felicity and me to bond. I know she hasn't fully forgiven me for not moving in with her."

"I'm glad this is happening soon. You don't need to keep living in that apartment by yourself. It's time to move on." He says all this without looking up.

"Yeah," I agree. "By the way, my parents are coming into town next week, so I might be held up with daughter duties and all."

Tina whistles teasingly. "Meeting the parents, huh?" There is no sarcasm in her tone. I see Colt turning red.

"No one needs to meet anybody's parents." I laugh, offering Colt a way out. I don't plan to rock the boat at this time. He hasn't looked up at me, not once, and I get it. He has already pushed his limits to get us where we are today.

"That smells fabulous, Colty!" Tina changes the subject and I appreciate her all the more for it.

"I'd see them, of course," he says, surprising both Tina and me.

"Whoa!" Tina screams with pure delight. The twinkle in her eyes is genuine, but as soon as it appears, I also see darkness clouding over her smile. I brush my uncertainty away. This is between Colt and me.

"You don't have to," I say, facing him.

"I want to," he replies, jumping back into chopping. I move to the counter and watch him. He notices me and smiles. He stops what he is doing, walks around the counter, and hugs me from behind.

"Go to your room, you rabbits!" Tina says.

"I want to meet your parents, Gabby," he whispers in my ear. "Baby, I'll meet your parents and you can't stop me."

⌐ℓℓ⌐

After dinner, Tina and I clear the dishes and start loading them in the dishwasher.

"I am beat," she says slowly, mid-yawn. "I think I'm heading to bed, sweet pea." She reaches for my head and kisses me on the temple. This is a new dynamic in my life that feels like I'm back where I was with Simon and Felicity again. Another threesome.

I dry my hands with the towel hanging on the stainless-steel refrigerator handle, and as I turn around, I see Colt sitting on the wooden picnic bench in the backyard looking straight at me. Bright strings of lights are wrapped around the poles on four corners, and the reflection of the soft swinging lights gives him a joyful glow.

It's almost ten o'clock, but what is time in New York City when you can always hear faint sounds of movement from a distance? There it is again, a sense of breathlessness. I can feel my cheeks turning red, and my body both heavy and weightless. I no longer need to pretend around Colt—I was totally naked in front of him when I bared my heart and my soul and told him I love him.

I grab my thick cardigan from the top of the desk next to the fridge. I put it on and pull it tightly around me. I walk outside slowly, descending the steps from the sliding door to the patio, and make my way to him. He has a glass of scotch in one hand and uses the other to grab my thigh. He then presses his left cheek against my stomach, and I gently run my fingers through his thick black hair. I move my hands to caress his shoulders, and I can feel his muscles relaxing.

"Thank you for dinner, my love." I don't care about self-preservation anymore. I've never loved like this before, and I want him to know that I'm proud of it, and that I'm proud of him. He has changed me. I am proud of the person I am with him. I don't want to go back to the uncertain, compromising person I once was. The courage that burns inside me today is the best gift he has given me. I feel fearless.

He lifts his head up to face me, and I look him straight in the eyes. I want him to see the pureness of my love. It is not enough that he knows. I want him to own it. I beam at him with my entire being, and I can feel the light glowing with happiness from within my soul. He doesn't say a word, he doesn't move a muscle, he just stares at me. I close my eyes, laugh a little, and lift my head to the sky. There I feel the autumn breeze in the air, and I let it touch my face.

"I love you . . . I love you . . . Gabby." I freeze. As I hear those words, I know that this is the most beautiful moment of my life. I look at him, hold his gaze, and kneel in front of him. He is hunched forward, his elbows on his thighs. I squeeze between his legs and cup his face with both my hands. He pulls me closer into a possessive embrace.

"I love you . . . and no matter what, I always will." I say it again. I feel him tremble lightly in my arms, and I am on top of the world. He smiles at me, and I know deep in my heart that right now, here, is his truth.

How can I be this lucky?

Chapter Twenty

I find Thomas waiting in front of the shop as soon as I turn the corner. I find it odd that he's standing outside at this hour when we're expecting the big lunch hour crowd soon. Something is up. Standing next to him is another older gentleman. From what I can see at a distance, Thomas appears to be turning customers away. His lanky arms sway in what seems like an apologetic gesture. I furrow my brows in confusion and quicken my pace. As I get closer, I can see that Thomas is anxious. This concerns me. I've never seen Thomas this unbalanced before. I turn my attention to the mysterious man, who is nothing like Thomas except, perhaps, in age. He wears creased denim pants, a plaid shirt, and brown loafers without socks—making me even more suspicious. He's tall, very tall. He probably had sandy blond hair when he was younger—you can still see a bit at his crown—but now it's gray. This is not the kind of man I can see Thomas hanging out with. They are visually polar opposites.

I see that the shop is, in fact, locked and the sign says "Closed." I give Thomas a quizzical look.

"Gabby, oh Gabby! Thank goodness you're here." He never calls me Gabby. He clasps his hands together at the sight of me.

"I'm not supposed to be here until one," I say. I look from him to the other gentleman and back at him with concern. Thomas appears even more unsettled, which is disturbing because he is the calmest and the most composed person I know.

"Yes, but I know you come thirty minutes early anyway."
Thomas is nervously wringing his hands.

I bite my lip, widen my eyes, and look Thomas straight in
the eye in hopes he can answer my ten thousand questions tele-
pathically, but I finally have to ask, "What's up? Is everything all
right?"

"Oh, everything is perfect. This is Arthur. Arthur, this is my
little waif, Gabriella," he says. I squint at him in pretend disgust.
The tall man smiles and his golden eyes liquefy into molten amber, willing me to like him.

"How do you do?" he says and reaches out to me for a handshake. His grip is firm, but his handshake hesitant.

"I'm well, thank you." At a closer look, I can see that he is as
nervous as Thomas. Who is this man and why are they acting
weird around me?

"Gabriella, Arthur and I are going to lunch. He made reservations at Rosa's for one o'clock. It's just around the corner." I've
been there before. It was where Colt took me to lunch the day
Simon's lawyers kicked me out of my home. I look at Thomas
quizzically, cocking my head, trying to figure everything out. I
don't want to be rude to this stranger, but I'm truly concerned
about Thomas. This is so unlike him.

Thomas is acting oddly giddy. Thomas never acts giddy.

And then it dawns on me, and my eyes widen. This man in
front of me is the love of Thomas's life.

"Oh! Arthur? Yes! Oh!" Arthur looks at me like I've gone
insane, more so when I grab him by the shoulders for a tight hug.
I have to jump up to reach him. "Yes, yes, go . . . go, young ones
and be merry!" Thomas's face softens. Arthur's smile widens.
They have both visibly relaxed.

They don't need to explain themselves to me. They don't need to explain themselves to anyone.

"Thank you, Gabriella," Thomas whispers and kisses me gently on the temple.

"You're welcome," I whisper back with all the love and support I can muster. I squeeze the hand that's resting on my shoulder. The beautiful man next to him waves goodbye.

I watch them walk away from me. They don't hold hands, but they are close enough that their shoulders touch at each step. And with every step, I see them look at each other, a little shyly at first, and then, when they are farther away, they let out a carefree laugh. I sigh at the sight of this love. There is nothing more magical than to see it happen right before your eyes. Love is strange that way. You can't touch it with your bare hand or see it with your naked eye, but you'll know it—like the universe telling you what your heart is destined to experience.

As I stare dreamily at the lovers with a silly grin on my face, a woman in her fifties taps me lightly on the shoulder, bringing me back to the present. She regards me impatiently as I search for the keys in my backpack and unlock the door to the store. It's almost one o'clock.

Thomas left the lights on, and so I walk mindlessly to the counter feeling all the love. Love is truly in the New York air. Did I have this kind of giddy love with Simon? We'd been together for so long that by the time we got married, the excitement had fizzled between us. There was nothing new to be discovered, no mysteries about each other to unfold. I'd like to believe that we loved each other, but I don't think we were ever in love. And we both deserve to feel that, even if it means feeling it with other people. No one should live life not knowing how it feels to be in love—to feel like this. Like Thomas and Arthur, and like how I feel about Colt.

⸎

I go back to reading *Grave Sunshine* as soon as the lunch hour crowd has left the store. I finally have some quiet time to catch up. I'm perched on Thomas's favorite recliner like a throne behind the counter. I like the view from this spot. This is going to be my retirement plan. I will own a little independent bookstore someday, and I will be a female, half Filipina version of Thomas. I beam at the idea.

I ring up a couple more customers and realize that it's almost three o'clock. Thomas is not back yet. I get it. I think about my lunch with Colt at Rosa's where time was nonexistent. I really don't mind being by myself. Being here is like second nature to me now, and Thomas deserves this. Also, I completed the first half of the inventory last night, so I'm just chilling this afternoon. Thomas can take as much time as he'd like to be with Arthur.

"Is that Colt James's book?" asks a girl approaching the counter with a perky smile.

"Yes," I say. "He's my professor of Creative Expressions."

"So, who's the flavor of the month in your class?" She winks and then laughs. "Or the semester, I mean." I pretend to laugh along with her. "I can't blame these girls, you know. He's the hottest thing to hit this town. It's interesting that he's gone under the radar these days. I follow him, you know, on social media." I didn't know Colt was on social media, but I smile anyway. "I was one of those foolish girls a year ago." She winks at me again and hands me three books to ring up. I reach for them with shaky hands. I can't help but steal a look at this attractive girl and feel a pang of jealousy. I don't like it. Colt and I have been easy and honest and drama-free the past three months, and I don't want to complicate things with jealousy. It also doesn't help that this girl resembles Tina, the exact opposite of who I am. She's wearing an off-the-shoulder sweater, black bra strap showing. Her blond hair is tied behind in a neat ponytail. Her eyes are clear as a blue sea. And she is, of course, skinny, which I'm not.

"Your total is $47.35," I tell her. I pull a brown paper bag from beneath the counter, bending down to hide my face because I feel like crying. My insecurities are getting the better of me. I reemerge from the counter with a fake grin, a paper bag, and a racing heart.

She hands me her credit card. I look at it and try to remember her name. I tell myself to stop. What will I do with her name? Ask Colt about her? That seems childish. I remind myself that she is part of Colt's past, and I shouldn't bother myself with it.

"These are good titles," I finally say.

"I know. They'll do. I've been looking for a book like Colt's, but he hasn't written anything in over a year because of his painting, I guess. Has he said anything about a new book? I was his student when *Listening* came out. He was pretty pleased with himself." I can sense a dreamy tone in her voice.

"I haven't heard anything." I hand her credit card back with the paper slip for her signature. Her nails are well manicured in bright pink. I look at my fingernails—bitten, unkempt, and nothing like hers.

"Maybe there's a new woman in his life right now. Too busy

screwing her. That girl is one lucky bitch, but she has to enjoy it while she can because nobody can keep Colt James forever."

"He loves me," I say under my breath, conjuring the memory from last night when he said so.

"Thanks for your purchase, Brittany. Enjoy your new books!" I say through gritted teeth.

But I already know everything she said about Colt. He never tried to mislead me.

She turns around and waves goodbye, leaving the shop under a dark cloud.

I hear my phone vibrate next to where I set Colt's book on the counter. It's a text message from him. I sigh as if I'd been holding my breath the entire time one of Colt's blondes was here.

"Going to a meeting in Midtown. You at work?"

"Yup." I push the little letters on my phone with meticulous care. I want to savor a moment like this with Colt. It's silly, I know. But I also know that these are the little things I will remember forever, the texture of the moments when I feel his love, the sights and sounds of my breathing as I find solace in his attention.

"See you tonight?"

"I'm moving tomorrow. I need to stay in the apartment tonight."

"Do you want me to come over?"

"Nope." I do, but I need to be on my own tonight. Colt's presence in my life right now is a welcome surprise, but I need to make major changes that I can accomplish on my own. The mistakes of my past should be a learning experience. Depending on someone is not always a great option. I will finally say goodbye to my past. And I need to do this on my own.

"Why?" He sends this with a sad emoji. Never in my wildest

dreams have I envisioned Colt James using emoticons. Felicity taught him once, and apparently taught him well.

"Just. But I love you anyway," I reply.

"And I, you." There it is, right there. He says he loves me.

I receive another text message, this one from my mom, telling me that she has made reservations at Per Se for six people next Saturday night. I shake my head at this. I still think it's ridiculous to spend that amount of money for dinner. I could throw a medium-sized party with that kind of money. She's invited Felicity, Thomas, and Colt.

"Mom says you are coming to Per Se next Saturday night. Dinner. 7:30."

"Scary," he sends, this time with a worried emoji.

"Whatever. I told you, you don't have to come if you don't want to.

"Talk later, heading to my meeting now. Love you." He says it again. And whatever worries I had when I was talking to little miss sunshine Brittany here earlier, they've all disappeared. I just have to trust that Colt loves me today and that I should take him at his word.

⚬⚬⚬

Thomas waltzes into the shop around five o'clock wearing a silly grin. I stand in the middle of the shop to welcome him with my arms akimbo, like a parent waiting for her love-struck teenage son.

"But you should be happy for me, Gabriella." He continues waltzing, not caring that there are about a dozen people all over the store. Some look up and scowl. Others are smiling with him.

"It's so nice to finally meet Arthur," I say.

"I am glad you met him too. He has been my joy the past fifty years, Gabriella."

"You are so strong, Thomas."

"Love makes me strong." He stops dancing, walks to the corner by the window, and gazes outside, suddenly in deep thought. "I shouldn't be happy. It's selfish." I let his words soak in for a bit. And I wonder why. But I don't push Thomas. I let him take his time. I inch my way next to him and stare out the window. "His wife has been in the hospital for months now. She has cancer. They can't treat her anymore. Her body is too frail." He whispers this without moving a muscle.

I don't know what to say.

"I had a son, Gabriella. I lost him to cancer last year. It was sudden; we didn't know until it was too late. And he died three months after he was diagnosed. He was forty years old. He was single, an actor on Broadway."

"Thomas . . ." I whisper, putting my hand over my heart. Though I know this fact from the queens at Lips, it's still heartbreaking to hear it. No parent should ever bury a child.

"Arthur helped me through it all. And now, it's my turn to support him. I feel guilty, Gabriella." He turns around to face me.

"You did nothing, Thomas." He nods at me and gazes back out the window.

"I'm happy that Arthur needs me."

"Thomas, I don't think Arthur ever stopped needing you. Maybe he needs you more now, but he's always been a part of your life through the years and through everything. That is a beautiful kind of friendship, you know, the kind where there is true love."

"You're right." He smiles slightly and puts his hand on my shoulder in gratitude. "You've spent a few months in my company and now you are a wiser duck." His tone has changed, and Thomas is back to his usual jovial self.

Love is nobody's fault. Love is someone's magic. And no one should feel guilty for loving.

~♪♪♪~

I'm nostalgic as I walk into my empty apartment. I look around and soak it all in. I let the quiet envelop me. I'm no longer lonely or afraid or fragile. I set my purse on the kitchen counter, and I sit there in deep thought. I think of Thomas and his life. I think of Felicity and her new relationship. I think of Simon.

When Thomas talked about Arthur this afternoon, it made me question the possibility of a friendship that can stand the test of time. Me and Simon? Maybe. But with Thomas, Arthur never really left.

In one corner of the living room are piles of what's left of my belongings. There's really nothing much else to do. I just want to spend the last night on my own. This is goodbye.

Although there is no more space for sadness, I feel a weight settle on my heart. I have lived in this apartment for almost a decade. Ending a chapter in life is never easy. I close my eyes and recall the happier times, and then I think about the many nights I spent waiting for Simon to come home and those feelings in my gut that something was amiss. I knew he was having an affair before I was ready to admit it.

The doorbell buzzes and startles me. I'm not expecting anyone. I don't really want to welcome a visitor tonight. I try to crank up the window. I slide my torso out, clutching the rails, trying to get a glimpse of my visitor. I see the top of his blond head and hit my head on the window jam coming back in. Anxiety swirls around me. After the long conversation I had with Felicity the other night, worry snakes through me. I don't think I'm ready to see him yet.

I don't buzz him in. Instead, I take the two flights of stairs down and slowly open the door.

Simon's sunken eyes grip mine, and I freeze.

I can understand the nostalgia. It's the reason he's here, I tell myself. I take a step outside, and he glides to the side to make way. I touch my jeans pockets, making sure I have my keys before closing the door behind me.

I descend the steps, waiting for him to join me. I see disappointment written on his face as we stand face to face on the sidewalk, no one saying a word for a minute. I pull my cardigan tighter around me, and I'm glad I have not changed out of my jeans. The air is chillier tonight than it was yesterday, and the wind blusters with stronger force.

"Do you need my jacket?" Simon asks, ready to take off his navy coat for me.

"I'm fine, thanks." I lower my head, not knowing what else to say.

"Is this your last night? You don't need to rush moving out, you know." He draws in a long breath.

"My apartment is ready. I move in tomorrow. I'm excited about it." I nod my head a few times, showing him that I'm no longer upset.

"Gabby, I'm so sorry. . . ."

"We're well past that." I lift my shoulder in a half shrug.

"Do you think you'll ever forgive me, Gabs?" The boy I used to love stands right here in front of me, and although our romantic relationship has ended, I will always care about him. Perhaps someday we can move past this.

"I'm not mad anymore."

"I don't think you ever were." He avoids my gaze and jams his hands in his jeans pockets.

A gust of wind is the only sound on this quiet street, which is unusual. This is a busy residential area, with people walking their dogs at all hours, and people jogging or biking by. No one is around tonight. And in the quiet, I feel the loud beating of my heart.

"I was."

"Shout at me, Gabby. Be mad at me. Throw things at me," he begs. I notice that tears are forming in his eyes. Sadness pierces my chest. I'm sad for our childhood and the friendship we had through it all. But I'm not in love with him anymore, and I'm not sure I ever was—at least, not the way I know now.

"That's not who I am."

"I know." He moves toward the steps and sits down slowly, holding the rail to support himself. I turn slightly to face him, still standing on the sidewalk. I close my eyes and think about Colt. I left my phone upstairs, and he could be calling right now. But I can't just cut Simon off and ask him to leave. He was my husband once. We had some good times. He took care of me and loved me the best way he knew how. He didn't treat me badly during our marriage. His parents are right. What happened to us was both our faults.

"Simon, why are you here?" I hug myself tighter.

He doesn't answer immediately.

"I made a mistake, Gabs. I screwed up." He threads a hand through his hair and lets out a heavy sigh. I don't move but I avoid his gaze.

"What do you need from me? I'm not the same person you left almost a year ago. That person was weak, she didn't know who she was, and she thought you were the only thing in the world going for her." I can hear my voice getting louder.

"I want you back, Gabs."

"What are you talking about? You can't," I say in frustration. I want him to stop because I don't want us to hurt each other any more than we already have.

"Maybe you're just saying this now. Maybe you'll find it in your heart to forgive me, and we can be happy again. Maybe we needed this break, for us to realize we truly belong together. I belong to you, Gabs." I shake my head, trying to block his voice.

"Simon, it's too late. . . ."

"Gabby, you're my best friend. And yes, I admit, I was stupid, and I thought I could be with some carefree woman and be wild and experience things we never did because we got married so young. But you're home to me." He bends his head, covers his face with his hands, and tries to stifle a sob.

"I dreamed of this happening for months after you left. I cried myself to sleep every night. On the nights I couldn't sleep no matter how I tried, I listened to every sound hoping that you'd come back home to me. I thought I was going to fall apart. I thought I was going to die without you." I say this in a whisper, as I look down on him. "Then I got into grad school and made new friends and got a job, and I realized there are so many things I need to learn about myself. You'll be fine. We'll all be fine." I sit next to him and put my hand lightly on his shoulder, letting him know I still care about him. He turns and lifts his head to face me. He looks deeply into my eyes, searching. I stay there frozen, looking back at him. This is the face I have memorized through the years, the face I know so well, the face that once was mine. And sorrow shreds inside me. Goodbyes are still hard. Endings are still painful. There is no way around that.

Then it happens. He leans to me and places his cold lips on mine. I let them stay there for a little while, trying to summon the feelings we once had for each other, sinking into nostalgia.

I pull away, pushing his shoulders lightly. I smile at him, hoping he gets the cue that this is no longer what I want. And just like that the silence disappears. New York City makes its presence felt again. I hear the sirens blare in the corner, the laughter of a couple walking hand in hand, a motorcycle engine revving angrily at a distance.

Chapter Twenty-One

"What the fuck is in here, Gabby?" Felicity stops at the bottom of the stairs, panting and staring at me with annoyance—this, after dragging down two flights of stairs and immediately dropping on the ground a box full of my favorite books. I agree that we didn't plan this right. I should have borrowed a wheelbarrow from someone. I sent Colt a message twice last night to see if he has one to lend, but I have yet to hear back from him.

"My books," I say, stopping next to her with a large comforter bundled in my arms.

"There are two guys who are hopelessly in love with you, both offered to help us with this move, and you said no. What's wrong with you?" Felicity looks silly, clutching her chest and leaning back on the rail like her very life depends on it. "This is heavy shit you've got there! How are we getting this up to your new apartment?" She has a point. I wrinkle my nose and silently laugh. She gives me the evil eye.

"Maybe we should just open the box and take them up a stack at a time. Yes, that's a great idea!" I clasp my hands together, very proud of myself, but Felicity is unimpressed.

I feel my phone vibrate and extract it from my back pocket, expecting it to be from Colt. It's a Facebook message from my mom, with a photo of her and my aunts at the new MGM Casino at the National Harbor, which is apparently just a twenty-minute drive from our house in Virginia.

"My mom and my aunts at the new MGM." I show Felicity the photo and she starts laughing. Phew! She's no longer pissed off. The photos show my mom and her sisters wearing funny hats at a row of slot machines, looking very serious as they play. No one is looking at the camera. They are all preoccupied with their game. I hold my stomach to keep myself from laughing. I can guarantee that my dad took this photo.

"Mom's a riot! And your aunts, geez! Oh, how I miss all of their banter. Are you going home for Christmas?" Felicity asks. Christmas is our thing—Simon's, Felicity's, and mine. We've never celebrated Christmas in New York. We all go back home to our families, and we end up hanging out the entire week doing nothing. Last Christmas, Simon and I pretended to be okay —but everyone could tell that something was up. A few months later, he moved out.

"I haven't really thought about it." Felicity can sense that I'm not ready to talk about this and immediately backs off.

"You know what, this sucks! Let me call Phil. I would prefer for you to meet him under more formal circumstances, and believe me I am so into this women's equality shit, and that we are tougher than men and crap like that, but right now I want someone to carry this shit for us." She always knows when to change the subject.

❦

A burly guy with brown hair is waiting for us on the steps of my new apartment building. He is exactly how Felicity described him. Wearing cargo pants and a light sweater, he waves at us as we pull up. He walks to Felicity and opens her car door. He immediately bends down and plants a kiss on her mouth. I get out of the car to give them some privacy, and slowly walk around to meet them.

"Hi, Phil. I'm Gabby! I can't believe it took us this long to finally meet!" I reach to him for a hug, and comfortably, he hugs me back.

"I'm so, so happy to finally meet Felicity's best friend."

"One of," I say, thinking about Simon and knowing that they've already met. "Thank you for coming to the rescue."

"My pleasure. I was working from home today and got bored, so I was glad Felicity called." Felicity gets out of the car and joins us.

"Aww, that's so sweet." I can't help but smile playfully, giving Felicity a little shoulder nudge. She makes a face, and I tease her some more. "But it is the sweetest!"

"Okay, let's get this hauling show on the road. Where are your keys? Let's go up to your apartment first before we start carrying stuff in," Felicity says.

I search for my Louis Vuitton key ring, a gift from Mom, inside my backpack. It's easy to find it inside the black hole that is my backpack because it holds about a thousand keys. I need to mail my old apartment keys to Simon's lawyers first thing Monday morning, I remind myself. And then I see Colt's key, which I've attached to its own key ring—an "I love NYU" chain I bought at the stall next to the shop.

The three of us make our way up three flights to my apartment. My apartment. I'm the only one who's going to live here. I'm paying the rent, and I can arrange it without asking anybody's permission. This is all mine. I draw a big sigh and unlock the door.

I take my first step in, and to my surprise Felicity tosses sparkly confetti on my head.

"Welcome to your new home!" Phil and Felicity shout together. I turn around to face them both and I can't help but tear up.

I think of Colt and regret not inviting him to come join us today.

Felicity and Phil rush in hand in hand, inspecting my new home. I pull out my phone from my pocket and send a text to Colt.

"Hey, where are you? Haven't heard from you today. Hope you're having a good day. I love you." I shove my phone back into my back pocket.

"It looks like they cleaned," Felicity mutters, brushing one finger on top of the kitchen counter. She opens the fridge and the smell of lemon fills the air. "Oh, and they have cut up lemon pieces and baking soda inside the fridge too," Felicity adds, looking impressed. It matters to me that she approves.

"This is not a bad size, Gabby," Phil says, looking around the tiny apartment. What I like about this place is that the owner installed see-through French doors to divide the main area and the bedroom. This is supposed to be a studio apartment but the way the flooring is configured, it looks like a one bedroom. There's also a small fireplace in the living room/dining area next to the window. I'm lucky that they were able to fit a washer and dryer on top of each other inside what I assume is supposed to be a coat closet by the entrance. They also left a coat rack for me by the door.

"I liked it the moment I saw it. I mean, it's a fifth of my previous apartment, but I'm by myself now, and I don't really need that much space anyway." The walls are white. I have some art that Simon let me keep, so I have enough to fill them.

"Felicity, give me the keys to your car and I'll start carrying stuff up. You ladies take a break for a little bit since you've already done a lot of carrying this morning." Phil is the sweetest. I give Felicity a knowing smile. I'm so happy for her, I really am.

Felicity pulls open the French doors that lead to a tiny bedroom and is surprised to see that there is no bed in it.

"You don't have a bed?!"

"I'll get one. I mean our bed was king size, and it won't fit in here. I don't mind using a sleeping bag for a few weeks until I figure this out."

"No! We are getting you a bed today."

"Don't worry about it. It's like I'll be camping every night."

"Well, you stay at Colt's a lot anyway. There's really no need for a bed here," she says.

"I plan to stay here a lot during the week. The commute from the Upper East Side to school is just horrible. It always takes me forty-five minutes. From here, it's a ten-minute walk." I open the window to get some fresh air inside the apartment.

"Do you know that this is the first time I'm actually going to be living by myself, not counting when Simon moved out. I mean this is the first time that it's mine. No one else will call it home but me. Imagine that." I touch the side of the window and look outside, staring into space. I snap out of it instantly and turn to Felicity, who's looking at me with such pride.

"You've come a long way, Gabs. If you'd asked me eight months ago if we'd be here today, seeing you so independent and so sure of yourself, I would've said it was never going to happen. Not because I don't believe in you, but because back then you didn't seem to believe in yourself." She gave me a big hug.

"Thank you," I say with all my heart to the best person who has always stood by me and always has my back.

The door opens with a noisy bang as Phil gives it a kick with four of my big bags in his arms. Seeing us like this, he smiles, drops everything on the floor, and joins us in a group hug. We all start laughing. Right here is another milestone in my life that I need to celebrate.

To new beginnings. . . .

~ ❧ ~

It's almost two o'clock when we finally decide to take a break. I don't know how I would have managed moving without these lovebirds. Most of my books are now on display in the built-in bookshelf right outside the bedroom door. It isn't much, but it's enough to hold my favorites. Felicity unpacked my clothes and made them all fit perfectly in my tiny new closet. This is not even a fraction of the closet Simon and I once shared. I've had to store my shoes next to the washer and dryer in the coat closet, but I don't care.

I've been so used to perfect, to what's right and accepted, that throwing things somewhere that doesn't make sense is now my new perfect, and I love it. I adore my new space. It's like a part of me always knew I'd end up here. It doesn't matter that there is a tiny chip in the kitchen counter and a crack in the bathroom door, what matters is that I rent this chip and crack all on my own. I can't wipe the proud grin off my face.

"I'm starving," Phil declares in a bit of a growl. I see the spark of affection in Felicity's eyes, so we lock my tiny apartment and head down to Maharlika on First Avenue.

Maharlika, a specialty Filipino restaurant, is just over a ten-minute walk from my apartment.

"You are about to gain a few extra pounds, my friend," Felicity says as we enter the restaurant, taking a sniff of the unique aroma of Filipino food. She knows my weakness for Filipino dishes, and the reason I never learned to make them was because I'd finish them all in one sitting. It smells of heaven—although all should be warned that once you enter a Filipino restaurant, chances are you'll exit with that distinct smell lingering on your clothing. I see Felicity sniff her sweatshirt before we walk in. She sees me and we both laugh hysterically. Phil gives us a weird look.

"You are in for a treat, Phil!"

"I'm game! Bring it on!" Of course, I don't intend to traumatize Phil by serving him *balut*—a bird embryo boiled and eaten from the shell. It's a famous Filipino street food that only the brave can consume. I can't even do it, and neither can my mom. My dad tried it once and almost threw up right in front of all my mom's relatives. That was a good time.

The restaurant is packed. It normally is on a Friday afternoon and into the weekend when Filipinos from all over New York and New Jersey come down here for a treat. After about twenty minutes, we are finally seated at the far back of the joint where long wooden picnic tables are set up to be shared. The Filipinos at our table all stare at me, and I smile back. I always get that. I take more after my Dad, but you can definitely see my distinct Filipina features. I have a small nose, my lips are thick, and my hair brunette. I give them a big smile that says, yes, I'm *Pinay* (Filipina) too.

Hearing the crackles of sizzling plates at the next table makes my mouth water. We take our seats and read the menu.

Felicity knows Filipino food like the back of her hand, so I don't need to recite and explain each item. I see confusion on Phil's face though and nudge Felicity to help him.

"Filipino food is complicated. But tell me what interests you on the menu, and I'll help you decipher it," Felicity says, sliding closer to Phil.

I let the lovebirds be as I read through the familiar Filipino fare that my mom cooked for me. But my thoughts wander far away—to Colt, and how it's almost a full day since his last text message. I reach for my phone on the table and I scroll through it. There are no new notifications. I reread my last message to him this morning and it only says delivered. Looks like it has not been read.

～✦～

When our food finally arrives, Felicity has already given Phil instruction in Filipino Food 101— the number one point being that only Filipinos, and those who love Filipinos, love Filipino food. I think I have to agree with that, although I must point out that Simon hates Filipino food with a passion. I remember the first time my mom offered him our traditional Filipino breakfast of *daing na bangus*—fried milk fish marinated in vinegar and garlic—with an even more garlicky fried rice and egg, and he nearly puked at the sight of the fish at the breakfast table. "Who eats fish in the morning?" he asked in disgust. Simon quietly complained to me once at my aunt's birthday party where they served steamed fish with mayonnaise dressing, "That dead fish is looking at me. Can't you see the eyes are still attached? Also, am I the only one smelling that stench coming from the fish?"

Felicity looks like she's ordered half of everything on the menu, reciting the names to Phil as the waiter serves us each dish.

"This is *adobo*—pork marinated in soy sauce, vinegar, garlic, and lots of whole peppercorns. Oh, and this is *kare-kare*. You said you're game, so this is oxtail in peanut sauce, and you can add some *bagoong* to make it a bit salty."

"Whoa! What's that?" Phil asks, jerkily moving backwards from the table.

"That's the *bagoong*. It's shrimp paste." Felicity reaches out for his arm to get him back closer to the table. "Dude, c'mon. You said you're tough. This is nothing," Felicity teases. "I didn't even order the bird embryo inside an egg yet." Phil's eyes widen in horror. Felicity and I can't help but giggle. A white girl talking about Filipino food like an expert is a sight to behold. I giggle some more.

"I'm so sorry, Phil. Filipino food is not for the faint of heart." I reach across the table to touch his arm apologetically.

"It can't be that bad, right? I mean, I've heard of the Bad Saints restaurant in Washington, DC, that got a Michelin star. Let me try that pork soy sauce thing and stop scaring me, you two."

As it turns out, Phil actually loves the food, which is another boyfriend test he passes. Felicity is over the moon about it. Phil loves the *kare-kare*, minus the *bagoong*.

~ℓℓℓ~

"So, I have an announcement!" Felicity booms gleefully after the waiters have cleared most of the dishes off our table. But we order another round of San Miguel beer.

"What's going on?" I ask excitedly. Phil and I look at each other.

"Well, I decided to go back and write for *The New York Times*." Felicity spreads her arms wide in pride.

"As a reporter? You hated being a reporter, Felicity," I say, worried.

"Exactly. So when they called to ask me if I want to come back to write, I said I'd do lifestyle. Book reviews, literature, or art. The things I like to do, really. And they said yes."

"Oh, babe! That's good news!" Phil gently touches the back of her head and turns her to him for a big kiss. I don't feel uncomfortable. I've done this to Felicity a number of times. I can see her turning red.

"Felicity!" I get up and reach across the table to give her a hug.

"Well, you know my parents helped me buy my apartment, but my mortgage is brutal, and my salary as a professor at a public university isn't really enough. I mean, I've had this romantic notion about being in academia forever and finishing my PhD, but I don't think I can survive in New York by doing just that. I've accepted that now, so I am restrategizing."

"This will be great, babe!" Phil holds her hand tight.

"You'll be great! They called you back because they know that you're meant to write about what you truly love. I'm so happy for you!"

"So, Phil and I are now both real writers!"

"Congratulations!" I beam.

I find out that Phil works as an editor for a publishing company. He says he focuses a lot on mystery novels, but would like to diverge into science fiction and fantasy. I agree. It's the hottest genre right now. He's also writing his first novel during his free time.

"Gabby used to write these short novels when we were in middle school, and my classmates and I would devour them overnight. And when we were done, we'd all ask her when she'd write the next one. They were all love stories, like Sweet Valley High."

"Yeah, that was before . . . you know . . . sometimes priorities change." I smile at him like it's not a big deal, but I know now that it is. I can rewrite my life from here on out, and it's not too late.

"Gabby, you should start writing again!"

"You should," Phil encourages, shoving a spoonful of *sisig* and vinegar in his mouth, the only dish still left on our table. Felicity and I look at each other and chuckle. "What?" Phil asks before taking a big swig of his Filipino beer.

"Babe, *sisig* is made from pig's head and liver, seasoned with lemon and chili peppers," Felicity says.

"Ha! I don't care because it's sooo good." I have a feeling this relationship will actually last.

Chapter Twenty-Two

I wake up this morning feeling anxious. My entire body is sore from all of yesterday's activities. I don't want to get out of my newly purchased mattress from Costco. I reach for my phone, which says it's nine thirty, and I scroll down my text messages, missed calls, and even Facebook messenger, which I barely use.

Still nothing from Colt and it's been almost two days. I leave the house in a hurry to make sure I get to class before eleven.

I played the past week over and over inside my head last night. Did I miss something? Did Colt mention anything about being busy this weekend? He wanted to spend Thursday night with me, the day before I was scheduled to move. It doesn't make sense. I know it's only been a couple of days, but this is the first time I've not heard from him this long. I'm sure there's an explanation. He's probably locked up in his studio painting or in his office writing his next book and couldn't get out of his creative trance. I tell myself there's nothing to worry about.

I sit in my usual spot and try to ignore Heather. I'm not in the mood for small talk today. I'm sweating despite the autumn chill. I can feel my heart beating fast under my sweater.

A man in a plaid shirt and jeans enters the room. "Good morning, Colt is out today. I'll be covering for him this morning. My name is Benedict Donovan."

My heart sinks.

"Hey, Gabby, are you okay?" Sophia asks from across the

table. I nod at her. "You look really pale; let me know if you want me to take you to the clinic," she whispers.

"Where is Mr. James?" Heather asks with genuine curiosity.

"He's in Los Angeles." I jerk my eyes up in surprise. Colt would have said something to me if he were going to L.A.

Something's definitely wrong.

"What is he doing there?" Heather continues her questioning.

"That I cannot say because, honestly, I don't know. Anyway, let's start with the class discussion." As Benedict starts talking about creative expression in the time of social media, I zone out.

Why hasn't Colt answered any of my text messages or any of my phone calls? Even if he's in California, it's only a three-hour time difference.

He just told me he loved me, for Christ's sake. We made love Thursday morning before I left his apartment.

I exhale forcefully.

Benedict turns in my direction, and I lower my head.

I can't focus in this class. My mind is a mess and I don't want to go where it's taking me. I get up, excuse myself from class, and grab my phone off the table in a hurry. I can feel ten pairs of eyes follow me out of class, baffled.

The hallway is empty, which is just as well because I need to gather my thoughts. I grip my phone and stare at it, trying to conjure up a message from Colt. I try to remember our last conversation. I scroll to his name.

"Talk later, heading to my meeting now. Love you." This was his last text message from Thursday. I look at the words inside the green thought balloon, to try to read between the lines, to decode what I could have missed. I knew he was meeting his

agent, but I don't know what it was about. He's been meeting with his agent every week for the past month or so, but he's never mentioned anything to me about going to California. And again, even if he's in California, I don't see any reason why he couldn't keep in touch.

I pace back and forth outside my classroom door. There has to be a good reason for this because if there isn't, then it only means one thing—Colt is avoiding me.

I punch his number on my phone again and my call goes straight to voice mail. I'd like to think that maybe his phone is turned off. It's only eight o'clock in the morning in California. But I also know that he's a morning person.

I sit down on the bench next to me as I feel my head start to spin.

❦

I leave the building after an hour and I walk toward nowhere. I'm tempted to call him again, but I don't. Maybe I got this all wrong, or maybe I fell so damn hard that I forgot what I know is the truth—that no one can own Colt James.

❦

I'm back at the same spot three days later after Benedict, Colt's teaching assistant, sent an email yesterday saying he wants to see us today, Thursday, to substitute for next Monday's class, which he would have to cancel due to scheduling conflicts.

Benedict walks in with the same excuse—that Colt is in Los Angeles. Nobody in the room seems as affected as I am, except maybe for Heather, who also seems a little anxious at Colt's desertion.

"When do you think he's coming back?" Heather asks. I've known about Heather's little crush on Colt since the beginning of the semester so I'm not that surprised about this. In fact, I'm grateful that she's asking all these questions for both of us.

⁓⁓⁓

"Still nothing from Colt?" Thomas asks as soon as I walk in the shop for my afternoon shift. I shake my head. Thomas looks at me with concern and walks around the counter to give me a hug. "Colt is a creative spirit, Gabby. Maybe he just needs some time to be left alone, to gather himself."

"Do you think he got scared that we're moving too fast?"

"Perhaps. But that's for him to answer. We can't assume anything, Gabriella." I close my eyes tight, holding on to Thomas. I don't want to break down in the middle of the shop. I can feel my heart breaking piece by piece every day that I don't hear from him.

"It's been a week, Thomas."

"I know, my darling." He brushes my hair lightly with his hand. "You've had your heart broken once before and look how far you've come. If you break your heart again, pick yourself right back up and start moving along. No one can stop you from loving someone, not even yourself. But you can choose to do something about it."

Thomas walks me toward the sofa by the fireplace, and we sit down together with his arm wrapped around my shoulders. I can feel tears forming in my eyes. I try to control a sob. How can I be going through another heartbreak? It doesn't seem fair.

"Do you think this is love, Gabriella?" I look up at him like it's the most ridiculous question he's ever asked, because he knows full well what the answer is. He knew from the moment it happened.

"Yes."

"Then just dwell on the good and beautiful times you've had with him."

"It still hurts though."

"That won't really go away." And the tears start rolling down my lifeless face.

⌇⌇

I'm like a zombie at work this afternoon. Thomas doesn't leave the shop today, missing his daily walk. I do like having him close by. I don't trust myself right now.

I'm slowly stacking some books on the shelf by the window when I see Tina walk by. I drop all the books on the table behind me and run out the shop. I can feel Thomas follow me with his gaze.

"Tina! Tina! Hey!" She turns around and sees me immediately. I can see the shift of expression in her eyes. She stops in her tracks, carrying a fancy denim Chanel tote on her shoulder and a stack of binders in her arms.

"Hey, how's it going?" she asks but doesn't come to me for the usual hug.

"Have you heard anything from Colt? I heard in class that he's in L.A., but he's not answering my texts or my calls." I feel very vulnerable. She hesitates for a second and shifts her weight from one leg to the other. I can tell that she's hiding something.

"Yeah, he's in L.A." The chill in her voice confirms that something is definitely off.

"Do you know when he's coming back?" I'm almost begging.

"No. I don't, I'm sorry."

"Tina, what's going on? Why is he not returning any of my calls?" I say this in a whisper.

"You tell me, Gabby." There's obvious irritation in her voice as she speaks.

"I seriously don't know what's going on, you have to help me understand. If . . . if he wants me out of his life, all he has to do is say so . . . and I won't bother him again." I want to scream but I don't. I try to keep my calm.

"Look, I don't know what's going on either, okay? All I know is that he is in L.A., and he's been there a week. And I don't know when he's coming back. I spoke to him the weekend he left, and he was really out of sorts. Pissed off." I can see her muscles tense, and anger is written all over her beautiful face.

"Why?" I search for anything else in her posture, hoping for sympathy—but I know that at the end of the day, she is Colt's ally and not mine.

"All he told me was that . . . it had been a . . . mistake." She looks away as she says it.

"What was a . . . mistake?" I can hear my voice quiver.

"I don't know what you did or what you said when I left you guys in the kitchen Wednesday night. But whatever it was, I can tell that he wasn't happy about it."

I give her a blank stare, replaying the moment in my head. And then it hit me. He's pulling away from me. He wants me out of his life but doesn't know how to do it—all because he opened his heart to me.

He made a mistake.

What he said to me was a mistake.

"Look, I have to go. I have a five thirty class that I'm late for." She turns around and walks away, not even saying goodbye.

Colt James's interest in me has expired. It was a game, and Colt James has won.

Colt James didn't love me. I was a fool to believe that a guy like him could actually love a girl like me.

Chapter Twenty-Three

Seventh Avenue is bustling with tourists coming out of Penn Station and lurking around Madison Square Garden tonight. The air feels icy but clammy. I don't want to be here. I want to go back under my covers and hide in darkness. But I can't. I have to meet my parents at the bus station tonight.

Felicity and I, both bundled in thick puffer jackets and heavy scarves, are waiting for them at the corner of 7th and 38th. No one says anything. Our dejected faces say it all. I appreciate Felicity's respect for my silence. We've been here once before.

On our walk from her apartment, I gave her a rundown of my conversation with Tina. She didn't offer any opinion either, though I'm sure she has plenty. I'm waiting for her to say, "I told you so," but it doesn't come.

"Do you want to talk about it some more?" She stands next to me with her head bent down, her UGG-clad foot awkwardly kicking around a pebble on the ground.

"Not really," I whisper, shaking my head slowly, my face full of misery. I look like I'm about to cry any minute.

"You have to try to get this out of your system before your parents arrive."

"I know." My head nods in agreement, and I sigh in defeat.

I've been dragging myself through my routine since I got up this morning, trying to find the courage to get through the day without bursting into tears. I don't want crying to be my default setting. That person is supposed to be gone. I'm supposed to be stronger now than I was a year ago.

"God, I didn't want him to be this predictable." Felicity throws both her arms up in frustration. I know what she's getting at. The bad boy will always be the bad boy. We both knew it was coming, and it did. She and I both hoped that we were wrong—but we predicted it well, and I suppose everyone who knew would have seen it coming.

"We both knew." I shrug as I say this.

"I guess so but, my god, how I wanted so much for both of us to be wrong."

"Yeah, well, I guess this time we won the jackpot for knowing in advance." My sarcasm is bubbling onto the surface.

A black Toyota Suburban starts honking its horn loudly right in front of us. I welcome the noise because I don't want to listen to the painful speculative voices in my head.

"What do we do now?" Felicity looks straight into my eyes. Amidst the sadness, I also see love and courage and faith in her stance. This is who she is in my life—all that.

"Nothing. We go on living."

"God, I'm angry and sad and fucking pissed off!" She throws her arms up, stomps, and turns around in rage. I pull her away from the perplexed pedestrians, and she hugs me tight.

"Don't. I can't cry here. I can't be crying when they arrive." She gently pushes me away. And I close my eyes. The pain is torrid, real, and physical. I can feel the cruel nips at my heart. I've not eaten in days. Have not slept. I can feel myself wasting away. I feel sick constantly. I just want this to be over. This feeling. I'm not even expecting anything to turn around at this point. I just want to move on.

We are silent again. The more we talk about it, the more vulnerable I become.

A few minutes later, the bus from DC arrives. My heart starts pounding. Felicity reaches for my hand, balled into a fist, and squeezes it. I need to give the best performance of my life tonight and the next few days because that's how much my parents mean to me.

Mom is the first one off the bus. She runs to me like we've not seen each other in years. She hugs me tight, and I hug her right back, the top of her head resting well under my chin. This is what I need right now. Seconds later, Felicity joins in. My dad appears from nowhere and envelops us all in his long arms. Home.

God, I want to collapse in their arms, but I don't.

"You've lost a lot of weight!" My mother finally pulls away and looks at me with great delight. I know she's been wishing that I'd shed all the pounds I've gained over the years. I give her a big pretend smile. Dad plants a kiss on top of my head.

"Hey, kiddo." My dad greets me with the kind of big wide grin that makes everything better, that makes all the bad things go away. I beam with enthusiasm because, truthfully, having them here somehow gives me solace.

My mom and dad then turn to Felicity and give her a tight bear hug, like a lost daughter they've not seen in years, and she hugs them right back with all her might. She's closer to my parents than she ever was to her own—and growing up, it was like having a real sister.

"Look at you, little cupcake! You've grown an inch or two," my dad says to tease Felicity. "Let me get our luggage, Maria." He walks back to the bus where a group of people are waiting.

"So, where is this new boyfriend of yours?" Mom asks. Felicity looks at me and immediately turns away.

"He's not in town, unfortunately." It is the truth.

"What?" My mom is so dramatic. I don't know how she'll react if she finds out that my so-called new boyfriend has gone missing without a word. Not even a goodbye. The painful truth hits me again like a heavy brick.

He didn't even say goodbye.

"He's in California. Selling his book in Hollywood!" Felicity steps up her game, pretend pride in her voice, and gives my mom a sultry, mysterious glare. My mother chuckles at this bit of exciting news.

"Wow! My daughter is dating someone famous." My mother is not easily impressed, but she seems besotted at the prospect of Hollywood fame. "It's a shame I won't get to meet him," she says with a pout. I smile weakly.

"I'm sure you will, at some point," Felicity says. And we both know there is no certainty to this declaration.

$$\sim\!\!\mathcal{L}\!\mathcal{L}\!\sim$$

It's midnight by the time I leave Felicity's apartment. My parents tried to convince me to stay, but I couldn't. I can't pretend around them anymore. It was exhausting. I am exhausted. I need my space to gather my thoughts.

It's about a forty-five-minute walk back to my apartment. Time flies when you are in deep contemplation. Like a video collage of beautiful moments, I think of the months Colt and I were together. It brings me even more pain because up until a couple of weeks ago, everything was like magic. And then puff, it's all gone like a dream. No word. No explanation. No good-bye.

❧

Felicity and my parents show up at my tiny apartment this morning with coffee and a bag of my favorite cheese Danish. I haven't slept well. Felicity looks at me with wide eyes, silently telling me to get my shit together or we'll get busted.

"This apartment is cute, babycakes! My ever-positive dad walks in, stands in the middle of the room, and inspects every corner with enthusiasm.

If there was one person I failed when I married young, it was my dad. I knew that if he had his way back then, he'd have wanted me to be more independent, to aspire more, to be more. Of course, he didn't say any of these things to me because he's considerate and kind like that, but I sensed his strong disappointment when Simon and I announced our engagement during our freshman year. But like the great father that he is, he welcomed Simon with open arms and accepted him as his own son.

"Isn't this tiny room suffocating you when you sleep at night?" my mother, always the fusspot, asks. She doesn't mean to insult, it's simply the way she is. Her family, they are tactless like that. One time when Simon gained some weight after our vacation in Hawaii, my mother told him that he'd gotten fat. Fat is not a taboo word in my mom's vocabulary. I smile at the memory, and I am grateful that she's here.

"Maybe you're not getting enough oxygen in here. Do you have those carbon monoxide detection devices? Chris, you have to get her one of those later," she tells my dad, who's still standing in the middle of my tiny room, which now looks even tinier with him in it.

"Oh, stop it, baby." He still calls her that. "This place looks spectacular! I'm so proud of you, sweetheart." And I can tell that he truly is. He reaches out to me for a hug. And then it happens. My tears start to roll down my cheeks. All I want is to just cry in my dad's big strong arms—the only man who has not broken my heart. "Oh, sweetie . . . are you okay?" He pulls away and looks at me with genuine concern, searching for an answer.

"I am ju— . . . just . . . happy . . . that you are both here to see me . . . on my own. Independent." I reply in between sobs. He pulls me back in his arms and holds on to me tighter.

"Oh, babycakes . . . I'm proud of you no matter what." And I cry some more, letting all my tears out, my emotions overflowing, and hoping that my repressed sorrow will eventually go away.

⁓⌇⁓

By afternoon I have given up on the thought that Colt will eventually show up. He knew how important my parents' visit was to me, and how they were looking forward to meeting him at dinner tonight. I try to summon any emotion other than sadness, but there is nothing. I want to be angry. But it doesn't come.

I'm so glad to see Thomas waiting for us outside Per Se at seven o'clock in his debonair attire, complete with bow tie and pocket square. To see him there waiting is comfort to my soul. I introduce him to my parents, and I can tell that my mother is really taken by him. She's examining him like he's from another planet, and it's absolutely hilarious to watch. She arches her head to one side and gets close to his face. Felicity and I exchange amused glances because of this. My dad, in the meantime, is smiling like a lovestruck schoolboy—ever the biggest fan of my mom. It's actually very endearing.

"You've lived here for more than fifty years and you still have that sexy accent?" My mother is never shy. It's funny that she says this since she has not lost her accent either, and she's been in the States more than forty years. Thomas gives me a secret wink.

"No, ma'am," Thomas gallantly replies, indulging my mother. I've only known Thomas for a few months, but I cannot imagine life without him. His friendship keeps me afloat.

Thomas then turns to my dad and gives him a firm handshake. I can see that my dad doesn't know how to navigate this— Thomas is old enough to be his father, but he's one of his daughter's best friends. I give them both a big loving smile. My heart is full as I see them like this.

As soon as we walk in, a nice lady at reception tells us our table is ready. She walks us to a large table at the center of the room. I don't know how my parents were able to get this spot. It's the kind of table reserved for celebrities in a PR stunt who want to be seen. And my mother looks dumbfounded in an excited way, which is really important to me.

Once we are seated, the manager walks over to greet us. Behind him is a waiter holding an ice bucket with a bottle of champagne. Another waiter carries a tray of flutes. My mother looks confused—but I can also see how much she's enjoying all the attention.

"Welcome to Per Se," the manager begins. "We hope you are

comfortable here. This is our best table for a large group such as yours. We always take care of Mr. James's guests here." I look up at the mention of Colt's name. The waiter holding the tray of flutes starts serving each of us a glass of what looks like a very expensive bottle of champagne. "We hope you enjoy the complimentary champagne." I look at Felicity and then at Thomas, questioningly. Felicity slightly shakes her head to let me know she doesn't have any idea what's going on. Thomas, sitting next to me, reaches for my hand under the table and squeezes it.

"Your boyfriend is very thoughtful, Gabriella!" Mom squeals, clasping her hands in front of her in amusement. I can feel my heart racing. I'm totally perplexed about all these grand gestures. I don't know what to make of them.

"Mr. James already covered everything. He left specific instructions to provide you the very best our restaurant can offer. So Carlos and Bryan here are your servers tonight; just let them know what you want, and we would be most delighted to oblige." I start to get dizzy. I put both my elbows on the table for support, nearly toppling my water. Thomas, for his age, has very fast reflexes and rescues the glass.

My dad is impressed too. There's a glued smile on his face.

"This is marvelous. Oh, my goodness, Gabby, please thank Colt for us." My mom can't stop beaming.

I want to throw up. I put both my hands under the table, clutching it tightly. I feel Thomas's hand reach out to me again, and Felicity's rests on my knee for support. I have to show a brave face.

"Goodness, I need to go to the girls' room already," I say with a fake jovial tone in my voice.

"I think I'll join you," Felicity says, wearing a fake smile. I know that my parents are in good hands with Thomas, so I dash off with Felicity right behind me. As soon as I reach the corner of the restaurant, I stop and look around.

"Where the hell is the goddamn restroom?" I ask loudly. A waiter sees me, and directs me to the farthest corner. Felicity is running behind me to catch up.

I slam the door open, run to the nearest cubicle, and vomit. Felicity follows me inside the stall and closes the door behind us.

"Gabs, are you okay?"

"No! I'm not okay," I say and start retching again. I feel Felicity's hand on my back, soothing me.

"What the hell is his deal?" she says.

Still hanging over the commode, I start to cry. I wipe my mouth with the back of my hand, not caring what it will do to my lipstick. I'm angry and confused and in pain. I stand up and face Felicity.

"He called me a mistake, Felicity. Tina said he called me a *mistake*." I say this in between sobs, looking into my best friend's eyes just in case she knows something I don't. "Please, if you know something, anything, please tell me." She shakes her head and reaches out to hold my hand.

"I don't know what's going on either, Gabs. I really don't."

Chapter Twenty-Four

I sigh in exhaustion as I wave goodbye to my parents at the bus stop. They're both all smiles as they look at me out the window. I'm glad that they enjoyed their visit, and I'm glad it's over because I can no longer keep up the façade. After two failed relationships, I simply can't be around people who are so in love. I feel guilty about this, of course. I'm grateful that my parents are the way they are. It just makes me wonder where I went wrong.

My mom and dad are the ultimate sweethearts, a fairy tale, a genuine love story. My dad loves my mom more than anyone can ever understand. She is his whole world, and he is hers. To love like they do, which I thought I had with Simon, is something to aspire to. I don't think most people are that lucky.

My mom blows me a kiss as soon as the bus starts rolling away. I dig my nails into my palms to hold myself together and blow a kiss right back with a big smile.

"I love you, babycakes," my dad mouths.

"I love you too," I say in a whisper. And as the bus turns onto 37th Street, I let my tears go.

I don't have anywhere to go. I feel totally detached from everything, and yet I feel trapped. My tears won't stop flowing. My sobs are getting louder, and I'm gasping for breath.

The big red double-decker tourist bus is my friend this morning. Its brightness cheers me up inasmuch as it could any broken soul. It's there. It exists. It's loud. It's tangible. It belongs. It's red. It does not make sense. But I stare at it as it wiggles its way through traffic jams. I wipe my wet face on the sleeve of my thick wool jacket. I welcome the brashness of its texture on my face. I can take anything, feel anything, if it means helping me numb the pain inside me.

I'm broken again.

When I moved to New York City with Simon and Felicity, I moved because of them. I didn't have a grand plan or a vision. I didn't move for the sights and sounds of New York or the big red double-decker buses. I moved along with what they wanted out of their lives. I was happy and content. There was nothing to fix because life was perfect. But I was at a standstill with nowhere to go. It was a perfect life, yes, but I was not really living.

So, I suppose, as I think this through—I do, in fact, needed to be broken. Like the laws of physics, a glass ceiling, or a glow stick. They are better when they are broken.

I unlock my door with the precision of a new lodger—clumsy, unfamiliar, and frustrated. I have to shove the door with my shoulder a few times before it finally opens. I close the door behind me and lean against it as I stare at the emptiness of my apartment. Boxes are still all over the place. The only space I make sure is picked up each day is my bedroom. I toss my keys on top of the kitchen counter, walk straight to the bedroom, throw myself on the mattress, and bury my face in the pillow.

I stay this way for a few minutes.

I want to go to sleep, but it doesn't come.

I reach for my phone from my back pocket and see Mom's message.

"We had the most wonderful time, Gabriella. Daddy can't stop talking about dinner. Hopefully, next time we'll get to meet your generous hotshot boyfriend." This is one of those rare occasions, ironically, where she can't find anything to complain about. Well, I'm sure she could, but Colt's generous gesture trumps everything else. It's all she could talk about.

I didn't lie. I simply omitted some truths.

I scroll through my messages. There's one missed call from Felicity. Nothing else.

I scroll down to Colt's name on my text message inbox. I reread the last message he sent me.

"Hey . . ." I start typing and immediately delete it.

"Thank you for dinner." I finally get the courage to send him this. Immediately, it says *read* under the text. He has seen it.

I look at the screen closely. I see the three moving dots icon, which indicates he's typing. Then it stops. Seconds later, it's back on. Then it stops again. I sit upright and I stare at my phone attentively. *Should I call him?* I ask myself this though I know it will be a dead end.

"I hope your parents enjoyed it." A text. Colt. I immediately get out of bed. It's the first message from him in more than a week. It's our first real conversation.

I stare at the message. It's cold, but at least it's personal. He did it for my parents. I'd like to think he did it to spare me from more shame.

I don't answer.

It's not Thomas's usual place to visit, I know, but I don't want to be alone tonight. So, this afternoon, I called in reinforcements—Thomas and Felicity—and asked them to meet me at The Skinny on Orchard Street. Colt knows the owner, and we've been here a couple of times before. Although it's a party scene on weekends, it's typically pretty quiet and mellow during the week. The art on the wall is the reason Colt and I enjoy it here very much. A small tidbit: it's called The Skinny because it is a long narrow hall where art is beautifully displayed on both sides.

I'm at the bar on my second pint of IPA when Thomas walks in. He looks around the bar with an arcane expression. He and his bow tie are out of place. He gently pulls out the bar stool next to me, and sits on it as slowly as possible, looking pained. I'm sure he had to resist pulling out his pocket square to clean the chair and the bar in front of him. This makes me smile. Thomas makes me smile. He is just a joy to be around, even when he's looking grim like this.

"What are you having?" the cute, young African American bartender asks. Thomas looks at him with concern.

"Do you guys do cocktails?" I ask this for Thomas.

"Yes. Even if it's not on the menu, I can make it for you. What would you like?" the bartender asks with an endearing grin. He is years younger than I am, but I can't help flirting a little. I give him a coy smile, complete with the hair tucking behind my ear technique. I look at Thomas, who looks at the bartender and then at me and back to the cute bartender, and rolls his eyes. I laugh at him.

"Are you okay, my dear?" he asks. His wide-eyed worry fills my heart with gratitude.

"Yes," I say and brush his hand with mine. "Hey, can we both have cosmopolitans, please?" The bartender turns around and does his thing. I can feel Thomas staring at me intently. I don't want him to see the storm in my eyes. He gently grabs me by my shoulders and pulls me to face him.

"Sweetheart . . ." He smiles tenderly.

"Thomas, I've been through this before." I stop him before he says more. "What's another heartbreak to an already broken heart?" I laugh weakly. "You can't make this stuff up, you know."

"We don't know that."

"We don't know what? That Colt has moved on? He has, Thomas." I bow my head and feel Thomas's hands tighten on my shoulders. "Let's not talk about this tonight," I add.

Felicity walks in, grabs a chair at the other end of the bar, and drags it over to us with a screeching sound. She is not apologetic about it, and her tiny frame even makes it look adorable. My Felicity always draws attention to herself whenever she makes an entrance. Tonight, she is wearing a black-and-white polka-dot dress with a bubble skirt, ruby red four-inch heels, and matching red lipstick. She is a sight to behold. Just looking at her already makes me a little less depressed. I consider my own careless getup—jeans, NYU sweatshirt, and my old pair of checkerboard Vans—and feel rather self-conscious.

After taking a seat, Felicity turns to me with sympathetic, sad eyes like I'm about to break again. She brushes my hair off my face with her delicate fingers as if I'm a five-year-old in need of consoling. I pretend to laugh. She and Thomas look at each other, and Thomas rolls his eyes again.

The bartender breaks our awkward standoff and serves our pink drinks. Thomas reaches for them and hands me mine with meticulous grace.

"I'll have one of those too," Felicity tells the bartender without taking her eyes off me. "I don't know what to say about all this, Gabs."

"You don't have to say anything. I just want to spend tonight with my very best friends in the whole world." The two pints of beer have made me a little floaty, and I like it.

⁓

After a few more rounds of cosmopolitans, Thomas and Felicity have relaxed a bit and finally stopped worrying. The music has started to pick up, and the eighties dance tunes blare at full volume. A boy who looks like he's about fourteen mans a tiny DJ booth in the corner. And the three of us start dancing on our spot by the bar, oblivious to the stares around us. Caring about what other people think is not high on our list of priorities tonight.

The cute bartender gives us a free round of drinks, passing us each another pink concoction. "Woo-hoo!" Felicity shouts in gratitude.

"Thank you, my dear!" Thomas reaches for the drinks in obvious delight. He even winks at the bartender, who welcomes it with a charming grin. Something is clicking between these two, I can tell. For an older gentleman, Thomas is not a bad-looking fellow. He's a spitting image of Ian McKellan, and we all know he is still a hot ticket. I giggle at this, and Thomas gives me the evil eye. Felicity laughs along with me, quick to understand what is happening. "Oh, stop it . . . I am too old for these things."

"But are you really, Thomas?" I drape my arms around his neck and bend my body backwards, swaying to the song "Take on Me" by a-ha. Thomas firmly holds my waist for support.

"I am not as sturdy as I used to be, Gabriella. Be careful!"

Felicity skips around with her arms spread wide, as if waiting for someone to come for a hug as she sings at the top of her lungs. Then she stops moving, closes her eyes, crosses her arms on her chest, and shouts the "Take on Me" chorus.

I'm still in Thomas's arms when I feel a hand pull me away, giving Thomas a much-needed reprieve. I turn around and find myself face to face with Simon. Instead of fear and worry, which I always thought I would feel if I ran into him, I'm surprisingly glad to see him here. There are no jolts of excitement or longing, but there is a sense of home and comfort in knowing that he is close by. I let him hold me. I let him steady me with his hands. And I let him treat me as if I'm still his.

"Simon! You came!" Felicity stops dancing and jumps up and down when she sees him. Simon pulls Felicity with his other hand and steadies her next to me.

"What the hell are you both up to?" he half scolds, half teases. Simon looks good tonight. He's less wound up than the last time I saw him. He's wearing jeans, which is far from his usual Wall Street getup, and a white shirt folded up to his elbows. I have never seen him in folded sleeves before, and I've known him all my life.

"I am so glad to see you, Si!" Felicity lands straight on his chest, her face flat on it and her arms around his waist. Felicity is like a little sister to Simon, and I can tell how happy they both are to be together like this again. And I jump right in with them. I lean my body behind Felicity and put my arms around them both. Simon steadies me with his strong hands. Thomas looks curious upon introductions. I don't blame him for being less than cordial after all the painful stories I've told him through the months of our divorce. He accepts Simon's handshake with reluctance. I want Thomas to be okay with this, like I'm okay with it. Colt helped me transition in my relationship with Simon from being an ex-wife to this—whatever this may be. Simon is no longer the cause of my heartbreak, and I welcome his presence again in my life.

"Don't you think this is a bit surreal? Us, hanging out with your ex-husband," Thomas finally asks as he dances next to me, close to the DJ booth on what passes for a makeshift dance floor for those in dire need of it—like us.

"Let's just enjoy tonight, Thomas," I say. "Tomorrow is another day. Let's worry about this tomorrow, okay?" I look earnestly into his eyes and then I smile. My love for this old man happened swiftly, and I know that he loves me back just as much. Our friendship is peculiar, I agree, but friendships are truer and more enduring if they are undefined. Friendships are no different from love at first sight, and ours was definitely one like that—I fell in love with him the moment I met him.

"Okay, little one." He reaches for my head and plants a kiss on my forehead. In my peripheral view, I can see Simon staring at us. I move my head to face him, and the sparkle in his eyes is undeniable. He's staring at me like he's seeing me for the first time. I see him take a deep breath and smile at me like he has never done before.

"You three are all pretty lit, huh?" Simon asks, breaking his stare. He moves next to me. "Do you need anything, Gabs? Diet Coke?" Diet Coke is my go-to drink when the three of us are in bars and clubs together. I was never a heavy drinker. Actually, I was never a drinker at all.

"I can use another cocktail, maybe," I say, and Simon looks at me like I've grown horns.

"Are you sure? You seem pretty tanked already." He twitches his lips as he says this, teasing me. And I like it. This is new for both of us. I feel myself flirting with him a little. I don't remember flirting with Simon this way before. I didn't need to. He was mine, and I was his. I put my hand on his chest and give him a knowing smile and wink. He raises his head and chuckles before walking back to the bar and ordering another round.

⸻ ⁂ ⸻

"Holy shit! What the hell is going on?" I put my hand over my mouth and rush straight to the bathroom as soon as I shove open my apartment door. I raise the seat and puke my guts out. Finally, I feel acidic bubbles rising from my stomach to my mouth, but nothing is coming out but the stench of alcohol and white saliva. I stay like this for a little while.

"Here, have some water, Gabs." Simon. Simon is in my apartment. I almost forgot about him. I sit crisscross on the floor and close the lid of the toilet seat. I rest my head on it and reach for the glass of water. Simon sits next to me and leans on the tub. In the twenty-odd years I've known Simon, we've never been in this situation. There are still many firsts to be had, I guess.

"Thanks. I'm fine," I say between hiccups. "You should go home."

"I want to make sure you're okay." I don't want to be mad. I don't even want to sound cynical. But I want so much to point out that I've been okay on my own for a year now.

"Simon. I'm fine . . . you don't . . ."

"He's gone?" He cuts me with these hurtful words.

I don't say anything. I want to make up excuses, or use Colt's trip to California as a reason that he is missing, but I don't say anything. I don't need to justify anything to anyone.

"Were you like this when we broke up?" It's almost midnight and it's eerily quiet. The only sound is the sequenced drip of water from the sink. Simon rakes his fingers through his hair, and I can tell that he's anxious. I hope he isn't. "Did it hurt you to lose me the way it hurts you losing him?" He bends his head in embarrassment.

"Simon . . ." I whisper his name. "A few weeks ago, you asked me if we could be friends again. Tonight proved that we can be."

"You're right." I exhale as he agrees. Simon is not an unreasonable man. He sees things the way Felicity and I see them, and hopefully he accepts what we are at this time. "I'm glad that I spent tonight with you and Felicity, and—okay well, Thomas too." And with that we both start laughing.

"Thomas is like my fairy godmother," I say, pushing myself upright.

"You work for him?"

"Yes. But he's more than just my boss. He made my new life my new home. I know it doesn't make sense, but he makes everything better."

My stomach has settled for the time being. I see Simon look around my tiny bathroom. I'm glad that it's still relatively clean from when I moved in. I laugh a little.

"What?" He looks embarrassed.

"Nothing. I can tell you are disgusted about how tiny this bathroom is." I laugh some more. "I'm fine because I'm tiny. Having you here is like a giant invading a dwarf's home." I laugh even louder.

"Funny . . ." We are quiet for some time. We try to enjoy the calm of our newfound relationship. Simon stretches both legs on the floor, which takes up the entire space from the bathtub to the door. He leans back against the tub and clasps his hands together in his lap. "Are you feeling better?" I nod. I'm starting to get really tired. I can sleep on the floor right here in the bathroom. "Get up," he says. "C'mon. Don't stay here another minute or you'll fall asleep. We both know you can fall asleep anywhere." He bends his knees and pushes himself up. He then reaches for both my hands as if to pull me up too. I try and fail. And we both end up laughing. "Gabby, try."

"I had a lot to drink! Geez! This bathroom is swirling!" I say this as I steady myself in his arms.

"Yes, you did." Simon walks me out of the bathroom and into the bedroom. Then we both stop. Our eyes meet. I can see questions in Simon's eyes and immediately look away. These are questions I don't want to try to understand tonight. "I'd better go," he finally says. "Are you going to be okay on your own? I'll wait here while you change and get into bed, and then I'll go." And I do as he says.

I'm in bed in my pajamas when Simon knocks on the bedroom door. He walks in with a glass of water in his hand. He puts it on the side table and sits next to me on the bed. He pulls the covers up to my chin. This is the side of Simon I love, the part of him that shows how much he truly cares about someone who means a lot to him.

"Here's your water, and I'm off."

"Thanks, Simon."

"Gabs?"

"Yeah?" Simon towers over my tiny apartment, which makes him look so out of place.

"I love you." He's staring into my eyes, and I stare back because I'm no longer afraid of him, or of our circumstances.

"I know. And I love you." He bends his head in sadness and I'm glad he gets it. He understands that although I love him, things are different now.

Chapter Twenty-Five

"I am going to the doctor, yes! I'm on my way." I'm on the phone with Felicity who's been nagging me to see a doctor since I started complaining about headaches, dizziness, and nausea a week ago. I blamed my heartbreak. Sometimes sadness also manifests through physical illness. But I'm past the sadness. I've not heard from Colt in a couple of weeks, and I don't expect him to just show up and all will be well. We've definitely broken up. Definitely.

"I'm jumping on the train. I'll talk to you later," I tell Felicity, and I hang up. But I don't take the subway. I will enjoy Manhattan today and take my time. Midterms are over and Thanksgiving was challenging with my parents inviting Colt and me to Virginia for the holiday. I still don't have the heart to tell my mom that Colt has ghosted me. Instead, I stayed in town. Felicity hosted Thanksgiving dinner at her apartment with Phil as doting cohost. Thomas and Simon were there too, and two of Phil's single friends, Trish and Matt, from work. I had a great time, and I felt that Simon and I, and Felicity too, have all moved past the divorce.

I walk toward Bryant Park. For days I've been craving pistachio cake from Lady M Bakery located next to the park. There's usually a long line on the weekend, but hopefully I won't have to wait too long on a Wednesday morning. I walk under dangerous construction stands to cross Broadway. These scaffolds all over this area of Manhattan are a pain to pedestrians, really. It's like *Super Mario Bros.* world out here; you need to watch every step and turn or you'll end up inside a manhole or under a precariously low construction platform. I take my sweet time.

Lady M Bakery doesn't open until nine, so I head straight to the park. It's a lazy Wednesday morning, but the coffee stand is in full swing with people lined up all around the small booth. I get a copy of *The New York Times* and spot an empty table next to two older gentlemen having a serious chess match. I read there for a few minutes. My doctor's appointment is not until ten. I read Page Six, my guilty pleasure. After I finish the lifestyle section, I fold my newspaper, shove it into my tote bag, and head toward my favorite sculpture in the park—Gertrude Stein.

Gertrude Stein was an exceptional author in the 1920s who defied traditions. Her statue is located behind the New York City Public Library.

I've been visiting Gertrude for more than a decade now. I look at her seated bronze figure and I feel her speak to me. Gertrude's statue shows her as a contemplative, heavyset woman who represents strength. They call her the modern Buddha because she was larger than life, and there was more to her than met the eye. She was mentor to many writers, artists, and musicians during her time. And I come to her here because I can still feel the magical pull of her history. I wish I had her strength and her cadence—to be in tune with herself despite the expectations of her time. Perhaps there was always this part of me who wanted to be bigger than I was, who wants to be bigger than I am. Perhaps I admire Gertrude because she was unapologetic about who she was, and I have always been uncertain of my next step. I can look like her someday. I can cut my hair short and I'll definitely be in the heavyset category by the time I turn fifty. The thought doesn't frighten me. In fact, it makes me smile.

"Hi, Gert. . . ." I whisper into the wind, and then I walk back to the Lady M Bakery on a mission to satisfy my pistachio cake craving.

~✤~

"Are you sure?" I look at Dr. Sharma with furrowed brow, at her perfectly coiffed hair and flawless olive skin, trying to understand the foreign language she seems to be speaking.

I stare at her for a good thirty seconds. She smiles at me, letting me process this diagnosis. Her smile is sweet and encouraging. She has one of those faces that is unforgettable, striking. I'm sure she's used to this—wide-eyed stares, uncertain reactions, and shock.

"This is not something you need to worry about. You have options." She says this with a tender voice. "You're only eight weeks in, so you have time to decide what would work for you." She leans back, letting me take my time.

I'm still as a log. I feel myself holding my breath and waiting for someone to crack a joke and say "Gotcha!"

It doesn't come.

"Let me get some stuff for you and I'll be right back." Dr. Sharma gets up and walks out of her white-walled office, plastered with expensively framed Ivy League diplomas as evidence of her expertise in general medicine.

I sit here and try to process this news. I feel my palms sweating, my throat drying out, and my eyes welling up. Finally, I feel a tear roll down my cheek, and my hands start to shake. The fear that came when I heard the news has been overpowered by the happiness of knowing that this can and is actually happening to me—in my life, in this lifetime. I had almost given up and have long squashed the dream of holding someone in my arms, of putting someone to sleep next to me, of someone calling me *Mommy*.

I think of Simon and all the times I'd secretly hoped to be pregnant when we were together.

Then I think of Colt.

Instead of sadness, I feel gratitude. I now understand why he came into my life when he did. I can't think of any other explanation, and here it is. My love swells over for this man I haven't known long. I don't need to forgive him for anything. I'm glad I had the chance to love him and know how it was to be loved by him.

I put both my hands over my tummy and stare into space, perfectly still. Then I bend my head to look at my midsection.

"Hey, you. I'm going to be your mommy," I whisper as I stroke my tummy. Then I break down in tears, and all my emotions finally decide to escape at the same moment.

I'm going to be someone's mom.

⁓

"Wow! Wow! Wow!" These words are said exactly three seconds apart. Thomas's eyes are brimming with excitement. I can tell that he's trying to discern whether this is good news or bad news. He walks around the counter and gives me a tight bear hug. The lunchtime crowds have dissipated, and the store is empty. I hold onto him like my life depends on it. I bury my face in his chest, inhaling his scent that has become a comfort to me—a place that is like home. His chin rests on top of my head. He strokes my hair and kisses me on my forehead like I'm his own child.

He holds me at arm's length and looks at me. I also see tears in his eyes. I see encouragement. I see happiness. And most importantly, I see life.

"You've been splendid at rocking your boat, Gabriella. This is your best work yet," he says, and we start cackling. He lets me melt in his arms once again. And I do.

Thomas closes the shop, makes some tea, and moves us to the sofa. He turns on the fireplace. British people think they can solve every problem with a cup of tea, so I indulge him. I sit slouched on one side of the long leather sofa. I put both my legs up as Thomas hands me a cup.

"I put extra milk and honey in there, dear." I nod in thanks. He sits opposite me on the other side of the lounger and crosses his legs with finesse and precision, like he has rehearsed for this moment his entire life. This is another reason I adore Thomas. Even after decades of life's many painful twists, turns, and punches, Thomas glides through it like a ballerina—determined, brave, and graceful.

The sun is shining today. I didn't notice it earlier when I walked out of Dr. Sharma's office, but I see it now, and I feel its rays on my face through the window. I lean my head backwards and close my eyes. I drown myself in sunshine.

"Do you want me to be a friend or a father?" Thomas asks. I open my eyes and see him gazing at me in deep contemplation. His concern is clear.

"Both," I whisper. My eyes are puffy from incessant crying,

my nose is starting to tingle from all the blowing, and my hair is a complete mess.

"Cut your hair," Thomas suggests. I look at him, puzzled. "That has nothing to do with all this." He gestures toward me. "I just think it's time for a little bit of change, don't you think?"

"I guess. But is that the father or the friend talking?"

"Both and neither. Being a father is my life's greatest work, Gabriella. There is nothing more valuable than to be someone's parent." Thomas is deep in thought as he stirs his steaming cup of tea. He finally takes a sip and looks out the window. "As your friend, I will shake you and ask you if this is what you want. As your father, I will tell you to take this responsibility seriously. Childcare is not cheap in the city, hospital bills will be outrageous with no insurance, and your apartment is not conducive to raising a child."

"I know."

"Is this good news?" he finally asks.

"Yes. God, yes." I say this in a whisper. I pull myself up and put the cup of tea on the coffee table in front of us.

"Well, let's start with your insurance. You can get some from me. We can figure out how you and the shop can share the cost. You don't need to worry about that."

"Thomas . . . " I stifle a sob.

"Let's discuss childcare. Are you staying in school? Are you going back to Virginia? Are you going to let the father know?" I've been thinking about this very question. "Have you heard from him at all?" I shake my head. "I'd like to say it's unlike Colt, but I don't know him well enough. I'm pretty sure you've seen stories about him in the press." I slowly nod. When Felicity mentioned a few weeks ago that she got news alerts on Colt's book and art events in California, she also mentioned that there were many photos of him with this one blonde girl on his arm. Felicity was angry, but I didn't need to see them.

I put my head in my hands and stay like this for a little while. Thomas doesn't say anything. All I hear is the crackle of the fire. When I open my eyes, Thomas is holding his cup on his lap and looking at me affectionately. I give him a weak smile, not because I'm unhappy but because I recognize the tangled mess I'm in.

"Gabriella, when I became a father at twenty-eight, I didn't know what I was doing. But one thing I was certain of—my life was finally complete. There was nothing else I could ever ask for. I tried to be a good father to Harry." Thomas pauses. "Unfortunately, I could never be a good husband to his mother. And you know how the saying goes, the best thing you can do for your children is to love their mother. I loved her the best way I could." Thomas is deep in thought as he continues to stir his steaming cup of tea. He takes another sip and looks out the window again.

"What happened to Harry's mother?" It's good to talk about something else other than me.

"When Harry was three years old, she left us for another man. Harry was devastated. By the time he was five, he had forgotten about her. I never wanted to put her in a bad light, so we didn't talk much about her. I had many faults too, as you can imagine."

"Did she ever come back to try to have a relationship with Harry?"

"She did, but Harry didn't want anything to do with her. By then she'd been married for fifteen years and had three other children. I wanted us to be friends, but she hated me."

"Thomas . . ."

"When Harry was diagnosed with cancer, she helped me care for him. For a time, she stopped hating me. A child can make you do things you didn't think you could. Matilda, that's her name, stayed with us for months until Harry passed away quietly one night." I move closer to Thomas and rest my head on his shoulder. "A part of me died with him. That boy, that beautiful boy, was my everything." I hear Thomas stifle a sob. He lowers his head and lets go of his sorrow—and the tears that have been welling up inside finally escape. I reach for his hand and hold on tight, and we stay like this until almost nighttime.

Chapter Twenty-Six

The surprise on Mom's face when Simon drops me off in front of our house is priceless. I walk past her at the door with my rolling duffle as she stares at Simon's car drive away with her mouth half open. She doesn't even welcome me. My dad, on the other hand, grabs my stuff, gives me the squinty-eye look, and pulls me into an embrace. This man still looks great at age sixty, and his positivity about life makes it better for the people around him. I don't remember seeing my dad mad or sad—pensive, yes, sometimes, but never angry. He floats through life like a ray of sunshine.

"Welcome home, princess," he says. My mom is still at the door. I think it's hilarious. But I let her figure it out.

"Hey, hey, was that Simon?" she finally asks, her Asian glare piercing my soul. I give her a nonchalant nod as I walk to the kitchen. I can smell adobo cooking. It's nearly dinnertime, and she promised me a full Filipino spread.

"Hey, Gabriella! What was that about?" She's relentless in her inquisition and blocks my path, hands on her hips. Mom is a full foot shorter than me, but that doesn't stop her from being a warrior. I have a tiny feisty mother, I think affectionately.

"Mom, it's no big deal. He was driving here anyway. We do it every year. Felicity was with us in the car." I roll my eyes, and I get a slap on the shoulder. "Ouch!"

"Tell me what's going on, young lady. I don't like surprises."

"If you're asking are we back together, the answer is no." I get out of her way and she trails behind me. I hear the pitter-patter of her slippers on the hardwood floor.

"But that means you've forgiven him after all he's done. And his parents, my goodness! I saw them at the grocery the other day, and I had to hide. I don't like to be buddy-buddy with those people after all the things they've said about our family." I honestly don't think she's as mad as she's letting on.

"Maria, let your daughter rest and have dinner first." My mellow father is no match for my boisterous mother, but he tries.

"Gabriella!"

"Mom . . ." I start to laugh. "Stop it. There are no surprises. Simon, Felicity, and I are back together again—as friends. Like middle school." I walk to the stove and check on the simmering pots. The lingering smell of vinegar and garlic is proof of Mom's famous chicken and pork adobo.

"When did this happen?" She stands next to me, her hands still on her hips. I take a small sip of the adobo sauce and I can't help but be transported back to my childhood. Here, exactly where I am right now, with my mom cooking this very concoction while I play on the floor. As an only child, I was constantly with my mom. She never left my sight, and we were totally inseparable. When I was around twelve years old, I longed for a sibling to draw her attention away from me. But that doesn't bother me now. The three of us, like this, is perfect. I couldn't ask for anything more.

"A couple of weeks," I say. "Can I eat now?!"

I feel my phone vibrate in my back pocket. It's Felicity.

"Yup. C'mon down!" I tell her. "Felicity is coming to dinner."

"I already know. I think her parents are out tonight and

won't be back until tomorrow morning. They said they're getting a tree somewhere in Shenandoah. Why they need to get their tree there, I will never understand." My mother rolls her eyes. Dad, on the other hand, is sitting at the breakfast nook, looking at us like we are pure entertainment. "Christopher, can you please talk to your daughter?"

"What do we need to talk to her about? It's not rare that ex-spouses can actually be friends after their divorce." He leans back in his chair and crosses his legs, a wide grin on his face. I can tell how much he's enjoying this.

"See, Mom . . ." I move toward Dad and pull up a chair next to him.

"Whatever. I'll set up the table in the nice dining room—"

"No!" Dad and I interrupt her in unison. We never use the nice dining room. We're the kind of family who hangs out in the kitchen. That room is only ever used when we have visitors— visitors who aren't family. It's really just for show. And every time we do, we never hear the end of my mother's complaining about it. Most of the time, Dad and I end up cleaning invisible messes and nonexistent smells just because Mom imagines them. This house is her sanctuary. She is proud of the home she's made of it—and we're grateful to her for it.

"Don't you guys want to eat there?" Mom is definitely irritated.

"I'm fine here, Mom. And I'm sure Felicity is too."

"Babe, we're fine here in the kitchen."

"Mom, this is what I look forward to—being here in the kitchen with you guys, eating your awesome cooking."

"Fine. Do you think Simon is coming too?"

"He didn't say, and I doubt it very much." I can sense Dad

looking at me, sizing me up, trying to figure out this thing with Simon. But there is nothing to tell—well, at least where Simon is concerned.

Now, how do I tell these two beautiful souls that they are going to be grandparents? The thought stuns me. I've always been a model daughter. I always try to do the right thing. Even the divorce wasn't really my fault. Sometimes, it's simply in our stars.

"Mom, can you sit here please?" I ask, pulling a chair next to me. She looks at my dad nervously and slowly takes a seat. "Let me just start by saying, there is nothing going on between me and Simon. Period." I see my mom and dad nod in understanding. "The guy who paid for dinner at Per Se, remember him?" Mom and Dad nod together again, slowly, nervously. "Well, he's also no longer in the picture." My mom's eyes widen in panicky surprise. Then I stand up and face both of them, like I did a thousand times before in this very room when I had either good or bad news to share. My mother, ever dramatic, puts her hand on my dad's shoulder for support. I can sense her anxiety. My dad hasn't taken his eyes off me. I pause because, quite honestly, I don't know any way to break this news gently. I clasp my hands together and start swinging them uncomfortably from side to side, like the little girl I once was.

"For crying out loud, Gabriella, tell us!" Mom jumps up and Dad gently pulls her back to her seat.

"You guys are going to be grandparents!" I smile tentatively. And both my parents turn a lighter shade of pale.

Just as I'm making this announcement, Felicity walks in. Behind her is Simon. All four people around me are frozen. I smile and I frown, and I make faces, because I don't know what else to say or do. Simon walks away. Felicity looks like she is about to explode. Mom is speechless, and we all know that's impossible. Dad is the first one to push his chair backward and rush to me for a hug. Felicity slowly puts her hand over her mouth and is almost in tears. Mom is still sitting there motionless. I can see the wheels in her head turning. I can tell she is rationalizing, analyzing, deciding. I'm thirty-six years old, and by the time this baby is born, I'll be thirty-seven. I got this. They should know that I got this.

"Oh, sweetheart!" My dad envelops me in his arms. This big burly man made everything possible for me, loved me unconditionally all my life, has given me anything and everything I've ever wanted—and I don't see any remorse or disappointment, only joy. My heart swells with so much love for him. "My baby is going to be a mommy. How is that even possible? I have waited for this moment all my life." I hug him tighter.

I pull away from my dad a little to look at my mom, and there she is, silently crying in her corner. Maria doesn't cry, she never cries. She's the toughest cookie I know. Then she rushes to me and hugs me tight. There we are, in a circle, my life—the support system I need. Felicity finally walks in, closes the door, and sits on the stool next to the kitchen counter. And then she starts crying too.

"Come over here, Felicity. You're going to be an auntie!" my dad says, and welcomes Felicity in our embrace. We stay like this for a while.

After we break away, Felicity starts jumping up and down, and so does my mom.

"I'm going to be Grammy!" my mom screams and starts laughing. Felicity gives her a big hug and jumps up and down with her in excitement.

"And I'm going to be Tita Felicity! I'm finally going to be Tita Felicity!" She's still jumping and screaming with my mom.

"Felicity, you already have five nephews and nieces," I remind her.

"Yeah, but this one I'm sure to see all the time!" She comes to me, bends, and puts her ear to my tummy.

Dad walks down to the basement and comes back up with several bottles of his expensive champagne. "I was keeping these until Christmas, but this big happy news calls for a big celebration! I'm going to be a grandpa!" He pulls out champagne flutes from Mom's china cabinet in the nice dining room and pops a bottle in one swift go. We all scream in glee.

The door opens and Simon walks in. I can tell he was able to gather his composure and come to terms with this new reality. We all stop and stare at him.

"Congratulations, Gabs." And he walks right to me for a hug. I can sense my mom's irritation. Felicity shrugs her shoulders in a heavy sigh, and I can feel how much this is pleasing her. I hug him back because he is Simon, because he is one of my best friends, and because he is still family.

We move to the family room, and the champagne keeps flowing. I've been nursing the same glass the entire night. Mom is drinking more than usual, but I can see happiness in her eyes. The stress of hours ago has vanished. There is laughter and excitement all around. My parents, who love both Simon and Felicity dearly, do not question this new dynamic among the three of us. They treat Simon like they've always treated him—as their son.

Simon, in turn, behaves like he always has. Now, as I look at us all, I can't believe that our divorce became final only a few months ago. Perhaps a part of my distress back then was losing Simon as family. But tonight his laughter is carefree, and I can tell how much he has missed my family and vice versa. Maybe I can actually do this—maybe Simon and I can actually do this.

He gives me a sideways glance as my dad tops his glass with more champagne. He smiles at me and sighs. I understand that we will need to talk about all this later—not because I need to explain, but because he cares enough to want to know how everything is for me. I give him a wide smile, letting him know I'm fine, because I am. I raise my glass to him, and he raises his back—nobody notices this because my parents and Felicity are busy sorting our Christmas decorations, which are scattered all over the family room. My heart is full.

"Let's go to Camelot!" Felicity stands in the middle of our family room, screaming at the top of her lungs with both arms up in the air. She's not talking about the magical, mythical place of King Arthur, obviously, but the elementary school a few blocks away from our house where the three of us went for our primary education. Simon and Felicity were already friends then—they'd been friends since they were in diapers—but I didn't encounter them until middle school at Jackson. Felicity used to wiggle her way through an opening in the backyard fence between their houses. She was a handful even as a child.

Sitting on the floor next to the fire, still nursing my flute of champagne, I look at my home, my family, and I am glad that this tiny beautiful seed inside my tummy will share this with me.

Simon gives me a contemplative smile. Perhaps he is also feeling nostalgic, reminiscing about the past and at the same time thinking about what lies ahead—for all of us. I no longer blame him for all the changes that happened in the past year. If not for them, I would not have this gift.

My mom is radiant. I can see excitement coursing through her, and I'm glad. I've never seen her this carefree or buoyant, and I know that it has something to do with my news. My mother is not an easy woman to please. Dad knows it, I know it, and she certainly acknowledges it—but tonight, she is different. She smiles at me from across the room, and she pours champagne freely, which is totally unlike her. She usually scowls or tells everyone to be careful with their drink because it might spill and ruin the carpet. My Asian mother is not one for petty niceness, which is in total contradiction to her Filipina nature—Filipinos are always, always polite—but tonight, I can feel the lightness in her heart through her unguarded smile.

"Go ahead, young ones," my dad says, leaning next to my mom after topping everyone's glass but mine. Felicity takes one of my arms and Simon the other.

"C'mon! Let's go to the playground. I'll carry a flask. Do we have a flask?" Felicity looks at my parents, and my mother, still totally out of character, goes to the kitchen to find us a thermos for the remaining champagne. She pours the golden liquid into the container and hands it to Simon.

"Don't get caught, okay?" And there she is—my Asian mother is back with her stern warning—the very tone I know and love.

Simon helps me up. I can feel my dad observing us, and I sincerely hope they are not thinking about Simon and me getting back together as a couple. I glare at my dad, and he throws his head backwards and laughs heartily.

⚬⚬⚬

They've upgraded the school, and it's pretty impressive. The once half basketball court is now full-sized complete with side bleachers and an electronic scoreboard. There's also a new build-ing adjacent to track and field, and the playground, which used to consist of a monkey bar, a swing set, and a merry-go-round, now boasts giant slides and seesaws and three different levels of rock climbing by the wall close to the gym. I see myself as an olive-skinned girl in pigtails, walking these very grounds, a girl who was always uncertain of herself because she was different. There were not many Filipinos in this area back in the day. There still aren't in this part of town. My cousins live farther away in Leesburg and Fredericksburg, so I seldom got to hang out with them. But I'm looking forward to seeing them all this week for Christmas lunch.

"God, it's cold. . . ." Felicity is shaking. She opens the ther-mos, gulps some champagne, and hands it to Simon, who takes a swig. I sit at the end of the shortest slide and pull my coat around me tighter.

"Ha! Do you remember our last fun run here, Felicity?" Si-mon asks, looking around the dark field. The only light is the dim glow from the basketball court.

"Yes, you threw up!"

"Ha! *You* threw up!"

"Whatever." Felicity rolls her eyes and settles next to me, squeezing her butt next to mine. Simon sits on the sand in front of us, stretches his long legs, and leans back on his elbows.

"You were always so quiet, Gabs," Simon says.

"Yeah," Felicity agrees. "God, I loved your backpack so much and begged my mom for months for one like it, that pink cloth one. It was so punk rock, which was so unlike you, but you pulled it off perfectly."

"I remember that backpack! I used to adore it. But I fell in the river with it, and it was a total loss. I cried for days. Mom couldn't find a replacement."

"I thought you were the coolest girl in school," Felicity adds. I look at her in surprise. I've never considered myself cool, not in the slightest. "You were just always so aloof the way you are now. You came to school, didn't talk to anyone, and left like you couldn't be bothered by our childish antics. So when you helped Simon and me fight off those cowards at Jackson, I was so happy you finally noticed me—us."

"You're nuts!" I say, giving her a playful shove.

"Yeah, we talked about you for weeks after that," Simon adds. This is news to me. I've always been grateful that they took me in, made me part of their little pack, and not the other way around. "Remember that eighth grader who asked you to the dance? Geez, what's that dude's name again, Felicity?

"Ranger or something weird."

"Ranzel," I offer.

"Who names their kid Ranzel?" Simon and Felicity say in chorus and laugh. I didn't realize how much I missed this until tonight. The three of us like this.

"He wasn't your first kiss, was he?" The horror on Felicity's face is comical.

"I was her first kiss, dumdum!"

"Ha!"

"I missed you guys! I missed you guys so much!"

Felicity reaches out to Simon, hooks his neck with one arm, and mine with the other. She kisses my cheek and pulls us all together in a tight embrace. I feel Simon awkwardly put his hand on my back. I do the same because, although our lives have changed and we're moving on in different directions, this is still the family I've known all my life.

～ℓℓℓ～

Christmas Eve is a big deal to the Pableo side of my family—my mom's side. When I was growing up, my mom and aunts and uncles would tell us kids about their childhood in the Philippines and especially stories of their Christmas Eves. My mom is one of seven kids, so their household was always in constant chaos. Tonight, all seven siblings and their spouses and their children and grandchildren are gathered at the Stevenses' household. They each brought their own Filipino dish, so our house has food everywhere.

"Woo-hoo! Can't wait to try them all," Felicity exclaims upon seeing the Filipino food spread all over the house. It's a wide variety of my ultimate favorites—*lumpiang shanghai, menudo, morcon, pancit palabok,* and *dinuguan at puto.* Tomorrow, at my Aunt Rosie's house, there will be a much larger feast with *lechon*—suckling pig—as the main attraction, or as Simon calls it, the heart attack.

"Go get a plate," I say. Felicity has talked about nothing but food since this morning. She stayed the night and woke up to the smell of Mom's *calderatta*—beef cut in cubes simmered to perfect tenderness in spicy tomato sauce—cooking in the kitchen.

"Hey!" Simon walks up behind us. Mom and Dad didn't need to invite him tonight—it's been a tradition for almost two decades, and they talked about it last night like he was expected to come. I did have to forewarn him, though, that it's best not to allow his parents and mine in the same room at this time. We agreed to work on that.

Felicity grabs a plate and piles it with an array of delicacies. I see that look of disgust on Simon's face—and nobody is taking any mind because we all know that he hates Filipino food with a passion.

"You're weird," Felicity says as she walks past Simon to go to the living room and join the throng.

It's surprisingly warm in Virginia for this time of year. My dad was able to put up the string lights this afternoon without a coat and said he was almost tempted to wear shorts. He grew up in the Midwest, so Virginia winters are nothing to him. For the first time this season, the sliding door leading from the living room to our big patio is wide open. It gives the house extra space, allowing the party to flow outdoors. My loud Uncle Roger just opened a bottle of Johnny Walker Black, and my cousin Mickey poured everyone a shot of tequila. Felicity loves hanging out with these guys. They treat her like one of us, although her skin is white as snow. Seeing her with them always warms my heart. I'm blessed to have the best friend in the world.

"Feliza, come on over here! We're starting soon!" My uncle Roger baptized her with a Filipino name because, he explained, she is more Filipina than any Filipina he knows.

"Game!" she screams. And when Uncle Roger sees Simon next to her, they freeze. Of course, they all know. My mother is not one for keeping secrets. Uncle Roger looks at Simon, then at me, and back at Simon. Mickey looks at my ring finger, probably to confirm we're no longer married.

"I guess this is how kids do this divorce thing these days. I will never understand you young people." Uncle Roger makes this pronouncement with such a thick accent that Simon looks at me for translation.

"He said you guys are weird," Cousin Mickey offers. Felicity, Simon, and I laugh a little nervously.

By nine o'clock, the party is in full swing. My cousin Joanna and her boyfriend, Patrick, arrive with a big platter of *chicharon bulaklak,* deep-fried pork innards—and although it sounds disgusting and a little dangerous to your health, I can devour it with vinegar and garlic in one sitting and totally without guilt. I jump up to hug her. The thought of this delicacy is making my mouth water. Patrick, originally from Nebraska, is not a fan, but his love for Joanna makes him willing to try anything. Nevertheless, the look of fear on his face is hilarious as we remove the cover and the smell of grease permeates the air.

"Gabs made me try those," Simon teases Patrick and pats him on the shoulder, almost like welcoming him into the family. I can see Simon tense up after speaking. It's a hard habit to break, especially since we've been together twenty years—and it seems so surreal that we're together tonight after finalizing our divorce not so long ago.

"Gabriella! Gabriella! Your boyfriend just sent you something!" My mom's voice thunders in the room, reverberating, getting everybody's attention as she stands at the other side of the house with the door wide open. Everyone, I mean every single person at the party, looks at her expectantly—and then at me

—and slowly they all turn to look at Simon. Felicity hurries over to my mom and talks to whoever is outside. I slowly make my way to them. As I peek outside, I see a big flower arrangement and an expensive three-tiered cake, the kind of cake you get for weddings that usually costs thousands of dollars.

The man carrying the cake hands me a heavy glossy card.

"For Ms. Stevens from Mr. James." I can't breathe. The mere mention of his name is like a brick sitting on my heart. I put both my hands on my tummy, trying to breathe normally, reaching for a place from which I can calmly navigate this scene. Simon is right behind me. I slowly take the card from the deliveryman. He gives me a huge Merry Christmas smile, but I don't reciprocate. I feel like throwing up. I want to run away and lock myself in my childhood room and not face any of this. My mom, who is oblivious, calls my dad and tells him to take the cake and make space for it on the kitchen counter. I stand there, motionless.

"Hurry, Chris," my mom says. "That poor man is having a hard time balancing this thing." She walks along with Dad slowly, admiring the cake inside a box with a transparent plastic cover.

"Do you want me to read it for you?" Felicity whispers. I shake my head lightly. In the background, I can hear my mom telling my aunts about my new boyfriend, and about the time he paid for a $3,000 meal in New York City.

"So generous, *diba*?" she tells her sisters proudly. I'm a little pissed off at her right now because she knows that my "boyfriend" and I are over. I begged her this morning not to tell anyone that I'm pregnant, not until I'm ready to tell everyone myself. It was hard to convince her, but thankfully she conceded. My dad helped me with this big-time.

With my mother commanding the conversation, everyone's attention is on her. Felicity takes my hand and gently leads me upstairs to my bedroom. I'm shaking. Does he think so little of me? Playing a trick like this?

I sit on the edge of my bed. Felicity is standing next to me in anticipation. I tear the envelope open. The paper is white, thick, and velvety—so uncharacteristically Colt.

Merry Christmas—Colt

That's all it says.

This insults me. I don't know what I've done to him to deserve it. I've stopped calling him and stopped trying to get answers. I just want to move on.

I just want to stop loving him.

It's so exhausting trying to stop wanting him.

But I have other priorities now. I hold my tummy. A spark of joy flashes within me—enough to see the reason for this pain.

I beg Felicity to head back down and enjoy the festivities with our families. I hear my mom's voice welcoming her parents and siblings not long after the cake episode.

I stay in my room the entire night and I welcome Christmas this way.

At around two o'clock, I hear a light tap on the door. I've changed into pajamas and have been willing myself to sleep ever since Felicity went back downstairs, but I'm still wide awake in the dark.

"Come in," I say in a whisper. I'm curled in a ball underneath my pink duvet. I don't move from my bed. The door opens. The light from the hall blinds me.

Simon walks in.

"Hey," he says, also in a whisper. He walks toward me and

sits on the bed. He brushes the hair off my face and looks at me with so much kindness in his eyes.

You okay?" he asks. He reaches for my bedside lamp and turns it on. I don't blink. I look at him.

"Should I hate him?" he asks. I shake my head again. He touches my cheek lightly, and it comforts me. This is not romance; this is friendship—the kind I want to have with him forever.

"Gabs . . ." He looks away from me, in deep thought. "I know this isn't the right time to say anything. I should let you be after all I've put you through. But I can't see you like this."

"You don't have to feel responsible for anything—for me— anymore, Simon," I say softly. He has to understand that I've forgiven him.

"But I do," he says, "feel responsible for you. I always have, and I always will."

"Thank you . . . but it has to stop." I don't say this with annoyance, but with affection.

"I didn't think I wanted children until I found out that you are pregnant. I couldn't believe how happy I felt when I heard you tell your parents, and when your dad hugged you. The irony is . . . we both know what the irony is here. Then it hit me. And it hurt." I reach for his hand and squeeze it gently. I can't think of anything else to say. "But if he's not around anymore, I want to be . . ."

"Simon . . ." I sound stern. I know what he's about to say. I'm grateful, yes, but this is not where we should be. I can't let him. I've grown up, and so has he. I'm a different person now. I can't see myself going back to where and what I used to be. His reality is different from mine, but I hope he is not mistaking guilt for love.

"I made a mistake, Gabs. . . ." He bends his head and starts sobbing softly. I can feel my heart breaking. There will always be a part of me that wants to protect Simon—always—but to give in to him would mean a betrayal of everything I've worked hard for the past year. "Is there any chance . . . you'll take me back?" He turns his head to look at me. I don't need to say anything. He has seen it himself. My eyes speak for my soul. But I don't look away because he is Simon. And because he is Simon, I don't want to hurt him, to reject him, or to ruin what we're trying to rebuild here as friends.

I get up, put my arms around him, and lay my head on his shoulder. We sit like this long into the night.

Chapter Twenty-Seven

"**D**oes he know?!"

I immediately turn around to look at the owner of the anxious voice. And right next to me is Tina, a troubled expression on her face. I close my eyes tightly in distress. This is not how I want him to find out. I haven't even decided if I want him to know. I don't say anything, instead I start gathering my prescriptions, prenatal vitamin samples, and pregnancy pamphlets on the nurses' counter, as well as my insurance card, which thankfully kicked in as soon as Thomas applied for it before the Christmas break.

There is no hiding from Tina now.

I walk away from her. She follows me into the busy reception area where more than half a dozen pregnant women are waiting to be seen. When she grabs my arm, I turn around to face her, unwilling to acknowledge what she's just seen. Then I continue to walk out of the clinic, trying to ignore her.

"Gabby, I don't want to see him hurt anymore." I stop and give her an angry glare. Hurt? Who is she to talk about hurt?

"You're kidding, right?" I say slowly, stressing every word. The hallway is quiet, except for a couple of people walking past us.

"Is it his?" She won't let go of my arm. I lightly push her away. I feel anger bubbling inside me. I give her a stare down—she doesn't have the right to do this. Neither of them does.

"It's none of your business." I want to scream at her, tell her how wrong I was to trust him—them. I don't deserve this. I deserve better.

"You don't have any idea what you've put him through." She turns around and curses, brushing her fingers through her beautiful blond hair.

I don't understand this reaction.

"You're kidding, right?" I say again. I'm never nasty and I don't want to start today.

"You don't have any idea, Gabby! I was there that night. He tore the apartment apart and wouldn't let me call anyone to fix it. He says it's a cruel but useful reminder of how stupid he is, and about making the mistake of trusting someone, of letting someone in. He never lets anyone in. So, please, help me fucking understand what happened." She's pacing back and forth in concern. "I can't even get through to him," she screams.

"Calm down!" I scream back.

"Calm down?" Her eyes are furious.

"He left me . . . without a word," I whisper. I'm ashamed of this reality—another man, apart from Simon, decided that I was not worth staying with.

"And you honestly think he doesn't have a reason for this? Come with me and find out." She grabs my hand, pulls me out of the building, and without a word hails a cab.

I need to find out, for whatever it's worth. I need to find something, anything, to justify why Colt just disappeared from my life. It has been a trying few months without a word except for a text and a hurtful Christmas present.

For selfish reasons, I do want to know.

No one says a word inside the cab, but I can hear Tina's

rapid breathing. She is livid. She stares into the distance with clenched fists.

I try to recall my last few days with Colt. I have come to terms with Colt having a change of heart. It's what a guy like him does. They conquer and break hearts—and although it hurt me to lose him, I made peace with the reason why he happened in my life.

But Tina's reaction doesn't make any sense.

The hubbub of New York passes us by in a blur. I look outside, trying to make sense out of things. He was too much of a coward to admit what he truly feels, or, as I suspect, he made a premature declaration and a huge mistake.

I was that mistake. Why am I always someone's fucking mistake?

Oh, New York, hold on to me tight—tighter, this time. I need your energy more than anything today. You are where I finally found my strength. You are where I fell. And you are where I learned to stand up again. I hold my tummy as I think about all this—if nothing else, you are where I finally learned how to be human and to understand that happiness and love are not simply about floating through life, but actually charging ahead with passion. You gave me that.

I turn sideways to look at Tina, who's staring back at me unblinking. I can't make out the expression on her face—earlier she was livid, but now I sense she is as bemused as I.

"Look, you were there when I needed you. . . ." She speaks slowly. There is a change in her tone.

"It's what any decent human being would do," I reply.

"But you chose not to leave me, or to pass me on to someone when I was bleeding to death. You stood by me, stayed with me, and made sure that I was fine before you left the hospital. Colt told me." We settle down together in the back of the cab in silence until we pull up in front of Colt's apartment.

I get out of the cab and nervously close the door behind me. I stare at the apartment—where the best moments of my life have taken place—and I feel panic overwhelming me. The last time I was here was that night we affirmed our love. *Our love?* I can't believe that was only months ago.

"Why are we here?" I ask. Tina simply looks at me and walks straight ahead to unlock the door. I climb the steps slowly behind her.

"Because," Tina says as she pushes the door wide open to let me in, "I owe you this at least."

I put my hand over my mouth in shock as I walk into the apartment. It's a disaster. There is a big hole on the left side of the wall close to the entrance. And as I walk through, I take a peek at the living room—with hateful graffiti on the wall and broken furniture.

"He wouldn't let me touch it," Tina says as she walks into the room. She stands next to the framed mosaic mirror smashed in the middle—I can see faint dried blood at the center. What have I done to make Colt this angry? I see his mom's Nobel Prize for Literature medal among the debris.

"That is his most prized possession, the only thing that is left of his mom." There is great affection in her tone.

"I don't understand." I am in shock.

"That morning, he left for Los Angeles."

"I don't understand," I repeat as I walk around the living room, expecting to find answers—any answer as to why Colt felt this way that night.

"To love him means to understand him, even if there are blind spots. You can never get the full picture with him. I know this because . . . well, because I've loved Colt all my life." This is not a surprise to me. I look at Tina as she says this, and I sense the understanding that passes between us. "He was crying when I found him and all this. There in that corner, like a child."

"Tina, I don't understand . . . this is probably not about me, or us."

"He saw you kissing your ex-husband. It was the night he wanted to be with you so badly, but you told him not to go to your apartment. He went anyway. He wanted to surprise you." My eyes widen in shock. I remember that night.

"Oh my god . . ." I put both my hands over my stomach. I feel sick. I tightly press my lips together, willing myself not to throw up right here. "It's not what he thought."

"Tell me what he saw?"

"He saw two very sad childhood friends who were finally letting go of their marriage. I stopped it before it went anywhere." Tina walks around the broken side table and sits on the piano bench. She crosses one long slender leg over the other, in deep thought, trying to grasp my explanation. I stay where I am, unmoving. I feel like I'm on trial for a crime I didn't commit. This irritates me. "Look. It's been two months. I've moved on, and obviously so has he, so I don't think we need to dwell on this." I can't believe I just said that. I am not one for boldness. I can hear myself talking, but I'm in some sort of a trance or an out-of-body experience. The expression on Tina's face shows disbelief.

"Who's giving up on whom now?" Her voice is sharp. "Colt is not over it. I know this. I know him. You were not just some fling to him. God, I wish you were." She rolls her eyes and throws her hands up in frustration. "We have a rule in this house. We don't bring home anyone until we're sure we want to spend more time with that person. You're the only person he brought home. The only one! I've met others at parties and such, but never here. Never. It made me nervous at first because it was very new for Colt, but I saw how happy you made him. The change had been astonishing. He drank less, stopped smoking, and he was home more—with you. He even started cooking, for crying out loud!"

"It's his . . ." I whisper, and Tina goes silent for a bit.

"I thought you were the antidote to the anxiety his parents caused him—the fear of falling in love." But I can't cure someone who doesn't want to be cured. I close my eyes, and the vision of him comes to mind: *"Hold on to me, Gabby. I don't know how to do this. Hold on to me."* I jolt back to the present and open my eyes. "Do you plan to tell him?" I bend my head because this is the question that I don't have an answer for.

"I don't know, Tina. I really don't."

"Do you still love him?"

"Colt will always be part of my life now. He's not just some guy I met and had an affair with. He's the father of my child. Do I love him for that? Yes. Do I love him for all of it? Yes. Did I deserve to have my heart broken this way? No." I feel tears roll down my cheeks and wipe them with the back of my hand. Tina nods her head. She's a woman too, after all. She gets up, walks toward me in calculated steps, and hugs me tight. I let my arms hang at my sides.

"I won't tell him anything, I promise," she whispers in my ear. "But he deserves to know."

I'm back at school today.

I'm still a little shaken from my conversation with Tina a few days ago, but life goes on. There are a lot of things on my mind and big decisions to be made. But I need to make them and still maintain a normal life. Thomas says the same thing. I shouldn't stay in bed all day and forget that I have a life to live. With a snarky phone call this morning, he prodded me to get up and go to school and then work this afternoon.

The hardest decision is whether I share this news with Colt. For the first time in weeks, I'm actually relieved that he's not in town. I don't need to make that decision any time soon. I trust that Tina will keep her promise of silence.

But being in school today brings back some memories of a past life. I can't believe it's been less than six months since I stumbled upon Colt as I was nursing a broken heart from Simon. The irony of my life doesn't escape me.

"Hey, hot momma!" I hear Felicity's voice behind me. I turn around and give her a wide-eyed warning. She dismisses me with an eye roll as she runs toward me in her sparkly pink UGGs and white popcorn sweater over blush-colored skinny jeans. She immediately links her arm in mine as soon as she reaches me, and I notice gazes of admiration from the students around us.

"I must say, your choice of outfit today is spectacular." I laugh a little as I say this, but there's clearly pride in my expression.

"I hate wearing black and gray in the winter. It's already dark and dreary; we don't need to join the gloom. Look around you, everyone's wearing black." She gives me a stink eye.

"It's depressing!" I reply with a sneer.

"So, how is this momma feeling, otherwise?"

"I feel good. Starting to feel a little heavier, but good."

"Do you have work today?"

"Yeah. Thomas has some tea party he needs to go to around four. And you? What's up with you today?"

"Well, I was thinking now that the band's back together again maybe we can all have dinner with Phil tonight—you know, since I'd like to keep him as my pet for a little while." I give her a teasing shove.

"I have to work until around nine, but I can catch up with you guys if you'd like. Have you asked Simon yet?" She nods and looks at me with pleading eyes. "I'll be there, but a little bit late," I say.

"I'll make nine thirty reservations at El Caminero. I feel like Mexican today. Is that good?"

"Whoa! Fancy, Mexican, huh? I'll be there, can't wait. I've not seen Phil in a while anyway." Felicity jumps me in excitement, putting all her weight on my shoulders for a big hug. Then she abruptly stops in mid-yelp, probably remembering my condition. It makes me laugh. Then she moves away slowly and lets go. As if she has seen a ghost, she turns white. I turn around to see what she's staring at and gasp.

His hair is longer, and he's grown a beard and lost a lot of weight. He's as breathtaking as the first time I saw him, and he glares at me. This time, I finally know why. But I also see something else. Relief. I don't know what to make of it. He breathes out a heavy sigh and walks away. Like a dream, he has vanished into the crowd.

I don't move. My heart is racing, and I feel a panic attack

coming on. I cling to Felicity because I'm dizzy. There are black spots in my vision, and my hands start to shake.

"Gabs?" With a look of concern, Felicity grabs my binder from my hands and leads me to the closest bench by the administration office. I sit down slowly and stare into space, in shock. I don't understand this feeling. I thought I had it all sorted.

Well, I guess not.

Chapter Twenty-Eight

T homas lets me leave the shop early to get ready for dinner. The day was a blur because seeing Colt put me in a chaotic state of mind. But I pushed on. There is no other way to do this.

I get home and change into my black jersey cocktail dress and black sheer tights. I let my hair down and style it in waves with my curling iron. When I finish, I stand in front of my full-length mirror. I like what I see. I touch the tiny bump on my stomach and stare at myself. I'm still me, but somehow different. I feel an overwhelming surge of happiness.

"I saw your dad today. He's as good-looking as ever," I tell the tiny seed inside me. I should try to make this a happy pregnancy. I read somewhere that it's important that the baby knows and feels that it is wanted and loved before it's born. From now on, nothing is more important than this tiny life I carry. It deserves a strong mom, and it deserves all my attention. I was weak for most of my life, letting the flow move me in directions I didn't necessarily want to go, or where I didn't truly belong. There is no more second-guessing. I need to start moving with purpose.

I put on some red lipstick to brighten up my mood. I'm excited to be spending the night with my friends, and I'm so glad that Felicity found love with Phil. She deserves it more than anyone I know.

Putting on a red winter coat that matches my lips, I slip into my black flats on my way out the door and sling my black Chanel bag on my shoulder—one more gift from Simon years ago.

El Caminero is packed tonight, even at nine thirty, but the dim lighting and the soft Mexican music playing in the background makes it seem serene and intimate. I see Felicity, Phil, and Simon in the center of the room, and there's an expensive bottle of wine chilling in a bucket next to the table. Felicity's face is relaxed and happy, and her pink off-the-shoulder dress makes her even more radiant. Next to her is Phil, in a white dress shirt and tie. And Simon—who will always be the Simon from my youth—looks handsome in his expensive suit. I'm glad I was able to change into something presentable for tonight.

Felicity's face lights up when she sees me walking toward them. Both men get up. Simon pulls out a chair next to him and plants a light kiss on my cheek. Phil gives me a comforting hug, and Felicity jumps up to kiss me on my forehead.

"I'm starving," I say immediately.

"Eat this! It's great!" Felicity pushes over a small plate of tiny duck tacos as soon as I sit down. I grab one and immediately swallow it. This is not something that I would normally do, but I'm starting to recognize this new, spontaneous Gabriella, and I like her a lot.

I can sense Simon observing me. I turn to him and smile. He smiles right back—a little uncertainly—but I know he's always trying to understand the new person that I'm becoming.

"How are you, Gabby?" Phil asks while pouring Felicity more wine.

"I am super!" I can feel Felicity and Simon tense up. "Oh, shut it, you guys. I'm fine." I figured Felicity already told Simon about this morning's encounter with Colt.

"Just making sure. You know pregnancy jacks up your hormones. One second you're entirely human, the next you are a crazy bitch from outer space." I make a face at Felicity for saying this.

"Do you want something to drink?" Simon asks.

"Orange juice is fine."

As it turns out, Phil recently got a promotion and has been planning to take everyone to dinner after the holidays. He's been made senior editor and is now heavily involved in a new imprint at his publishing house. Felicity is beaming as he reveals this good news, and I couldn't be happier seeing the evolution of this relationship. Simon gives him a big pat on the back and a massive handshake. I get up from my chair, walk around the table, and give him a congratulatory hug.

As I walk back to my seat, I look around and admire the wall on the far side of the restaurant, brightly decorated with colorful Mexican sombreros. It's a favorite of mine. A spotlight brings attention to one red sombrero in the middle with *El Caminero* written in script. The ceiling is another spectacle in itself, covered with Mexican-inspired draperies that connect to a vintage chandelier. It's exactly how I remember it. Simon and I used to come here often. It's our favorite Mexican restaurant.

Simon pushes my chair in for me as I sit down. "It hasn't changed one bit since we were here together last, huh?" He notices that I'm staring at my favorite wall. I nod in agreement.

"So, this promotion of yours. Will this get me a book deal someday?" I ask Phil.

"You are full of surprises today, Gabby!" Felicity lightly punches me on my shoulder. I swat her hand away. I start laughing, and she joins in.

"How were you able to manage these two growing up, dude?" Phil asks Simon.

"It wasn't easy, especially this one." Simon points at Felicity affectionately. "I was an only child, and my parents love her. We grew up next to each other. But my goodness, she was a handful." Felicity tosses her table napkin in Simon's face, and his look of shock is priceless. "What are we, six?" he asks. Felicity and I are laughing so hard we can't contain ourselves. I start coughing, and I can feel tears running down my cheeks.

"You see, when Simon became a hotshot Wall Street dude, he thought we all needed to mature along with him. I can't change who I am! Gabs, remember the time we went to his office retreat? Gosh, how I begged him to take me." Simon puts his hand on his forehead at the memory of that embarrassing weekend. I barely control a giggle as Simon gives me the stink eye. "It was at one of those fancy schmancy Connecticut resorts where all the rich old men take their mistresses. Anyway, it's got this nice big lake that you can go boating on. I channeled Bridget Jones and brought a bottle of wine with me on the boat with some dude. . . ."

"And then she decided to park her boat on the spot where we were having our office cocktails, started singing at the top of her lungs, and fell into the lake laughing like a crazy person! My boss looked at her in great disgust and asked who brought her. I wanted to shrink and disappear at that very moment, but I had to raise my hand and say . . . she's my best friend," Simon says.

"And I love you more for it!" Felicity and I do a high five and laugh loudly, much to Simon's dismay. Phil looks at the three of us with a wide, sweet smile of affection on his face, and I can tell that he's glad to be part of this, to be able to experience this kind of long-lasting friendship, even though two-thirds of this band has just gotten divorced.

"Oh, baby, you make me so proud!" Phil exclaims, reaching out to Felicity and planting a big fat kiss on her check. Simon gives both of them a childish scowl, and I touch his cheek affectionately to appease him. Some habits are hard to break. Twenty years of togetherness is not something you simply forget. Simon bends his head toward me and smiles weakly.

I raise my head from Simon's childlike smile and encounter Colt's angry glare.

I jolt backwards, like a strong wind just knocked me over. Felicity and Simon notice and watch the two figures approaching us. There is no mistaking that on Colt's arm is Heather, wearing a tiny red dress that matches her lips perfectly. Her blond hair bounces over her shoulders, and her perfect smile could launch a thousand ships.

"Gabby!" Heather screams. I sit there frozen with a fake smile pasted on my face. I'm barely holding myself together. Heather bends to me for a quick kiss on both checks. I can feel heat surging through me, but I reach for her shoulders to return the gesture. Standing next to her, I can feel Colt staring at me.

"Hey, Colt. How's it going?" Felicity tries to break the ice.

"Oh, you know, everything's just perfect," he replies with a veneer of sarcasm.

"Colt, this is my boyfriend, Phil, and my best friend, Simon. And of course, you know Gabby."

"Of course. How could I not? Also, I think I've met Simon before. . . ."

"Yes, at the Back Room," Simon says.

"Right."

"Nice to meet you, Colt." Phil tries to move past the awkward silence. Colt just nods, but I sense that his gaze is focused on Simon and me. Now, I understand what that means—his anger—after Tina's revelation. I want to grab his hand, pull him aside, and explain everything, but not with Heather clinging tightly to his arm.

"We should meet up for coffee some time, Gabby! There is a lot of catching up to do," Heather says with a giggle. I don't want to sound distant, but I can't find any enthusiasm for the prospect. I nod and remain seated. I look at Felicity and the flicker of concern in her eyes is clear.

"Sure. You have my number. Call me anytime."

"When are your classes?"

"I'm in school Monday through Thursday."

"Are you still working at Thomas's?" Colt asks. It's the first time he's addressed me. I nod my head. Our eyes meet. Everything stops. Our world is back to where it once was—just the two of us. The fury in his eyes disappears, and I can feel my tense muscles softening. Then we both smile— the kind we used to share, the kind we both know is infused with love and care and affection, the kind we know can make us the happiest—the happiest we've both ever been. And then it vanishes as quickly as it appears—because he's with Heather and I'm sitting next to my ex-husband.

"We have to get to our table, Colt." Heather's high-pitched voice painfully slices through the connection that binds Colt and me.

They walk away hand in hand.

Simon reaches for my hand to comfort me. Felicity touches my shoulders with great concern. Phil looks at all of us in confusion.

"Are you okay?" Simon rubs the back of my hand and squeezes it. I nod my head because I'm afraid to say anything that might break me.

"Do you want to leave?" I shake my head to let Felicity know I'm fine.

"I feel . . . I feel like I should talk to him." My voice cracks as I speak. The courage that suddenly engulfs me is a welcome surprise.

"Gabby . . . you don't need to do that now."

"But I do, Simon . . . I think I should do this now before I change my mind, before this bravery disappears. And you know I'm not always brave." He bends his head, avoiding my eyes, and finally nods in agreement.

Suddenly our waiter appears, asking for our orders. Felicity asks him to give us more time and bring another bottle of white wine. The one in the bucket is nearly empty anyway. The sweet young waiter happily obliges and leaves us alone.

"I won't be able to move on if there is this unfinished thing with Colt. I might not even get another chance, because I don't intend to make an effort to reach out to him. I'm tired of having to feel so uncertain and out of balance because of this big secret." I don't cry as I say this, I don't even falter. I'm like a phoenix rising from the ashes—gathering strength, pushing my boundaries. Simon and Felicity hold each of my hands—and I'm glad that they are here to help me see this through.

"Okay, then, let's do it," Felicity says with renewed confidence.

I get up, brush invisible dust off my plain black dress, and heave a heavy sigh.

"Do you want me to walk there with you?" she asks, and I shake my head. I need to do this now before I get frazzled and lose it again.

I turn around and walk toward Colt and Heather.

They are about five tables away. Colt is leaning backwards on his chair and wears an ambiguous expression as Heather chats away. He must have seen me walking toward them because he suddenly sits up at attention. Heather turns to look at me, and her face lights up.

"Gabby! C'mon, join us," Heather exclaims. I can't hate her. She doesn't know about Colt and me, and I can't hold it against her. I give her a bright smile, which I can only wish will do the trick. She doesn't deserve to be humiliated.

"Actually, I just need to talk to Mr. James privately. I need to ask for his advice on my new professor. I heard they've worked together in the past. This will take one second, Heather. I promise." What a lame excuse, I know. Colt doesn't move. And I can't drag him out of his chair. I give him a stern look, which I've never given him before. I can see that he is taken aback. He lifts the table napkin off his lap, drops it on his plate, and pushes his chair back to walk around the table to join me.

"Of course!" Heather says.

"I promise, it will only take five minutes."

"Take your time, I'll order us drinks. The usual, Colt?" She says this like they've done this a million times. I can feel my face burn, but I push it aside. This is no place for jealousy.

I take the lead and walk toward the bar. I look at our table, and I see Felicity, Simon, and even Phil watching me with concern. By now they must have already explained to Phil what's going on. I stop at the far end of the bar, blocking Heather's line of sight. I turn around to face him. He is mere inches from me. I can smell him, the wood and cider scent I once enjoyed. His closeness makes me dizzy, and I close my eyes to gather my sanity. I never said I stopped loving him. I stand in front of him now and in my heart, I can truthfully say that my love for him is more than I can grasp. It is much stronger than I can handle. Perhaps, this is how it's supposed to be.

When I open my eyes, I'm faced with the sadness on Colt's face. His anger is gone. His eyes have softened and become clear blue again. I want to reach out to him, but I stop my hand in midair. He notices it too.

"I'm sorry to take you away from Heather; this won't take long."

"So, when did you get back with your ex-husband?" I don't expect this from him. I thought I could simply say my piece and I would be free. I jerk my head up to look at him.

"We're not back together," I whisper softly.

"So, what is this—two old friends simply hanging out? You expect me to believe that."

"I don't expect you to believe anything . . . you left me, like he did. But at least he had the decency to explain and actually own it." His eyes widen in shock and he bends his head in shame.

"I saw you two together . . . I asked you to hold my hand, to help me make this work . . . instead I find you kissing your fucking ex—" He realizes he's starting to shout and stops himself mid-sentence.

"It's not what you think. But I was never given a chance to explain."

"You promised you'd help me," he says, softly now.

"Help you with what? Help you love me, help you keep me, help you understand me? The world doesn't owe you anything. I don't owe you anything. I don't need to help you love me. You should figure that out on your own. And if you're not brave enough to handle it, I don't think you deserve me." We're both quiet for a long time. Colt sits with his head bowed, uncertain. When the bartender approaches, Colt orders a scotch on the rocks. I don't say anything. When the drink arrives, Colt gulps it in one go. His face crumples as he battles with the sharp, bitter taste, but deliberately welcomes the challenge.

"I know you hate me. I get it. You saw me kiss Simon. I'm not here to talk about the past—you've clearly moved on." I jerk my head toward where Heather is sitting.

"Have you moved on, Gabby?" His gaze is penetrating my soul. I have to look away or I will never be able to help myself. I will never be able to lie. "Have you?" he asks again.

"I think it's pointless to talk about this now."

"Pointless for whom?" His anger is rising again.

"For both of us," I reply gently. "Colt . . ." The mere mention of his name on my lips sends my heart pounding again. I close my eyes, willing myself not to weep. The last thing I need is for Colt to see me weak. "I don't expect anything from you. I don't expect you to be part of my life anymore, or in any way. But you deserve to know this. I'm carrying your baby. I'm keeping it. And I've decided to do this on my own. This much, I think, I owe you, but nothing more. Now that I've said what everyone thinks I should tell you, I'm ready to move on."

Colt looks bewildered. I can tell that he can't seem to grasp what I just said.

"Goodbye, Colt. . . ." With all of myself, and all the courage that I've gathered, I turn around and walk away from him. The moment I reach Felicity, Simon, and Phil, a waterfall of tears starts rolling down my cheeks. Instead of sitting down, I gather my things and walk out of the restaurant. Simon is right behind me. I don't need to explain myself. I know they understand.

Outside, Simon reaches out for my arm and helps me into my coat. He is hailing a cab when I hear Colt call my name. I turn around to see him hurriedly walking toward us. Simon puts himself between us, and Colt looks disoriented. He buries his face in his hands and starts pacing.

"You can't tell me this and walk away. . . ." He's trying to reach me, but Simon doesn't let him.

"She can, man," Simon says, while shielding me behind him. "Look, give it some time . . . you and Gabby can talk about this later."

"Are you even sure it's mine and not his?" His words shatter my heart. But before I know what is happening, Simon smacks Colt in the face. Colt stumbles backwards. I put my hand over my mouth in shock but don't try to intervene. Thankfully, a cab stops right in front of us, and Simon and I get in, leaving Colt staring at us as we drive away.

Chapter Twenty-Nine

Inside the cab, Simon reaches out to me, pulls me gently, and envelops me in his arms. I can't stop crying. I let my tears run down my face.

"Shhh . . ." Simon cradles me in his arms as I whimper. I remember all of the past year's pain, and I need these tears to purge it.

It starts to rain. I can hear the light tapping on the roof of the cab. The sky seems to be mourning with me.

My god, I still love him. I cry not only for the events of today, but because deep down I know I will always love him. My strength is in him, the knowledge that I was able to experience how it was to be happy and to love with my entire being.

"You'll get through this. You're braver than you think." I remain limp in his arms. The rhythmic swaying of the cab as it traverses the New York City streets helps to lull my emotions. Finally, I move out of Simon's arms and stop crying. I look at him in gratitude, and he nods in acknowledgement.

"I hope you're right," I say.

"Of course, I am. You've always been a sturdy rock for Felicity and me. You're steady and consistent. That's why we've always depended on you. That's why . . . I still do." He says the last part in a whisper.

I stare out the window and watch as it starts to pour. I pull my coat tighter around me. Simon lets me be. He's staring out the window on his side, also deep in thought. We sit in silence until the cab stops in front of my building. Simon opens his door quickly and helps me out. We stand together in the rain looking at each other with sadness and understanding.

"Are you sure you're going to be fine?"

"Yes. And thank you."

"No, Gabby, thank you . . . for letting me." I give him a small kiss on the cheek before I run toward the door. I don't turn around to see Simon drive away. I'm too exhausted. I just want to collapse on my bed and forget about tonight and tomorrow. I'll probably miss class and call in sick. Thomas will understand.

When I get into my apartment, I strip off the soaking wet coat, dress, and tights in the foyer. I run to the bathroom for a towel to dry my face and hair. In my underwear, I walk to the kitchen to look for food. I can feel a headache coming, so I need food. We hadn't even ordered when Colt and Heather walked in. Now, I'm starving. I feel like a zombie, my mind in a trance. I can't think anymore. I just want to feed myself, take a bath, and go straight to bed. I open my tiny fridge and there's nothing but a cup of strawberry yogurt. I pull off the foil cover and squeeze the contents into my mouth. I finish it in three big gulps, and my stomach is still growling.

Perhaps, a hot bath will help me calm down. I go back to the bathroom and fill the tub. I strip naked and wrap a towel around me. I can feel my boobs growing tender, one of the many changes I embrace in my journey toward motherhood.

I hear my phone ring inside my tiny purse. When I pull it out, I see Colt's name. I don't answer it. I'm too exhausted to face this tonight—maybe tomorrow, or the next day, but not tonight.

A text message pops up next: "Please look out your window.

Please answer my call." I stand in the middle of my apartment motionless, uncertain of what to do.

The phone starts ringing again, and I swipe to answer. I walk back to the bathroom, turn off the faucet, and sit on the floor.

"Gabby . . ." I can hear the rain in the background.

"Hello . . ."

"Please come to the window." I don't say anything. "Please." And so, I get up and I walk as slowly as I can.

I see him outside in the rain with the phone to his ear. We look at each other in silence.

"I was a coward," he begins. Then I hear him start to sob. "I didn't know what to do, where to go, and I don't want to hurt you. I was so angry and so terrified of what I could do to you . . . like my dad did to my mom." I hear him hiccup, and I feel tears roll down my cheeks. But I still don't say anything. "My life is a constant heartbreak. There was not a day when I didn't feel my heart breaking, until you . . . and then I fucking blew it."

I see him wipe his face as the rain continues to fall relentlessly.

"I'm not asking you to understand, or to forgive me, or to love me again. But I want you to know that every moment you were away from me was like a punishment that I wasn't strong enough to endure. You gave me a dose of happiness I wasn't used to, and when it was taken away from me, I felt like I was drowning, and no one was there to save me. God, I need you. I need you to breathe. I need you to live. I just don't know how to fucking do this."

I put my hand over my mouth to muffle a howl as tears run down my face.

"Tonight, when you told me I was going to be a father, I was terrified. But when you walked away, I felt my chest tightening again. I can't let my cowardice take me down. You are all I think about. And I'm so tired of wanting and not having you in my life. I love you, Gabby."

I don't say anything for a few seconds as I try to compose myself. We stare at each other, my heart breaking.

"If I let you back into my life, I'm no longer just putting my own feelings at risk here. We're two souls now—your baby and me. I can't let this baby down because I wasn't strong enough for both of us. And so . . . though I love you with all my heart, and all my soul, and all of me, I can't let you back in like this." I control a sob as I speak. "Goodbye, Colt, and please know that I want you to find your peace and be able to love again, and hopefully the next time, you can do so without fear."

I draw the blinds down and walk away from the window. And then I break down and fall on the floor. I open up my heart, and I weep like my life depends on it.

Chapter Thirty

I see Colt at school sometimes. We smile and then we walk on. On a few occasions, I caught him staring at my tummy. Our eyes meet and then we walk on. We're strangers now. But I no longer question his reason for coming into my life because he made me a complete person.

My pregnancy belly is showing now, but nobody really cares to ask. And I'm glad. I don't want to lie and concoct some lame story after I blurted out on my first day of school that I was going through a divorce.

Felicity and Phil are still going strong. Thomas and Arthur are now open about their relationship since Arthur's wife passed away a month back. Simon is on Tinder, not because he's looking for a hookup, but because he is also ready to move on with his life and to find love again.

My mom and dad can't wait to be grandparents, sending me heaps of baby things almost every week. My mom calls me every day to check in. My dad sends me text messages every hour, which are mostly forwarded pregnancy or grandparent jokes.

I still haven't decided what to do next. For now, I plan to stay in New York, continue going to my classes as long as I can, and continue seeing Dr. Zaragoza, the OB-GYN I share with Tina, recommended by Dr. Sharma. Of course, my mom and dad keep on nagging me about coming back to Virginia where there is family who can look out for the baby while I finish school, which I can do at Georgetown. I'm also looking into the creative writing low-residency program at NYU, which I could do from Virginia.

My phone rings as I walk out of class. It's Felicity.

"Hey. So, hear this—Tina said she is moving out of Colt's apartment." Tina has become a great ally and friend. We meet for coffee every once in a while, but we have agreed not to talk about Colt. I was with her the other day and I didn't hear anything about this.

"Did she say why? Did they have a fight or something?" I ask, concerned.

"Colt is selling the townhouse." I feel a little prick in my heart when I hear this.

"Is he moving out of New York? Is he going back to L.A?"

"I don't know. I'm trying to find out some more, but . . . well, I won't if you don't want me to."

"I just hope they're both all right."

"Tina sounded positive about this change, so I gather this is for the best for both of them."

"You're probably right."

"Are you going to your doctor this afternoon?"

"No, I did that yesterday. I'll be at the shop around three today."

"What are you doing after class?"

"I have this paper I need to write, so I'll probably be at Washington Square Park."

"It's freezing out, Gabs!"

"I've got that covered. I have the thickest jacket *my* money could buy and the warmest tech-friendly gloves. I also have a thermos full to the brim with hot chocolate."

"Whatever!" I can sense Felicity rolling her eyes. "I'll see you at the apartment for lunch tomorrow. Phil is cooking."

"Yes, it's on my calendar. I'll be there for sure. What else would I be doing on a Saturday morning? Nursing my broken and sorrowful heart?"

"Ha! You're not there anymore. That's old news. You're a happy, single woman in the city now."

"Correction, happy, single, *pregnant* woman in the city. Is Simon bringing a date?"

"Yes. The same girl, Trish."

"Oh, I'm so glad! She's a winner."

"I think so too. So let's be the best friends that we are and make sure Simon makes this thing work." Suzanne, the woman Simon left me for, continues to stalk him. She has not given up on him although he has made it clear numerous times that he has moved on. After our divorce, I discovered that Suzanne ran after Simon when we were married and trapped him by saying that she was pregnant after one drunken night, when in fact she wasn't. When Simon discovered that she'd lied to him, he broke it off. She wasn't having it and continues to bother him. At one point, Felicity told her that we would report her to the police if she doesn't stop harassing Simon. The stalking has lessened a bit.

❧

I walk to Washington Square Park, and I'm glad to see from a distance that my favorite bench is free. I walk faster in case someone beats me to it. And to my dismay, someone claims it before me. I don't see his face, but he drops a large backpack on the bench and pulls out a computer. As I come closer, I realize there is also a bouquet of flowers next to him—peonies. They're lush and gorgeous. How he found them this time of the year baffles me. I walk past my favorite bench and try to find an empty one close by.

"You can share the bench with me," the man says. And I turn around to see Colt.

I can feel sadness in both our eyes. Regret. But we smile at each other nevertheless.

"It's okay. I'll find another bench," I say.

"Go, take this one, and I'll find another. This is your bench anyway."

"It's really not mine, but thanks." I'm about to walk away and leave him be.

"Gabby. Can you at least share a hot chocolate with me here?" I turn around to face him. My heart is still too fragile to be this close to my source of sorrow. I've been great at putting all the pieces back together, and slowly I've been making remarkable progress. "Please," he adds. His eyes are pleading. I stop in my tracks and sit next to him.

He moves the flowers to the other side to make room for me. He pulls out a thermos and two cups from his backpack, pours the steaming brown liquid, and hands one cup to me.

"Thanks," I say. He turns to look at me. We're mere inches away from each other. Face to face. God, he looks good, and different. There's something new about him, something light and positive. Peaceful. He smiles. The truest I've seen him since we broke up.

"How's the pregnancy going?" he asks as he pours himself his own cup.

"It's doing great, actually, considering I am a so-called mature mother." I do air quotes around *mature mother.*

"What does that even mean?" he asks with his brows furrowed.

"That I'm well past my prime child-bearing years." We look at each other and we both chuckle. "Oh, hey, I heard you're selling your townhouse. Are you moving back to L.A.?

He doesn't answer, and we're both quiet for a full minute. We let the noise of the city comfort us in the cold.

"Gabby, I want to be part of this pregnancy." It's been more than a month since our last conversation from my apartment window. Neither one of us has tried to reach the other. And so, this is a surprise to me.

"Oh . . . of course." I want this baby to know its father—its brilliant, talented, and loving father.

"Thank you." He exhales and beams with happiness, and his face lights up like I've never seen it before.

"You're welcome. I mean, I haven't really decided how to handle all this, but I'll keep you informed."

"Are you thinking of going back home to Virginia?"

"It's an option. I can't do this here on my own with the cost of childcare. It's ridiculous. I don't know how people manage."

"I can help, you know."

I don't answer. But god, I miss this face and his scent, his smile and his lips. I close my eyes to stop myself from remembering.

"Are you okay, Gabs?" He sounds worried, so I open my eyes and nod in affirmation. I take a sip of my hot chocolate and he does the same. We're quiet for a few minutes, enjoying the serenity of the park. The older gentlemen, despite the cold of winter, still find the courage to play chess here. There are moms with kids running around. And I look at these toddlers, and I feel my heart swell with love and excitement that I will soon be one of those moms. Colt looks at me as I stare at them.

"Gabs, I want to be part of this baby's life."

"And you will," I agree.

"But . . . I also want to be a part of yours." I pull my eyes away from the kids and look at his face—that beautiful, beautiful face that I still love. "I'm not the best person in the world, or the best boyfriend, and I kept you hanging, walking away without saying goodbye like that. I was such a coward. I'm so sorry." He holds my gaze with sincerity. And I realize that when he told me he loved me that night in his apartment, he was so unsure of himself. It was the first time he'd explored his feelings and was afraid to share them. I remember how I wanted so much to be strong for both of us. But today, as he speaks, I sense confidence and certainty. There is no veil of doubt.

"Colt . . ."

"I'm not asking you to take me back now, but I'm asking you if there's still a tiny chance that you still love me enough to at least think about it. I'm ready now. I'm not using my past as an excuse anymore. My past should be my reason to love more. And you made me see through all that."

"Colt . . ."

"I don't want to rush you. You can take your time. I just want you to know I'm willing to wait. I love you. I love you so much it hurts not to be near you. But at the same time, I'm trying to be a stronger man who deserves to stand next to you. I'm not promising that I'll be perfect, that I will never fail, but I promise that I will try every single day of my life with you."

I burst out crying, and then laughing, and then I put both my arms around his neck. And I kiss him because I miss kissing him so damn much. And he kisses me back and takes me into his arms—and it feels different, he's less guarded, more certain, more real.

"And when you're ready to take me back," he says as he pulls away, "perhaps, we can get married, spend the rest of our lives together, and make more babies."

"First, I need to know why you're selling the townhouse and how long you've been seeing Heather."

"Hmm, that's tricky," he says as he covers both my hands with his.

"Tell me now!" I pretend to be angry. "Fine, I'll understand if you slept with her while we were on a break."

"Wait, what . . . did you see other people while we were on a break?" He looks at me seriously.

"We were on a break, does it matter?" I tease him.

"No. It doesn't. And also no, I didn't sleep with Heather. She showed up in L.A. one night and invited me to dinner. I was dead drunk and fell asleep at the bar. She had to ask the bouncers to help us get into a cab. The next day, I woke up in my hotel room with a note that said to call her at her parents' house."

"How about the townhouse?"

"There are so many ghosts in that house—starting with my parents. I want to let go of that. And . . . well, that house is also not great for kids. So many stairs." I beam at this. "I mean, it's such a big house to babyproof—you know, if we decide to have babies every year from, well, when you decide to take me back. . . ."

"I love you, Colt James."

"Gabriella Stevens, I don't think you know how much I love you."

"Are those flowers mine?"

"Yes," Colt says shyly.

"Well, you have the rest of our lives to prove it. . . ."

THE END

ACKNOWLEDGMENTS

Seven years ago, I made a promise to an author friend that I would one day get a *real* novel published under my name. She said she made the exact same promise to another author friend. Two years after our conversation, she published her first novel and a second followed a few years later. Now, you are holding this book as a promise fulfilled to Eva Zsuzsa Trembacz. Thank you for caring enough to ask me to commit to this dream.

This book would not be made possible if not for my publisher, Brooke Warner, who gave me this amazing opportunity to put my heart and soul to paper for people to read. Thank you to my editor, Jennifer Caven, who made this book pop like I didn't think possible. My gratitude also to Shannon Green, who was always around to answer my questions, kept me on schedule, and made sure I got it all right—*Salamat*. Big thanks also to my publicity team at Booksparks, who made me feel like a star. Oh, and of course, Julie Metz, who created the most beautiful cover design for *After Perfect*, capturing the very essence of Gabby. I literally cried the moment I received the final version.

Forever grateful to girlfriends! I want to say thank you to Andrea, who was my first real reader, telling me that I should pursue my storytelling ambition. Maddy, for reading my terrible first drafts and getting really excited as if they were the best she'd ever read. Ioanna, thank you for listening to me talk about my writing ambitions over and over and actually believing that I could reach them all. To Bambi, thank you for loving me and for always being a constant. To Pam and Jeno, thank you for inspiring me with your creativity and for pushing me to be better at my craft every single day. There are so many women in my life that I am thankful for. Your messages of love and encouragement sustain my creative spirit. Please know that your friendship means more to me than you'll ever fully grasp.

Then there are the girls who knew me even before I became me—my college best friends and writing buddies. Mari Jojie and Lace Goodwin, you two have been stellar allies on this amazing journey. Who would have predicted that almost three decades after graduating college, we'd be authors together? And to my heart sisters Rascel and Jazel, and to Alex and Sarah, cheers to my *Kulasa* girls!

I would not have been able to do all the work without the support of my family. To my brother, Nico, who hates math as much as I do, I am glad we're creative together. To Arnie, making it possible for me to be at three places at the same time, thank you. I appreciate you more than you know.

My mom, Emely Gabriel—you are the reason I fell in love with books at a very young age. Thank you for taking me to bookstores instead of toy stores growing up. She swears she taught me how to read in English at age three.

Dad, I am you in more ways than one. You are the reason I do what I do. Thank you for showing me the world of news and the arts and live television.

To my son, Jack, my editor, the critic, the love of my life, the joy who lifts me up, the anchor who steadies me, and the beauty for which I forever will be grateful happened in my life. Thank you for making me a mommy. Know that I'll be by your side for all eternity whether you like it or not.

And yes, to my husband, Chris—my copilot, the constant

who showers me with love even in the most trying of times, the one person I am most certain has my back—you are my world. I have patterned Gabby's parents' love to the kind that we have: easy, light, and full of laughter. Thank you for walking this dream with me.

And to you reading this, giving me a chance to live a fantasy, thank you. My heart is overwhelmed with gladness because of you.

ABOUT THE AUTHOR

Photo credit: Kir Tuben Photography

"I dream of a world full of hope, where believing is as important as life itself, and where love can move mountains. This is at the very core of my stories, and I wish in more ways than one that I can inspire you to see the world as I see it . . . a fairy tale."

—Maan

MAAN GABRIEL is a mom, wife, dreamer, writer, and advocate for women's stories in literature. She earned her BA in communications from St. Scholastica's College in Manila and MPS in public relations and corporate communications from Georgetown University. She has lived in Manila, Brussels, Dakar, and Mexico City. During the day, she works in strategic communications. Gabriel, along with her husband and son, currently calls suburban Washington, DC home. *After Perfect* is her first novel.

SELECTED TITLES FROM SHE WRITES PRESS

She Writes Press is an independent publishing company founded to serve women writers everywhere. Visit us at www.shewritespress.com.

Center Ring by Nicole Waggoner. $17.95, 978-1-63152-034-1. When a startling confession rattles a group of tightly knit women to its core, the friends are left analyzing their own roads not taken and the vastly different choices they've made in life and love.

Stella Rose by Tammy Flanders Hetrick. $16.95, 978-1-63152-921-4. When her dying best friend asks her to take care of her sixteen-year-old daughter, Abby says yes—but as she grapples with raising a grieving teenager, she realizes she didn't know her best friend as well as she thought she did.

The Trumpet Lesson by Dianne Romain. $16.95, 978-1-63152-598-8. Fascinated by a young woman's performance of "The Lost Child" in Guanajuato's central plaza, painfully shy expat Callie Quinn asks the woman for a trumpet lesson—and ends up confronting her longing to know her own lost child, the biracial daughter she gave up for adoption more than thirty years ago.

Profound and Perfect Things by Maribel Garcia. $16.95, 978-1-63152-541-4. When Isa, a closeted lesbian with conservative Mexican parents, has a one-night stand that results in an unwanted pregnancy, her sister, Cristina adopts the baby—but twelve years later, Isa, who regrets giving up her child, threatens to spill the secret of her daughter's true parentage.

Shelter Us by Laura Diamond. $16.95, 978-1-63152-970-2. Lawyer-turned-stay-at-home-mom Sarah Shaw is still struggling to find a steady happiness after the death of her infant daughter when she meets a young homeless mother and toddler she can't get out of her mind—and becomes determined to rescue them.